FIGHTING CAPTIVITY

HUMAN PETS OF TALIN
BOOK 4

Copyright: RK Munin, 2022
Cover Illustration by RK Munin, 2022
ISBN–13: 978-1-962699-15-0

Warning: Author is dyslexic as hell.

The editing and beta reading team: Mary Alegre, Gary Anderson, Martha Collins, and Lauren Meghoo

Professional Editing: Amanda Brown Edits, LLC

Feel free to contact me with questions, requests, or comments: **author@rk-munin.com**

Check out my website for offers and free novels:
www.rk-munin.com

And, as with many writers, your reviews on Amazon, Goodreads, and/or Kindle help immeasurably, even if it's just clicking on the stars.

Thank you to all my readers!

CONTENT WARNING

One character is born deaf.

There is violence on page with several fight scenes.

There is talk of past trauma for both characters including bodily damage and scarring.

This novel is also meant for adult audiences and contains explicit sexual content.

Author's note: Several of the characters in this book will speak using the silent tapping language of the Norka. When they are doing this there'll be single quote marks (') instead of (").

To my anxiety-riddled brain: Thanks for making me so panicky all the time that I was always diving into books to avoid reality. That eventually led to me diving into my own head to avoid reality. Now have fun reading the results of my anxiety in this (and all) my books!

CHAPTER 1

Dots on the side of Zia's left eye blinked a light blue as her ocular implants made her aware that sound was coming from that direction. The pattern, color, and shape of the dots indicated the sounds she couldn't hear were made by multiple sets of footsteps.

Turning her head, she watched several processors hurry toward her. Although they were both Nimon, meaning their insect bodies were very dissimilar to hers, she'd spent enough time with the species to easily read their body language. These two Nimons seemed excited about something.

Everyone on board, as well as almost everyone in the entire universe, had an intercranial translator, or INT for short. They came with hundreds of languages preprogramed along with the ability to add even more. She had one too, but her INT was highly specialized because she was deaf. The owner of the ship had hired her despite her disability because her deafness didn't affect her work performance. Oh, and as a human, he could pay her less than the Nimon members of the crew.

She mostly worked alone, meaning her lack of hearing and unwillingness to use vocal language wasn't an issue.

Everyone on board knew if they wanted her to respond, they either needed to wait for her to type it out on an information square or download the silent tapping language of the Norka. It didn't seem to bother anyone on the crew much, which was why she stayed, despite the lack of a pay raise in three years.

Jerif was one of the excited Nimons approaching her. He'd downloaded the tapping language into his INT soon after she started working here, which made him her favorite Nimon on this ship. Judging by his excitement, he had something interesting to tell her.

Swaying her upper body slightly to display curiosity, she tapped out her question. 'What's going on? I thought you were off duty.'

Standing on his four lower limbs, Jerif moved his upper front limbs to reply. The great thing about tapping was that you didn't need a set number of limbs or fingers. The language worked in its simplified form as long as you had at least one limb and two fingers. But two hands with four fingers on each was the minimum needed for an in-depth discussion.

'You didn't hear? We came across some salvage. A ship exploded and all the lifepods emitting life signals have been picked up. There's no electronic banner on the ship, so it's fair game for us.'

While that was good news for any trawler that made a living by collecting salvage, their ship, Red Ore, was full. They were on the way to the trade planet Yarnetta to unload. They were so full that one crewmate complained his working space was limited due to an overabundance of salvage.

Straightening her body, she wiggled her shoulder to display surprise. 'That's great, but where will all the fresh salvage go?'

Her question made Jerif's foot dance with amusement. Nimons moved one of their two-clawed feet around to show amusement. The faster they moved their foot the more amused they were, and if they were rapidly stomping it, that meant they were laughing uproariously.

'We were told to take it ourselves,' he declared.

Her eyes widened with surprise. 'Crew salvage rights?' Now she was excited and forced to slow down because when she made the complicated gesture for salvage, Jerif didn't catch it the first time. Like any language, it took practice for the INT to transmit flawlessly, and even after years on board, Jerif hadn't had enough conversations with her to be fluent. She repeated her question with the more common terms. 'We are being granted crew salvage rights?'

'Yes! Crew salvage! You should come. I know you're maintenance, but you have as much right to collect as the rest of us.' Jerif lifted a rear leg and wiggled his toes in the air to back up his invitation with welcoming body language.

Good money might be made on salvage, but she couldn't do it by herself. 'Can we work together? I'll bring my tools so I'll be able to test if any of the tech we find is still working.'

Jerif looked over to his companion, another Nimon named Nalk, and spoke quickly. The implant in her right eye flashed their conversation across her vision. She was so used to it that she could easily read the words and follow their body language at the same time.

They made no effort to hide their conversation, so she unabashedly listened in. Unlike many species, most of the crew assumed she could hear them. Other crews on other ships thought she could only understand tapping, so she'd been privy to some interesting tidbits over the years.

The truth was, she couldn't "hear" them, but she could understand them. The implant hidden under the skin on either side of her head was better at detecting noise than fully functioning human ears would have been, or at least that's what she was told when her parents bought them. She wouldn't know. She was born with no inner ear.

Thankfully, it was cheap and easy to modify a regular INT to pair it with expensive eye and ear implants. Sadly, all her implants were old and needed to be replaced, but she still lacked the funds. She wanted the next ones to be top of the line, so she'd scrimped and saved for years. If they got enough good stuff from this crew salvage, it might mean she could buy them and pay for them to be installed when they docked and unloaded.

Crew salvage rights happened when a ship was technically full. The owner or captain gave the crew the right to find storage space in their work or private areas and then took a small percentage of what the crew made when they turned in their personal salvage. She missed out that last time this happened because she was in the middle of her sleep cycle and no one woke her up.

But it looked like she'd gotten lucky this time.

Their talk must be done because both Nimons regarded her in silence. Nalk's emotional body language told her that despite agreeing, he still wasn't sure about letting her join them.

"You're tiny," he finally commented out loud. The words moved quickly in Common across her right eye. Noises made dots or slashes flash in her left eye, and spoken words scrolled across her right eye. When she first got the implants as a little girl, they'd often made her dizzy, but now they were a familiar part of herself.

She had an answer ready before the last word scrolled across her vision. 'I'm strong for my size,' she tapped out, and Jerif translated.

Nalk still looked doubtful. "I don't see how you could be of any help to us. You wouldn't be able to carry anything but the smallest of items."

She pointed to her tool tote and then tapped her response. Jerif interpreted for her again. 'That's true. You'll need to do much of the lifting and carrying, *but* I'm quick and can take systems apart. And I have an entire shop we can store things in. I'm the only one who uses it right now, so there only needs to be enough room for me to fit. That makes my small size a bonus!'

Nalk looked nervous at her suggestion. "What if something big breaks and needs to be repaired?"

'I'll repair it in place,' she assured him. 'And we recently changed out the equalizer for the grav drive. That's the only thing I was taking into my shop regularly. It's doubtful anything large will break between now and off-loading.'

His eyes remained on her as Jerif translated. While Jerif talked, Nalk's body language relaxed. "Your shop would be good storage," he conceded.

"It will be excellent storage," Jerif agreed both verbally and tapped. "And I've seen Zia work. She's skilled. Don't let her small stature fool you."

"I was told humans aren't very smart," Nalk commented. By the way one of his antennae waved as he spoke, Zia knew he was baiting her. Those words were meant to get an emotional reaction out of her. Nimons didn't approve of emoting, and he was probably making sure she wouldn't be troublesome.

Considering she'd worked for years on this ship with a Nimon captain and alongside a majority Nimon crew, you'd think they'd stop testing her at some point.

Tapping the toe of one foot to denote amusement, she kept her eyes on Nalk as she tapped. 'I'd be honored to expand your knowledge of humans as we work side by side.'

There, a perfectly diplomatic Nimon answer.

Nalk made an affirmative body motion by scissoring his antennae back and forth. "Very well. You can join us. We will split all wealth equally. Standard crew sharing contract?"

Jerif copied the move with his palps. "Agreed."

Zia tapped. 'Agreed.'

Politely, they waited for her to pick up her tool tote before they headed to the retrieval bay. Predictably, the place was packed with crew. The three of them found a suitable spot and waited, their eyes on the front of the bay. Zia double-checked her tools and tucked a few of the smaller ones into pockets on her coveralls.

After a quick conversation, the three agreed that Jerif, the biggest of them, would pull items off the massive conveyer. If the items had an energy signature at all, Zia would check it for safety and disable anything if necessary. After they were sure it was safe, Nalk would run it to her shop.

Most of the crew were trying to do this by themselves, but with the three of them working together, they should be able to do a lot more. And with Jerif and Nalk being such big Nimons, they could grab larger items that others would have to let go by.

The warning bell sounded for the conveyer, and then it started up. At first nothing much came by. Nothing was left to be dumped back into space, but the three of them only pulled one piece off and kept it tucked behind them. It wasn't big enough to bother running it to Zia's shop.

Then a planet hopper shuttle lumbered up the conveyer.

Zia's eyes widen. The money they could get for that would be excellent. Even though the shuttle looked battered, the most important parts were still intact and didn't look damaged. If the hull integrity was still good, this could be their golden egg.

None of them even had to plan with each other; exchanged looks was all it took. They wanted that shuttle. Only one other team might take it, but they were on the other side of the conveyor, so the three of them should be able to get to it first.

She did a quick calculation in her head and then dug out her handheld uni-cutter. After she slung it across her body and checked the charge, she got Jerif's attention.

'Once we've got it on the platform, I can cut the broken stabilizers and maneuvering thrusters. Then it will fit through the standard hatches between here and my shop. With the grab stand in the front, we should be able to get it there without a problem.'

Jerif looked anxious. 'Are you sure it will fit?'

She made sure her body language was confident by tilting back a little. 'I know it will.'

It had to fit. All three of them would make it fit.

When it drew even with them, Jerif and Nalk wrestled it onto the platform. For their size, Nimons were incredibly strong, so she wasn't surprised they accomplished it although a third of it still hung over the conveyor. Now it was her turn to get to work.

With efficiency born of long practice, she cut off the parts of the shuttle that weren't worth much but made up a quarter of its overall size. Because the shuttle was so valuable, they tossed those less important pieces back onto the conveyer for someone else to snap up.

With those pieces gone, they relaxed a little because it was easier to move the shuttle more securely onto the platform. Nalk ran off to grab a stand from her shop, and without needing to discuss it, she and Jerif moved up to the shuttle's door. The next step would be to get the thing open while causing the least amount of damage possible.

She did a quick integrity scan and found out that not only was the hull not compromised, some of the internal systems were still on. The value of the shuttle kept going up. When she tapped out this information to Jerif, his reply wasn't a surprise.

"I could buy a wife with this," Jerif murmured to himself. It took a few misunderstandings when Zia first came to work on Red Ore before she figured out Nimon marriage customs. Jerif actually meant he would have enough money to attract a wife. The population disparity between Nimon males and females meant unless a male had a lot of wealth, he wasn't likely to attract a wife. At first she thought that was pretty mercenary of the females until she found out that couples needed a lot of funds to assure the survival of their offspring.

Much like Old Earth before, it was no longer habitable, so the Nimon homeworld was overcrowded and too expensive for anyone but the most elite to live on. That meant any Nimon who wanted kids needed to have enough money to build a cultivation room on a station, colony, or ship. Cultivation rooms mimicked their homeworld, and the offspring needed live in one for the first five years in order to survive.

Jerif often lamented that he'd never get to raise offspring. This shuttle might make both her and Jerif's dreams come true!

She finished interfacing with the shuttle, and the door unlatched with a hiss. 'Open the door,' she tapped out to Jerif. 'Then I'll go inside to double-check the systems and safely shut everything down.'

Jerif scissored his antennae back and forth in assent and hooked his claw into the edge of the door. The metal cracked and then slid open. The smell of blood hit her and made her wrinkle her nose. She hoped there wasn't a corpse in the shuttle. That would be nasty to clean out. Jerif and Nalk didn't react to the odor, and not for the first time she envied the Nimon inability to smell.

She was about to step up onto the door ledge when a sound from inside the shuttle made her hesitate. The way her eye flashed told her the sound the implants translated was a living sound. Judging by the dotted squiggles in her left eye, it was something like a moan.

Disappointment filled her. If someone was alive in the shuttle, that meant they no longer had salvage rights.

Placing her foot back down on the deck, she backed away and kept her eye on the shuttle. The shuttle system she interfaced with didn't register a life form on board, but that could be easily explained away by a broken sensor or damaged relay.

Movement at her side made her look over at Jerif. He quickly tapped out a question. 'What's wrong?'

'Someone might be inside,' she explained. 'My implant picked up a sound.'

Jerif moved both antennae in an agitated wave as he tapped. 'But our sensors didn't pick up anything alive.'

She pointed to the hull of the shuttle and then explained. 'That thing is meant to planet skip. It's triple plated to put up with heavy radiation *and* the pressure of a gas giant. Unless its computer can talk to our ship, there's no way we would know if anything was alive on board. I don't think the shuttle's computer and sensors are fully functioning, so our scans thought it was empty.'

The bristles on Jerif's shoulders sagged. 'This could ruin our salvage rights.'

The law was very clear when salvage ships like Red Ore picked up anything with a sentient life on board. They had to either deliver the person to the destination of their choice, or dump them back into space in the same container they were found in. In the years Zia worked on Red Ore, she'd only seen it happen twice. The first time the captain was going to dump the Leemron back into space in a ruined lifepod. But the Leemron knew the laws and how to wheel and deal around them. She negotiated a ride to the nearest space station. The captain got to keep the lifepod and was later paid under the table by the Leemron's family—a double payout for him.

The second time didn't end as well. They picked up a Hamlershin in a broken-down ship. When the Hamlershin wouldn't play by the unspoken rules, the captain shoved him back on his broken ship and left him where they'd found him. The captain stuck a beacon on the dead ship as the law required, but it was unlikely anyone found Hamlershin before he expired from lack of breathable atmosphere.

All that boiled down to the same thing. If someone was alive on that shuttle, none of them would get any money.

Jerif shook his head at a slight angle, a sign of determination. 'We can't stand here all cycle. We need to find out. You wait here. I'll look inside.'

Thankfully, the much bigger and tougher Nimon would be the first to encounter whoever might be on board. Zia placed the fingers of each hand to her mouth and crooked them inward to imitate palps. She tapped the tips of her pretend palps together in the traditional Nimon gesture of gratitude. Jerif waved off her thanks and turned his attention to the shuttle.

Cautiously, Jerif moved his upper body into the doorway. Her left eye registered him sounding a surprised exclamation. Then another moan with dots and squiggles went green to separate it from sounds Jerif made when he huffed with effort. She watched as Jerif grabbed something and wrestled it out.

Whatever Zia expected to come out of the shuttle, it wasn't the massive alien Jerif dragged onto the deck. Whatever species this guy was, he was massive and humanoid-shaped with two arms and two legs. He was only wearing pants, so she could examine most of his body. He was covered by thick, reddish-brown skin that was naturally armored in some places. The outside of his forearms bristled with quills, and it looked like the tips of his fingers housed retractable claws. If she pulled his lips apart, she would probably find sharp teeth too.

As her gaze moved up his sharply defined, muscled torso to the armor plating of his pectoral area, shoulder and neck, she was struck by the thought that she found him handsome. He was human-looking enough to spark her interest.

Or maybe the long time since anyone had shared her bed simply made anything without antennae and palps looks darn sexy to her.

When her gaze got to his head, sympathy filled her. An old mass of scars on took up most of the space on one side of his head, and the armor plating there looked damaged and oddly shaped. Whatever caused that trauma must have been severe, like a shuttle crash or mine cave-in.

He moaned again, and Zia's heart went out to him. Even though this male meant she'd lost the salvage that would have bought new implants with money to spare, she couldn't be angry.

It was obvious he was a stubborn survivor like her. Fighters like them needed to stick together.

First thing was to wake him up and explain to him how he needed to deal with the captain or risk being put back into a nonfunctioning shuttle to wait for death.

'He's breathing,' Jerif tapped out. Disappointment made not only his bristles sag but also his antennae. Glancing over to the conveyer belt, Zia saw that no more salvage was coming on board. They'd missed out.

Dragging the front stand behind him, Nalk skidded to a halt next to Jerif. His eagerness disappeared as he stared down at the unconscious stranger. "Who is this?"

Zia didn't bother paying attention to Jerif's explanation to Nalk. Kneeling next to the massive male, she touched his shoulder. His moan registered on her implant, but his eyes didn't open. She sat back on her heels and tried to remember if she'd ever seen this species before, but kept drawing a blank.

"What is a Talin doing in a dead shuttle in the middle of this sector?"

Nalk's frustrated question piqued her interest as the word Talin scrolled across her eye. Of course she'd heard of them. Who hadn't? Their powerful species seemed to be expanding by leaps and bounds, but they were only now traveling and trading is this section of the universe.

None of that meant much here beyond the fact that this male should have enough wealth to bribe the captain into dropping him off at some place safe.

Still kneeling, she waved a hand to get Jerif's attention. 'We should get the captain and the medic.'

Jerif scissored his antennae to signal agreement when the Talin suddenly moved. Alarmed, Zia scrambled backward until she was stopped short by hard, chitlin-covered legs. Fearful, she ducked between them as the Talin moved with fluid grace into a crouched position and roared. Even if the sound didn't register on her implants, she'd know it was loud because she could feel the vibration of that roar in her chest.

Another sound came out of him that registered as some kind of percussive noise as he bared his claws. The quills on his forearms were bristled with tension, and his lips were pulled back to reveal sharp teeth.

Forget getting the captain. They needed the medic to hurry so he could sedate this guy before anyone got hurt.

The Talin looked around, taking in the Nimons surrounding him. When his intense gaze sweep in her direction, those who were standing over her shifted back suddenly to reveal her. His eyes dropped to where she knelt on the ground. As their eyes met, a thrill of fear went through her, and then without warning, he launched himself at her.

With the dangerous spiked pad of the conveyer belt on one side and the mass of Nimon legs everywhere else, she had no place to go. Curling up into a ball, she closed her eyes and hoped the impact wouldn't injure her too badly.

This was not how this day was supposed to end!

CHAPTER 2

The world dipped and swooped, but she experienced no pain. Strong arms held her tightly against a powerful chest and her left eye registered a rhythmic sound pattern as she felt the vibrations throughout her body.

When nothing further happened, she risked opening her eyes, and the first thing she saw was spikes. It took a moment for her to figure out what she was viewing because her right eye filled with the scrolling text of excited Nimon voices all jumbled together and moving too quickly to read more than bits and pieces.

"What do we do?"

"…and the captain."

"…but what about…"

"…need a big weapon…"

"No, that would hurt…"

"Maybe a sedative?"

The barbs and the rest of the Talin's forearm blocked her from seeing much beyond. He held her in a way that those deadly quills faced away so anyone who reached for her would have to contend with the wickedly sharp points jutting out.

Two sounds were coming from him now—the gentle one she could feel where her shoulder and side touched his chest, and a louder, more threatening sound that was somehow emanating from behind him. She hadn't seen a tail before, but maybe he had one and was thumping it against the deck plates.

Between the voices and the sounds, it was all too much, so she wiggled a hand free and gestured in front of her eyes to reduce the sensitivity of her implants. Now only the loudest or clearest voices would register in her right eye and only sharp, sudden, or new noises would register in her left.

With that distraction calmed, she could focus on her situation. Craning her neck up, she could see the area around them. The Talin holding her had his back to the shuttle, and he was watching all the Nimons gathered with intense eyes and teeth bared. He was acting as if under threat of attack.

What worried her was the trickle of blood coming from one of his ear holes and the slight difference in the size of his pupils. Those two things clued her in to the fact that this guy had suffered a blow to the head and probably wasn't truly aware of what was going on around him.

That he was being so gentle with her was a surprise. He cradled her to his chest like a child. Could he be mistaking her for a child of his species? Maybe Talins' young were born without natural defenses like quills or armor plating. To his unfocused gaze, she might resemble a juvenile of his species just enough to trigger a protective instinct in his damaged brain.

Right now he wasn't attacking anyone and was obviously not inclined to hurt her. That meant she had a good chance to help him. With the way he kept shaking his head as if to clear it and swaying slightly on his feet, she was going to need to advocate for this guy before the captain had him sedated and tossed back out into space in his shuttle. From what she had seen so far, she doubted the hopper even had a working atmo-generator.

Spotting Jerif, she wiggled in the Talin's grip, trying to get both hands free so she could tap to him. The Talin looked down at her, his eyes with their different-sized pupils blinking and struggling to focus. She froze, wondering what he would do. The rhythmic sound coming from behind him stopped, and he closed his mouth to cover up sharp teeth. The other sound increased along with the vibrations coming from his chest. Then, almost reverently, he set her down on the deck. When her feet hit the deck plates, he urged her to stand between him and the shuttle.

More and more, she was getting the impression he saw her as a youngster to be protected. She could work with that. Instead of letting him move her, she took one of his clawed hands in hers. The moment her smaller fingers reached around his, the claws retracted and his hand relaxed.

Because he was swaying so badly, she sank to the floor, tugging him down with her. His focus on her was so absolute that he seemed to forget they were surrounded by Nimons he'd been threatening only moments before.

When she'd started moving in the Talin's arms, all the Nimons had gone silent. They'd stayed quiet until the Talin was sitting. Now they all started talking again, and judging by the brightness of the scrolling text, she could tell they were whispering.

"Are you hurt, Zia?"

"The captain and security officer are on their way. They're bringing sedatives and weapons."

"Hold tight and we'll get you free." Because she programed his voice into her implants' limited database, Jerif's words showed up a different color than everyone else's.

Without breaking eye contact with the Talin, Zia used one hand to talk to Jerif. 'He won't hurt me, but keep everyone away.'

"He can't stay here," Jerif answered after translating what she said to the few crew members who didn't have Norka downloaded. "If he can't even talk, no way will the captain let him stay."

Zia tilted her body back a little to display confidence to the Nimon. 'I know. That's why I'm going to help him. Slide me the information square from my smaller tool tote.'

"He looks dangerous," Jerif commented as he moved. Out of the corner of her eye, she watched him dig around in her tote and find the old, battered information square. Setting it on the deck, he slid it to her. His aim was perfect, and it came to rest near her right hip. Still maintaining eye contact with the wounded Talin, she groped for it.

His gaze dropped to the information square, and she froze, waiting to see if he would react badly to the piece of tech. The next thing she knew, his muscular arms were picking her up and settling her in his lap. Startled, she went stiff, unsure what he was doing. Then he plucked up the information square and handed it to her. As she took it from his clawed hand, the vibrating sound started up again, reminding her of when her parents would hum so she could feel the pulses that sound created as they hugged her when she was a child.

She was half surprised he didn't pat her on the head.

When he dipped his head to run his cheek along her hair and the scent of vanilla filled her nose, she only half noticed because she was busy finding the appropriate blank contracts in the ship's Unibase. She named the guy Talin Male as she filled out the contract. She could call him Big Sexy Spikey Guy and the contract would still be valid because it used bio-sigs instead of names to finalize.

When she was done, she pressed a finger down on the corner of the information square to attach her bio-sig to the contract. A character showed up on the contract to denote her half was done. Now she needed the Talin's bio-sig.

She expected him to resist when she picked up one of his broad hands and separated out one clawed finger. To her surprise, not only did he not pull away, but he acted with indulgence and retracted the claws on that hand so she could press his finger to the corner of her information square and take his bio-sig.

Although like the Nimons, this species couldn't make facial expressions, she got the feeling he was bemused at her actions. After she was done with his hand and let it drop to rest on his leg, he went back to rubbing his cheek against her hair. She wasn't sure if the action was meant to soothe him or her, but she couldn't deny the smell of vanilla was pleasant and strangely comforting.

When she was finished filling out the contract, she looked up to find Jerif. She set the information square down on her lap so she could tap. 'I need you to witness the contract.'

The bristles on his shoulders waved around in agitation and he forgot all about tapping. "Contract? What contract? What are you doing?"

'If I own him, the captain can't hurt him because he granted us Crew Salvage Rights. I've drawn up a basic slave contract, and he signed it willingly. You saw him. Now all I need is for you to add your bio-sig as a witness that he is doing this of his own free will, and it will be legal.'

Now both the bristles on his shoulders and the antennae on his head were waving in extreme agitation. "If his people challenge the contract, you and I could get into big trouble."

'I'm going to set him free as soon as it's safe,' she assured him and then thought of something that would sweeten the pot. 'And we still get to sell the shuttle. It's a win-win. He gets to stay alive and we all still add to our wealth.'

"This seems unwise," Jerif grumbled even as he edged a little closer. "But you're right. It seems the best solution in a bad situation. Slide me the information square and I'll sign as a witness."

She slid the square to him. The Talin silently watched her movements. He didn't try to stop her, but he did eye Jerif warily. She was pretty sure if the Nimon tried to get any closer, the Talin would start objecting.

Jerif quickly signed the contract and slid the square back to her. Picking it up, she finalized everything and then uploaded it to both the ship's database and to her own data storage on Muki station. It would take a few days to make it through the ship's transmission queue to get sent, but once it was uploaded to Muki, she could access it from anywhere with a decent interstellar comm array. For those who spent their lives on ships, Muki was often the go-to place to store data and even physical items because their comm array was top-notch and their lock boxes had never been broken into. That's why she rented both forms of space from them.

Dropping the information square into her lap, she looked up at the Talin. He was wavering a bit, and his hand was unsteady when he tried to touch her face. This guy needed a medic.

Don't worry, she thought. *I'm going to take care of you and make sure you get back to your people.*

"What is going on here?" Zia looked up to find the captain standing next to Jerif and looking back and forth between them, his body language screaming that he was startled and concerned. Then his eyes zeroed in on the Talin. "What is your name? Who is your clan and family?" The color and size of the captain's words scrolling across her right eye told Zia the Nimon was shouting.

Not surprisingly, the Talin didn't answer. Not only did he not respond to the captain's questions, but after standing up and gently setting Zia down behind him, he faced the captain with an aggressive display of teeth and claws. Both the captain and the surrounding crew moved back. That seemed to appease the Talin because he retracted the claws on one of his hands and reached behind him to reassuringly pet her.

Right, it was up to her to defuse this situation.

Stepping a little to the side of the Talin so everyone could see her, she started tapping quickly. 'Sorry, sir. He was in the shuttle, but you don't need to concern yourself. I own him now, so the *living being* laws don't apply here.'

The captain went quiet for a bit as he thought about what she said and then spoke. "You know he's a Talin. Correct? His species are powerful and yours aren't."

No one needed to remind Zia that humans were one of the least powerful species in the universe. Reprisal from any species for making one of their own a slave was a genuine worry. But she'd get him back to his people before he figured out what happened and could get mad at her then. Now that she thought about it, keeping the contract a secret from him might be the best approach.

'Yes, sir. I know, but he entered the contract willingly and I have both his bio-sig and Jerif*'s* bio-sig as a witness.' Thank goodness the Talin had been mostly calm when she pressed his finger to the information square. Otherwise the device would've rejected his signature. Bio-sigs weren't valid if the device detected any body chemicals being released due to fear.

By the way the captain was moving his bristles, antennae, and back feet, he was feeling a combination of angry and disappointed. She was going to need to be careful since this Nimon wasn't above being petty.

Glaring at her, the captain slapped his hands together in agitation. "Fine! He's your responsibility. Be aware that as his owner, you're going to need to pay for his medical care and food. And if he causes any problems, you'll get the blame."

She was prepared for all of that but still winced. Getting the Talin cared for was going to eat into her profits. She could only hope his injuries were fixable by the tech on the ship so she wouldn't have to take him to one of the expensive medical suites on Yarnetta.

'Of course, sir. That's only fair,' she was quick to say.

But the captain wasn't done. "If he causes enough issues or damage, I could take him as payment. I have that right."

Now they were getting into questionable territory. The captain didn't have that right at all, but as a human, she had little recourse if he wanted to steal from her. 'I don't even know if he has any skills yet, Captain. He might be addle-brained and not worth feeding.'

That made the captain pause and examine the Talin more thoroughly. "Perhaps."

The Talin in question was looking back and forth between her and the captain while doing his best to stay on his feet. His enormous body swayed dangerously, and if the shuttle wasn't behind him to help prop him up, she was sure he would've already hit the deck by now.

'I'm going to take him to medical now, Captain,' she explained. 'Everyone should probably give him a wide berth until he's been seen.'

"Very well," the captain agreed and stomped off. Sighing out a breath with relief, she pushed the captain out of her mind and focused on helping Mr. Spikey.

The rest of the Nimons around them faded back to allow her plenty of room to leave the bay. Taking one of the Talin's hands in both of hers, she stepped back and tugged him after her. For the first time in her life, her deafness was a boon because it was clear this poor Talin couldn't understand anything right now. Using non-verbal communication came second nature to her, and this Talin responded well to her urgings. He remained vigilant but docile as she led him out of the bay.

The next hurdle was medical. After that, he could rest in her cabin until he was doing better. She hoped the damage to his head could be healed, otherwise she might end up with the goliath as a slave for the rest of their lives because he was way too sweet to send off to an uncertain future if he'd permanently lost his reasoning skills.

Of course, there were worse things to be saddled with. Having a sexy, gentle—to her, at least—giant at her side wouldn't be a hardship. And it wouldn't be difficult to find them both work. Heck, with him at her side, she could find them an even better-paying job on another ship. She could take care of him, and she wouldn't ever have to be alone again. They might even make enough that she could take him to visit her family.

Her family would think she'd gone crazy, but what else was new?

As she led him into medical, she found herself torn between hoping he could be cured and wishing she could keep him. In the end it wasn't up to her, thankfully, but to the medical staff and the Talin's body as to what would happen next.

CHAPTER 3

Everything hurt. Palforma was positive there wasn't a single spot on his body that wasn't screaming with at least discomfort, if not outright pain. Focusing on his human was helping, but no matter how hard he tried, he couldn't seem to make his brain work right, not that it worked well to begin with.

Historically, his clan produced soldiers and warriors, so he'd been proud to join the Talin military when he came of age. It never occurred to him to do anything else. He was a good soldier. He worked hard on his skills, obeyed his commander, and guarded those he served with as best as he could.

But after taking a round to the head on his last assignment, he'd barely survived and was never the same. He clearly remembered lying on the gray-dirt ground, his brain coming on and offline like misfiring electronics as he listened to shouting and weapons fire. He'd heard nothing but silence and then the sound of his commander, Dalt, surrendering.

But that wasn't the end. He'd been forced to remain there, unable to move or even blink as people were systematically tortured to death. Everyone but a handful of the soldiers he served with and a few of the civilians stationed there died that day in the most excruciating way possible. He could still hear the screams of those who were tortured while his trained and strong body did nothing but breathe.

He never blamed Dalt or the military that stationed them there without enough backup, but he had regrets. One of the biggest was that he survived.

Later, the healers told him he was lucky. The round cracked the plate on his head, which caused it to ricochet around his brain inside his skull instead of going right through it. He could be healed instead of dying outright. The problem was that while his body recovered, his mind didn't.

Talking was impossible at first and then very difficult. Everyone looked at the old damage to his head as they heard his stuttering speech and then dismissed him. He was a failed soldier and a disgrace. His family disowned him. To them it would've been better to have him come back a corpse rather than a stammering disappointment.

Thank the ancestors for Holian. Commandant Holian made Kalor, the colony his mother started, a safe haven for former soldiers. Scattered in the wild jungle of that planet were almost a hundred former soldiers who still trained but now felt more loyal to Holian than Talarian. Most dangerous of all, Holian's colony was a place where human-Talin couples and their hybrid children could live safely outside the laws and strict cultural taboos of the Talin homeworld.

As much as Palforma craved the soft touch and companionship of the humans at Holian's compound on Kalor Colony, none of them ever picked him. Some would spend time with him, but he could tell it was out of pity rather than any true interest.

But this little, quiet human not only wasn't scared of him, but she was willingly touching him. He didn't know where he was, who she was, or why his body hurt so badly, but he vowed to keep her safe and happy.

Someone tried to talk, but he couldn't make his throbbing brain work. Every sound caused pain to bounce around in his head.

And he didn't like all the strangers surrounding them. He recognized the insect-like species, but his mind couldn't produce a name. He wanted to growl at them and sound a threatening rattle with his back plates, but his little human didn't seem bothered by all the strangers. Taking his cue from her, he worked on keeping himself calm.

When she tugged him down to a sitting position, it was a relief to sink to the floor and rest his back against something. He noticed she wouldn't look away from him, her adorable human face focused on his. But she was trying to pick something up without looking at it and not succeeding. Wanting to make her comfortable, he put her on his lap and handed her the object. An information square perhaps? It didn't matter what it was because it made her happy to have it.

She did something with it while he emptied his scent glands into her hair. Ancestors, that felt amazing!

A strange euphoria shot through his whole body. For a moment the pain disappeared, and she became his entire world. He'd never scent-marked anyone before. On Kalor you weren't allowed to do it unless the human invited the action. But he couldn't resist with this little dark-haired human with the giant, soulful eyes. She was beautiful—more beautiful than any other human he'd met so far.

He lost himself in the scent of his bonding oil soaking into her scalp and mixing with her body chemistry to create a smell unique to the two of them. His heartbeat calmed. His skin tingled with pleasure, and despite the pain, he'd never felt more content.

When she presented him with the information square, he tried to read it but couldn't understand the jumble of symbols swimming in front of him. He hoped she didn't get upset because he couldn't respond to whatever was there. Wanting her to be happy, he didn't pull away when she took his hand in hers and pressed his finger to the tiny information square. Somewhere deep in his brain, he knew she was getting his bio-sig for something, but as long as she let him hold her, he didn't care.

When she passed the information square between her and one of the Nimons surrounding them, he didn't stop it. As long as she was content and he didn't see any overt signs of danger, she could do as she wished.

Later, he might wonder why his little human didn't talk to him. His ears were ringing and all the sounds around him were muffled, but he could still hear the Nimons talking to each other and the human. However, the human never spoke a single word. She moved her hands a lot, making her fingers dance in the air. The movement was graceful and captivating. He could watch it endlessly.

Then an important-looking Nimon showed up, acting loud and threatening. Palforma wanted to rattle the back plates that ran down his spine. He wanted to warn this Nimon to keep clear. But he didn't need to. Everyone kept their distance and his little human's dancing hands seemed to calm everyone down. Before he knew it, the Nimons cleared a path as she took his hand in hers and led him away from the shuttle.

Walking was almost his undoing. The euphoria vanished and agony engulfed him again. It was all he could do to keep pace behind his little human with the short black hair and soft manners.

He recognized the smell of the room the moment they entered. It was some kind of medical suite. Worry pushed some of the pain aside. Was his little human sick?

When they stopped in front of an exam table, he pulled his hand free of hers so he could carefully lift her onto it. Then he crawled on as well when she grabbed his hand again and kept tugging.

He had to admit, it was a relief to lie down. She tried to slide off the table, but he wrapped his arms around her and drew her to his side so they were both lying stretched out. As long as he kept her tucked up against him, they both fit. Having him here holding her should keep her from getting scared of the medics. A lot of the humans on Kalor didn't like to go to the infirmary, so maybe this human was the same.

Ancestors, he wished his brain would start working and not hurt so much.

A Nimon approached but he couldn't make out the thing's comments at first. Nimon was one of the thousands of languages programmed into his INT, but his brain felt swollen inside his skull.

"…remain calm. Zia won't leave you, but you need to stay still so I can assess and treat you."

Zia? Was that his little human's name? He put all his effort into giving the name a try. "Z-z-zia."

He couldn't hear his whispered voice over the ringing in his ears, but the human snuggled up against him jerked a little in response. Yes, that must be her name. Happiness flooded him to know her name even if uttering that single syllable made his body seize with pain. Closing his eyes, he concentrated on staying conscious.

"Open your mouth please, Talin," the hovering Nimon demanded. Why did this Nimon need him to open his mouth? Shouldn't he be paying attention to Zia? That thought got derailed when Zia reached up and pried his mouth open with her little fingers. Oh, she wanted his mouth open, and the Nimon was helping her explain. Could Zia not talk? Oh well, that made two of them.

He opened his mouth for her and felt a medical wafer slip between his lips. It dissolved on his tongue and the pain in his body eased, making him feel a little boneless. Closing his eyes, he concentrated on the feel of Zia against his side while he listened to the sounds of the medic moving around and medical equipment being turned on and off. When the Nimon talked, he ignored the words because it was such a struggle to understand.

Zia sat up and got to her knees next to him. Lazily he opened his eyes to watch her place a medical device against his head and hold it steady, her face tense with concentration. A Nimon beyond his field of vision was talking to her. The thing turned on and vibrated slightly. Not long after that, the pressure in his head eased. Instead of his brain feeling three sizes too big for his skull, now it only felt one size too big.

The Nimon talked some more and Zia moved the device to activate it again. Every time she did that, he felt a little better. By the time she handed the device back to the Nimon, all Palforma wanted to do was sleep. The pain was only a dull ache now, and his body craved rest more than anything else.

To his disappointment, Zia wasn't ready to let him sleep yet. Climbing off the table, she tugged at him until he reluctantly got to his feet.

"N-n-need re-re-rest," he stuttered out. Zia petted the back of his hand, her face kind even as she continued to insist he walk. Nimons were everywhere, watching them as they walked by. Palforma tried to keep himself from rattling with displeasure at their stares, but it was hard as their giant, domed eyes followed his progress, bright and unblinking.

When Zia led him into a small chamber, it took him a moment to realize it was her quarters. It was nice that she had a room of her own, but the poor state of her accommodations was horrifying.

The room was so tiny that the fold-down bunk took up almost half the space. Even worse, he didn't see a single plush, comfy pillow or soft blanket. Everyone knew human skin was delicate, and they needed soft things for their bedding. How his little human must suffer during her rest cycles!

The room was also nothing but dull colors, everything old and worn. Poor Zia was being neglected. But that was common with wild humans because no one appreciated or took care of them as the Talins did.

Fatigue was dragging at him. Giving up examining the room he collapsed on the bunk. Zia tried to pull her thin blanket over him, but he stopped her efforts by pulling her into the bunk with him. She only fit because he draped her much-smaller body across his. He tugged the pathetic blanket over the both of them, confident his body would keep her warm as they rested.

With a contented rumble, he closed his eyes and let his exhausted brain slide into unconsciousness.

CHAPTER 4

Zia contemplated the Talin under her. When he'd pulled her down on top of him, she hadn't fought and found that he made a pleasant addition to her bunk. He sure was nice and toasty warm and she even felt herself drifting off as she snuggled against him. He was already showing signs of improvement, so she had hope that he would regain his intellect.

But still, there was something about him she hoped didn't go away as he healed. Something primitive and protective that made her feel safe and cherished.

Her mom once told her about these scary animals back on Old Earth called pit bulls. According to Mom, humans would train these fierce animals to fight other animals or to guard people and property back on Old Earth. Yet, despite their ferocity, the beasts were gentle and loving to the human owner who treated them well. Her Talin reminded her of a pit bull. Tough, terrifying, and potently vicious to everyone else, but gentle and biddable with her.

To be entirely honest, she felt more than a simple obligation toward this Talin. He'd done nothing but try to protect her so far, and he'd turned out to be a wonderful snuggler. Even now, his muscular arm was draped over her back, and his chest was vibrating under her.

Occasionally, he would jerk a little and then move his head to rub his cheek on top of her head. The smell of vanilla would fill the air and he'd settled back down. She wasn't even sure he woke up during the process. And even when he twitched, his hand never tightened on her and his hold remained gentle.

The guy's body might be designed for battle, but he sure knew how to be tender.

The alarm on the small information square tucked in the left leg pocket of her coveralls vibrated to tell her an assignment had been posted to her work queue. The Talin didn't move as she pulled it out to see how urgent the task was. Too bad it turned out to be about the thrust manager on engine two. Anything less vital could have been ignored for a little longer, but steering was rather important on a ship.

It took effort to wiggle out of the guy's hold, but in then end she shoved a few lumpy pillows under his arm.

"N-no leave. No go. S-s-s-stay," he mumbled. "S-s-stay with P-p-palforma."

Palforma. She liked it. It was a strong name. A good name for her spikey giant.

She leaned over and nuzzled the top of his head. That seemed to calm him, and he fell back to sleep. Despite the urgency of the task, she gave herself a moment to study him.

After treatment in medical, he moved better and his pupils started tracking. They even matched in size now. The medic had assured her that his head would heal, but they didn't know what kind of long-term damage he'd sustained. Only time would tell.

When he tried to talk, it was obviously difficult, bordering on impossible. If it turned out he lost that ability, he could always use Norka like her. Not being able to verbalize wasn't as bad as many thought. She got along just fine after all!

The plan was still to return him to his people, but a small part of her wished she didn't have to. On top of her reluctance to be parted from him, she worried. What if, like many other species, Talin civilization wasn't very forgiving of someone with impairments? If it turned out he had reduced mental capacity, his people might not welcome him back. They might even cast him aside if they no longer found him useful.

No! No one was going to throw her Gentle Giant away!

Right then and there, she decided she had a second goal—to take care of Mr. Spikey if it looked like he was going to be abused or neglected.

If it turned out his people didn't want him, she wanted him. In fact, she owned him. She could keep him if she wanted to. She had the paperwork to prove it.

At that moment, she realized how lonely she was. It wasn't just about protecting this Talin. It was also about having a companion. She'd spent three years on this ship without even a close friend and two years on another ship before that. She hadn't been back to see her family in five years and hadn't seen another human in four years.

Hadn't been touched or held in over a year and that had been nothing more than two individuals looking for a little relief.

And now she was ready to make this poor guy into a slave for real. Shame washed through her.

The information square in her hand vibrated again, bringing her out of her thoughts. A quick glance at the message made it clear that her supervisor was anxious. Because he knew nothing about repair, he was always anxious until she explained to him that the malfunction wasn't a big deal, and she could fix it. On the plus side, his anxiety meant he listened to her when she told him something couldn't be fixed and needed to be replaced instead. She liked that aspect most about working on Red Ore.

The third notice buzzed as she grabbed one of the tool totes Jerif dropped off while she was in medical and hurried out. Normally she wouldn't bother jogging through the ship on her way to fix something, but now that she had a cuddly Talin waiting, she found herself in a big hurry to get her work done and get back to her cabin.

"That's really all you needed to do?" Manto asked the moment she emerged from the crawl space behind engine two's port side.

Getting to her feet, she tilted her body back in a sign of confidence and worked hard on not nodding her head. Head nods were used to signal hunger to Nimons. For the first month of working here, everyone thought she was always hungry until she trained herself to stop nodding "yes."

'The thrust manager wasn't broken,' she explained. 'But the retrusion manifold is getting old. I would suggest replacing it.'

Manto rubbed and tugged at one of his antennae, a sign of anxiety. "I'll tell Captain. Do you think it will hold out until we reach Yarnetta?"

Poor Manto was in charge of all the non-scrapyard staff, so he had to deal with all kinds of issues—from food storage and prep to engine maintenance. Some days he was so anxious she was sure an antenna might fall off from too much tugging.

'It will last,' she tapped out and kept her body language strong as she moved her fingers. Her confidence helped Manto relax. 'I'm probably being overly cautious, but I've seen retrusion manifolds fail before and it can become deadly fast.'

"No, you're absolutely correct. It's better to act well within safety margins. You're a competent human, Zia. I know I can trust your judgment."

She fought the smile that wanted to form from his praise. Nimons, like most species, saw the show of teeth as a threat display. It was one of the hardest natural impulses she had to learn to curb after she left the human colony she grew up on.

She arched her back and shrugged her shoulders to display happiness as she tapped out her response. 'You're not one to say such things lightly. Thank you for the generous compliment.'

Because Manto was always busy, she expected him to rush off. But he stood there, and the way he started tugging at his antenna again made her curious. Instead of reaching for her tool tote, she regarded him steadily. 'Do you have more questions for me?'

After a moment of hesitation, Manto spoke. "You have the wounded Talin in your quarters. Correct? I heard you own him now."

'That's all true,' she agreed, wondering where this was going. Nimons were a slave-owning species, so he probably wasn't about to object to the change of the Talin's status from free to slave. For the life of her, she couldn't think of what else he might be concerned about.

"You should know some things if you plan to keep him," Manto continued. "You probably haven't dealt with Talins before. They are new to this sector, and because of what we do here on Red Ore, we wouldn't come in contact with them even if they were more prevalent. I don't think any of their kind are kept as slaves anywhere. There could be reprisals against you if word gets back to Talin authorities."

'If that's your worry, you can relax. I plan to set him free. I wasn't going to keep him as a slave, but you know how the captain is about the Living Being Salvage Laws. If he stays with me, it will be of his own free will.' She paused for a second, worried that her crewmates might judge her harshly. 'You know I only made him sign the slave contract to save him. Right?'

"The entire crew knows what you did was to save his life," Manto assured her. "And I'm glad you will set him free soon. Talins are a dangerous group to interact with. The important thing is that you never go onto a Talin-controlled station or colony. It isn't safe."

That surprised her. 'It isn't safe specifically for humans or for anyone who isn't a Talin?'

"Humans!" Manto burst out. "Talins are a slave-owning species, but the only slaves they keep are human ones. I heard a human named Tani got kidnapped off the station he was working on. No one ever saw him again. But at the same time he disappeared, a Talin ship was docked there. I assure you, that's not a coincidence."

It actually sounded like a coincidence to her. There weren't that many human slaves out there. Because humans were so small and considered weak and self-destructive, they weren't seen as valuable enough to own. Besides, only a few hundred thousand humans were left scattered in small groups across the galaxy. It wouldn't be financially advantageous to specifically hunt down only humans to use as slaves.

Manto probably had heard rumors and expounded from there, but she wouldn't argue with the Nimon when he was only trying to look after her. Besides, if Talins were a slave-owning culture, she should steer clear of their stations and planets out of principle. Nothing was easier to enslave than someone with no viable government or political power.

'I'll see if I can get him home from Yarnetta.' Even as the words left her mouth, she hated that idea. Sending him off from Yarnetta would mean that within a few days she'd say goodbye and never see him again.

"That would probably be wise," Manto agreed, even as she was already thinking of an alternate plan that would give her more days with the Talin. Maybe she'd even have enough time to convince him to stick with her.

They would be docked on Yarnetta for at least eight days, which would be enough time to accompany him to a transport hub with a Talin contingent. That would allow her to assess how they would treat him and allow her ample opportunity to make sure she and the Talin would get along in the long term. If his people were unkind at all, she'd be ready to convince him to return to Yarnetta with her.

The closest major transport hub was a station controlled by the Delorta, so she'd be safe from being kidnapped by any Talins if what Manto was saying had any truth to it.

She grimaced as she thought about how cold the Delorta liked to keep their stations. It wouldn't be a pleasant trip, but at least she wouldn't need to put herself in danger. Not only did the Delorta abhor slavery, but they actively fought against it. A few of their colonies were even safe havens for runaway slaves escaping deportation. It was a sound plan for both her and Palforma.

"Before you go, I wanted to ask you about…"

Her information square vibrated in her pocket, distracting her from whatever Manto was going to say. Concerned filled her as she pulled it out because it was rare for anyone but Manto to contact her. When she saw the single line of text written in common, she dashed out of the room without even saying goodbye to Manto.

Rule 55 being broken in crew cabin 29/8.

Rule 55 had to do with willful destruction of ship property and was most commonly used when a few Nimons had too much to drink and got into a fight. But cabin 29/8 was hers, so the only explanation would be that the Talin had woken up and was upset to find her gone.

When she rounded a corner, she skidded to a halt. The corridor outside her room was full of heavily armored Nimons, all of them silently staring at her door. As she moved her eyes to the closed hatch, she watched as a bulge appeared at the same time her left eye registered a loud banging noise coming from the same direction. Her Talin was beating the hell out of the door.

At that point it hit her that her door was locked and keyed only to her. She never keyed it to the Talin so he could open the door. She'd accidentally trapped him in there and probably caused him to panic.

Hurrying forward, she touched the arm of Kifer, a Nimon she knew was fluent in Norka. 'He's probably confused. If all of you will back away, I'll open the door and calm him down.'

Kifer's body language clearly told her he was worried. He spoke out loud instead of setting down his weapons so he could tap. "I don't think that's a good idea." He gestured to the door. "If he can do that to a standard hatch, he could kill you with one blow."

The energy weapons Kifer and his fellow Nimons were carrying weren't normally deadly, but if all of them fired on the Talin at once, they could kill him. None of these Nimons were soldiers or even professionally trained guards. They were all paid a little extra to be ready if the ship was ever attacked. It was likely that even if the Talin did back down, they might start shooting anyway.

'It's my choice to try,' she argued. 'He's my property. That means you have to let me go first.'

Kifer knew he couldn't dispute that, so he didn't even try. Even as he gestured the other Nimons to move far back, he stayed. Once they were all too far to hear, he leaned over and handed her a Single-Use Personal Defense Weapon, colloquially known as a punch-stick.

"I'm going to report this missing," he told her as he thrust it into her hand. "Even if you're able to talk him down now, there might be a point in the future you need this. If anything goes wrong, don't even think about it. Just use it."

Zia didn't refuse the generous offer. The punch-stick looked like a short length of narrow pipe and was small enough to fit easily into her hand. It was a single use weapon with a slight point on one end and a flat cap on the other. All the user needed to do was press the tip against an attacker and then press the other end to deliver a small but powerful explosive round. The problem was if you didn't press hard enough, the thing didn't go off. That meant users often stabbed it into their opponent and then slammed their other hand down on the back, ensuring that the round would be set off, hence the slang name punch-stick for the weapons.

Fisting the punch-stick in one hand, she tapped a simple response with the other. 'I won't hesitate.'

With that assurance, Kifer backed away to join the other Nimons. The entire time they had talked, the Talin had continued to batter the door. She wasn't sure it would even slide all the way open now. Replacing that door would be her responsibility and would probably use up her entire next paycheck. But she felt so guilty about locking the guy in and causing this much distress that she didn't wince at the loss of funds. Served her right for not thinking about that before she left the cabin.

Touching the display next to the door, her left eye registered the beep of the door unlocking at the same time the pounding stopped. The hatch struggled to open and got halfway before freezing up. At first she thought she would slide through the half-open door, but then Palforma was there, squeezing his massive body partially through and reaching out for her.

Grabbing hold of her sleeve, he dragged her inside the room. Without a pause, he wrapped her up in his muscular arms and lifted her high in the air, hugging her to him, his chest vibrating strongly. Fearful that she would accidentally hurt him, she tucked the punch-stick into a pocket on the sleeve of her coverall and then wrapped her arms around his neck. Because her feet were dangling in the air, she wrapped her legs around his waist for good measure.

Much like a mother might do for a child, he started swaying back and forth a little as he held her. Giving herself this moment to enjoy such unguarded affection, she relaxed into his hold. When he started rubbing his cheek against the top of her head and vanilla filled her nose, a sigh escaped her.

She wasn't sure how long they remained like that, but when she felt him tense, she looked up to find a few Nimon faces peering in through the partially open door.

Her left eye registered a loud rhythmic sound at the same time Palforma set her down and pushed her behind him. Concerned dialogue from the Nimons scrolled across her right eye as she moved out from behind Palforma so they could see her tapping.

'It's fine. He's calm now.'

"I'm going to need to report this to the captain," Kifer warned her as he urged the other Nimons to leave. Palforma tried to step in front of her again, but her gentle touch kept him at her side instead. His teeth were still bared at Kifer, but the loud, rhythmic rattling sound had stopped.

'I know,' she said and then moved her hands up to her head and used her first fingers to mimic antennae, waving them in little circles to denote apology. 'I'm sorry for all of this and tell the captain I know he'll have to take the damages out of my pay.'

"Be safe. I'll tell everyone to steer clear of you and this Talin," Kifer offered.

'That would be for the best,' she agreed.

With a wave of antennae and a worried wiggle of his shoulder bristles, Kifer left, and no more sound registered in the hall. Her cabin was the last in the row, so no one bothered coming down this far unless they were specifically seeking her out.

With the last Nimon gone, Palforma relaxed slightly. He stroked a gentle hand down her arm and then tugged lightly on her sleeve, as if requesting something. Looking up into his face, she examined his eyes, noting that they looked clear and were tracking well. But even with this improvement, she could tell that his bout of panic and the assault on the door had taken a toll.

He was till tugging at her sleeve and it took her a moment to realize he was urging her to follow him back to the bed. He needed to lie down and was telling her to join him. She wasn't opposed to the idea but wanted the door shut first. She couldn't imagine any of the crew coming near her cabin, but she still didn't like that anyone could look through the half-open hatch.

She pulled his hand free of her sleeve and then held it in hers to lead him to the door. She placed a palm on the door and pretended to push it closed. He understood immediately and reached out to sink his claws into the tortured metal. With a casual strength Zia could only admire, he slammed the damaged door shut. Her left eye registered the locking mechanism whirring, trying to engage, but the door was too warped. It gave up after several attempts.

Not caring that the door wouldn't lock, Zia led Palforma back to the bed. The large male eagerly crawled onto her bunk and tugged her in with him. As she lay on her side, he curled his warm, muscled body around hers and wrapped one arm around her waist. His hold was firm, but not tight and his breathing quickly evened out, telling her he'd dropped back into slumber.

Closing her eyes, she relaxed in his arms with a smile on her face.

CHAPTER 5

When Palforma woke up next, his head felt like a new Talin. Thinking didn't hurt, and the earlier agony was nothing but a shadow. Looking around, he took in the small room that had quickly become familiar. Next to him, Zia slept peacefully, hugging one of his arms to her chest. Guilt hit him as he noticed that her clothing was stained and rumpled, and she had splotches of dirt on her face and hands. He'd been so possessive and insistent that she rest with him that he hadn't even let her use the cleansing unit. Had she eaten recently? His little human could be starving right now and it would be his fault.

But she hadn't fought him during any of it. In fact, she was remarkably calm when he'd unceremoniously pulled her through the half open cabin door, despite the way he was rattling with rage and had tried to pound the door open with his bare fists. She had even settled down with him in the bed so he could rest.

With his brain working, he realized what had transpired. No longer suffering from debilitating pain, he could see all the ways she cared for him. She had led him to the infirmary and helped the medics assess and treat him. Then she took him back to her own room so he could lie on her bed and recover.

She even risked her life to come into the room while he raged at the door trying to get out when the display wouldn't unlock at his touch. Armed crewmates probably stood in the hall, ready to disable or kill him. They might have even warned her not to enter the room, that he would kill her.

Yet here she was, lying next to him, asleep and trusting.

He would never hurt her, but she couldn't have known that. To all of them on this ship, he probably seemed like a raging, violent beast without access to reasoning or communication skills. He knew without Zia's intervention, he would have died either on the platform with the shuttle or later in this room.

She probably even had to take on extra burdens in order to care for him, either financially or contractually, with the ship. No way would they let someone just stay as a passenger. He didn't know for sure what they would have done to him, but it was unlikely they would have taken such good care of him if not for Zia.

Despite the trauma to his head, he remembered how he ended up on this ship all too clearly. On a mission to pass misleading information to the more militant members of a Talin political faction, he and a human named Nalia ended up captured. He was knocked out during the preceding fight, but when he came to, he was on board a barely functioning ship, and Nalia was under attack.

Between the two of them, they disabled the attackers, but by the time they'd accomplished that, the ship was disintegrating around them. Carrying Nalia, he sprinted down corridor after corridor, desperate to find the small human an escape pod. Despite his injuries, he stuffed her in the last one and held off the Talins who wanted to take it long enough for her to launch.

Dead Talins lay all around him and the ship was coming apart when he remembered an old shuttle he'd seen in the bay as he'd been dragged through it, half conscious. He made it there in time, and his large frame and muscle mass meant he could push the shuttle into position.

Although the engines didn't work, explosive decompression of the bay had launched the tiny shuttle into space and away from the dying ship. The shuttle held strong under the blast wave produced when the ship exploded, but Palforma's battered body shut down. The next thing he knew he was waking up confused, disoriented, and in severe pain, lying on deck plating next to that same shuttle and surrounded by strangers.

When he spotted the little human looking up at him with such fear, he reacted instinctually. *Grab her. Stand with his back to the shuttle. Defend. Keep her safe.*

But now he could see he was trying to keep her safe from her own crew. No one was going to hurt her, and the fear on her face was probably put there by him in the first place. She'd probably never even seen a Talin before, so the sight and sound of him must have been startling at least. Maybe even downright terrifying.

That made her kindness toward him even more significant. He wanted to reward her so badly. Shower her with trinkets and delights. Buy her soft clothes and bedding. Wrap her up in a plush, self-heating omnie. Feed her all kinds of things the humans enjoyed eating under Commandant Holian's care on Kalor Colony.

What if this was only the beginning? What if he could convince her to stay with him?

Other Talins might think nothing of simply kidnapping her, putting her in a collar, and expecting her to learn to be a pet. But Palforma knew too much about humans to do such a thing. Forcing a human would only lead to disaster.

But humans could be seduced. They could be wooed, and if done correctly, they would come to love their Talin as deeply and fiercely as they could love a human partner. He'd seen that happen but never dreamed he'd have the opportunity himself. However, in the midst of disaster, he'd found her.

What would his next step be? Maybe he could talk her into going back to Kalor with him. His home was modest but nice, far nicer than her cold room here on this ship. And he had funds he never touched.

Most of the ex-soldiers who lived on Kalor had wealth they never bothered using. Between the jungles and Holian, they didn't need to buy much. And every single one of them hoped to have a human of their own one day to spoil. On Kalor, the humans might wear the collars of pets, but they picked the Talin they wanted.

Between his size and stuttering speech, most of the humans were wary of him if not outright afraid. But not Zia. She confidently took him in hand. She'd trusted him not to hurt her. She'd fearlessly sat in his lap next to his shuttle, guided him to medical, and finally led him to her room. Without hesitation, his hurting and broken brain had immediately started bonding with her.

The evidence of his bonding was thick in the air around them. Looking at her head, he could see that her hair was saturated, so he must have emptied the scent glands in both cheeks. She couldn't know the significance of it, but the sight and smell filled him with satisfaction.

The scent glands in his cheeks had long since refilled and now ached. Moving his face close, he rubbed them on her head, letting more of his bonding oil soak into her hair. She huffed out a breath and rolled onto her back. Opening her eyes, she blinked up at him.

She didn't speak but gazed at him with luminous gray eyes that looked startlingly bright compared to her dark skin. Her short-cropped black hair was shiny from his bonding oil, and her generous lips were curved up in a slight smile, but he could tell she was being careful not to show any teeth. Although he was used to the human habit of smiling, he didn't blame her for being cautious. Not even some Talins reacted well to a human smile that showed teeth.

"Hello." He was proud he got that word out without a single stutter. Of course, it was only one word, and they were going to need to have whole conversations. That felt like a daunting task.

To his surprise, she didn't answer him. Sitting up, she started patting at her clothing, a little frown making her brow wrinkle. Leaning forward, she searched the room with her eyes, her expression becoming even more severe as she took in the chaos he had created. Shame filled him as he followed her gaze, seeing the destruction he wrought while panicked.

"Much sorry," he stated. "Can replace. Replace b-b-broken things. Add things. Nice things. Many things. No mad. No angry. Replace all."

She turned her gaze to him, her expression concerned. She still said nothing, but she leaned over so she could peer into one eye and then the other. He was confused for a moment but then realized she might think his poor speech pattern was because of a still-healing injury. He hated to tell her the truth, but she would figure it out soon enough.

"No talk. Not good t-t-talk. T-t-t-talker. T-t-talking." That level of stuttering was new and only added to his shame. He tried again, hoping to do a little better.

"Could t-t-talk. But no. Hard no. H-h-h-hard now. T-t-t-talk hard." Embarrassment was making it even more difficult to get the words out. Giving up, he clamped his mouth shut and waited for her rejection.

To his surprise, her expression didn't turn to disgust. Her concern gave way to a gentle smile, and she gave him a pat on his chest. Stunned by the touch, he watched in silence as she wiggled out of the bed and searched the mess of her room. She unearthed an old battered information square and brought it back to the bed.

He sat up as she crawled back on the bed and sat next to him with her legs crossed. Once seated, she activated the square and started typing with her nimble little fingers. When she was done, she handed the square to him.

Written on the screen in Common was a simple message that floored him. *Don't worry. I don't talk at all. And I can't hear either, so you're doing better than me.*

When he looked up at her, she was smiling as broadly as she could without showing teeth. He automatically sounded a questioning rattle, even though he realized as he did that not only couldn't she hear it, but even if she wasn't deaf, she wouldn't know how to interpret it. Actually, now that he thought about it, how had she heard his poor stumbling words to begin with?

She didn't miss a beat, though. He wasn't sure how, but it seemed she already knew what he was thinking because she plucked the square from his hands and typed some more before pushing it back at him.

I have implants connected to a modified INT so words scroll across my right eye and dots and dashes tell me there is sound in my left eye. We can keep communicating like this, or I can take you to medical so you can get the silent tapping language of the Norka programmed into your INT. Whatever affects your speech might not interfere with your hands speaking for you instead of your mouth.

Although he was quick to read what she wrote, it took him longer to comprehend the information. The first thought that hit him was that if she had been born among the Talin, she probably wouldn't be deaf. Talin medical technology could fix almost anything that could go awry in humans.

The next thing that occurred to him was how smart Zia must be. It would be hard enough for a human with no deficits to make a living out in an unforgiving universe. But not only had Zia found herself a job, she had one that allowed her a private room and enough influence that the captain and crew allowed her to keep an unruly Talin in her private quarters.

Finally, he realized he desperately wanted to "talk" to Zia in any way that would make her comfortable, and if having a language painlessly downloaded into his INT would do that, he was more than eager.

"P-p-push in… make in…put in my brain. The language. Put in. Yes!"

CHAPTER 6

Far from his faltering speech annoying or frustrating her, he could tell that his enthusiasm delighted her. She got out of the bed and grabbed his hand to tug him to his feet and then led him to the beaten door. Before she could even put a hand on it, he sank in his claws and forced it open.

As she stepped through, he tried to stutter out an apology, but she did some kind of complicated gesture with one hand so he stopped. Her fingers looked so graceful when she moved them. It must be the Norka language she was talking about, but it made her hand look like it was dancing.

She let him keep his hand twined with hers as she walked them down several corridors. They encountered very little activity, and the few Nimons they did run across ducked away quickly. Still, he kept his focus broad, ready to defend if anyone attacked them. He couldn't help it. He'd spent too many years first training and then at war to simply relax.

Living on Kalor hadn't helped. Although according to government records he was retired, he and the other ex-soldiers living on Kalor all kept up their combat training. It had come in handy last year when their colony was invaded and Holian was taken as prisoner. Dalt's human, Lakin, got aboard the ship holding Holian. Palforma and Dalt had followed her, finding a different way on board. Being physically fit and ready for battle had been a boon to both of them when it came time to fight.

His alertness was unnecessary. No one jumped out at them as she led him into the infirmary. Only one Nimon medic was inside, and he was doing something on a large information square propped up on a table. Zia dropped his hand so she could make her fingers dance when the medic looked up.

"I can do that, but will he let me approach him?" the medic responded after she finished. The Nimon's eyes slid to him, and Palforma could tell he was intimidated.

She tapped rapidly, and whatever she told him made him relax a little. "That would work. Have him sit over there and I'll give you the equipment."

Palforma tamped down his annoyance at the fact that the Nimon wasn't speaking to him directly. He reminded himself that these Nimons didn't get the best first or second impression from him. At least he wasn't in chains locked up in a brig or empty cargo bay. Without Zia to intercede, that probably would have been his fate. Or even worse, shoved out an airlock or killed with energy weapons.

Obediently, he sat where Zia pointed, but when she tried to move away from him, he snaked out an arm to grab her hand back. Her expression seemed startled for a moment, but then it settled back into a closed lipped grin. She didn't fight his hold, instead stretching her other arm out to the Nimon who was staying as far away from the two of them as he could get. Extending his own arm as far as it would go, the medic handed her the transfer puck and then hurried away to stand by a wall display at the other end of the room.

Moving up to stand next to him, she looked over to the Nimon with a questioning expression.

"Press it against the skin about three bristle lengths up from his earhole," the Nimon told her. Palforma didn't know what a "bristle length" was, but Zia must have because she confidently pressed the puck against his thick skin. While she held it there, she never let go of his hand and even moved her thumb back and forth in a soothing motion.

"Do you only want the basic Norka program or the advanced with all the slang and nuances?" the medic asked as he pressed a few things on the display.

"All," Palforma stated before Zia could wiggle her hand free to tap at the medic. "All tap. Put all in my head. M-m-make m-my hands dance. Dance like she. Hers. Z-z-zia."

The medic eyed him with pity at his halting speech, and the combination of embarrassment and humiliation made his heartbeat speed up. No matter how many times others displayed pity toward him, he'd never learned to brush it aside. It was bad enough when those he served with would rumble out sounds of disappointment at his state, but when his own parents deemed him a failure and dismissed him, he was devastated. Although he could have found solace with other families in his clan, he ran away to Kalor to live among men who understood what it meant to sacrifice and live with the consequences.

Without the ability to easily convey his thoughts with words, he'd turned introspective during his years on Kalor. He learned to be observant and, despite his large size, learned to be far stealthier than most of his fellow soldiers.

But none of that mattered as yet another person looked at him with pity.

Suddenly Zia was in his face, her expression fierce. Without letting the puck move or letting go of his hand, she brought her forehead to his and gently knocked her head into him. Then she lifted her face and kissed the spot she'd bumped. He wasn't sure, but he thought she was trying to tell him to pay attention to her. That her opinion was the only one that mattered.

He could do that. He could make her his world.

"Right, I'll upload all of it into his INT. Everyone, hold still until I'm done," the medic warned. Zia turned her head and rested her cheek against the top of his head. He realized her action was a very Talin thing to do. But she didn't have scent glands, so she didn't rub back and forth to release oil. Even so, it felt like she was shielding him from the world as best she could.

The puck vibrated and grew warm against his skin. He wanted to rumble out a pleased or soothing sound as they stood so close, but he worried he might startle her. Although she wouldn't be able to hear his rumble, he knew she'd feel the vibrations emanating from the soundbox in his chest.

The skin under the puck tingled and he could feel the familiar moment of vertigo as information was processed in the INT. It only lasted a split second and then new impulses were pushing him to move his hands.

"That's it," the medic announced. "After he stands up, you can put the puck on the chair and leave."

Her hand holding the puck dropped away from his head as she straightened up. He hurried to stand so she could drop the puck on the chair. Letting go of his hand, she raised her own and made her fingers dance. But this time it was more than random gestures. Words registered in his brain, making him rumble with delight.

'How do you feel?'

Bringing up his large hands, he stared at them for a moment, thinking about the words he wanted to say. Often, hearing a language through the INT was a lot easier than speaking it and most didn't bother. They spoke their own language and let the other person's INT do the job. But it was important to him to try "speaking" this new language.

At first his hands did nothing, and he despaired. Would his brain not let him talk with his hands? Then movement came to him, hesitant but there. 'Is this…correct?'

She was quick to answer him. 'Yes! That's it exactly. Try some more. And tell me if I use a word you don't understand. Some of my gestures are from when I spoke with my parents growing up, and they don't exist in Norka. Occasionally I forget and mix them together.'

'I understood all of that,' Palforma replied, gaining confidence. 'You're the most beautiful thing I've ever seen.' The words flowed from his hands as easy as speech used to come from his mouth. Astounded and excited, he continued. 'This is brilliant. You're brilliant. You saved me. You kept me safe. And now you've given me the ability to talk again.'

Unable to contain his emotions, he snatched her up in a hug. He was sounding a rumble of affection so loudly they could probably hear it in the next room. He heard a huffing sound.

When he let her slide to her feet and they parted, he realized the huffing sound was her version of a laugh.

She was so happy she forgot to keep her teeth hidden when she smiled. 'You're picking it up faster than most. Usually it takes a few days for the program to completely integrate.'

He waved off her compliment for more important matters. 'I'm used to learning things quickly. Are you hungry? Have you eaten this rotation? You shouldn't skip meals. Humans don't do well when they skip meals.'

'Yeah, I'm hungry. And you're probably starving. Let's go hit the galley and see what's there. I hope you like Nimon food. That's all they offer here. Only three of us on the crew are non-Nimons. That means if we want anything special to eat, we have to buy it ourselves and store it in our room.'

She looked healthy enough, so Nimon food must be suitable for human digestion, but she probably didn't like it much. He knew from hearing others talk that the humans on Kalor all had very specific things they liked to eat, and a few items were almost universally adored.

He wanted to introduce her to all the tasty things he could offer her back on Kalor, but that would have to wait. He didn't have his Identification Cube, or any means to pay for anything, including passage to Kalor or time on an interstellar comm array. Until he could access his funds or contact someone from back home, he would have to rely on Zia.

But all those worries faded away as his little human took his hand and led him out of the infirmary. He might be a stranded Talin far from home, but he was the luckiest damn Talin ever born. He's stumbled upon a human who not only appeared to like him but gave him the gift of talking. He would have never thought to be so fortunate in his wildest dreams.

He would willingly follow her anywhere.

CHAPTER 7

It was satisfying to watch Palforma wolf down his food. Although the portions in the galley were generous, Zia was never tempted to overeat. The Nimons only cooked a few types of food, so her choices were always limited. After working on Red Ore for a few years, she had long since gotten sick and tired of eating the same fare twice a day. She always picked up snacks and stashed them in her cabin, but those had run out a week ago and she needed to restock.

Palforma must have been ravenous because he consumed three plates full of food, both cooked and uncooked. He didn't even pause when he got to the dish that was allowed to partially rot before being prepared. The smell alone made her nose wrinkle, but it didn't bother Palforma at all. Either Talins were a lot less sensitive than humans or this guy was a particularly adventurous eater.

Either way, she watched him plow through the food at a record pace. Impressed, she sat back with her steaming cup of

Delorta sweet tea and watched him eat. She'd never felt responsible for someone before, and being able to provide him with food made her feel all kinds of happy.

The galley was empty except for one Nimon asleep in the far corner. Nimons ate one meal a day and often slept while they digested. If they weren't careful, they'd end up falling asleep at the table. She had helped her fair share of crewmates to their cabins over the years as they struggled to stay awake after indulging in too large a meal because they had a good haul.

Some species drank alcohol to celebrate; Nimons overate.

She was eager for Palforma to finish eating so she could start asking questions about how he ended up in that damaged shuttle with such terrible injuries. And what caused him to struggle with speaking so much before the shuttle?

But she also couldn't wait to offer him a partnership with her. To travel and take jobs together. The thought of no longer being alone was so tantalizing that it was a fight to keep sipping her tea and not interrupt Palforma's meal.

She smiled into her cup as she remembered how adorable Palforma had been when he started tapping. He reminded her of a big kid, excited and full of delight. It all made her even more impatient to get him to agree to stay with her.

Palforma had finished his last plate of food when Jerif walked in. He hurried to her but stopped a respectful distance away from the table, eyeing Palforma warily. Setting down her tea, she waved a hand to get her crewmate's attention.

'He won't hurt you,' she assured her friend. 'Do you need to talk to me?'

'I won't hurt you if you don't threaten Zia,' Palforma tapped, his full attention on Jerif.

Jerif startled and then stomped his leg on the ground to indicate a laugh as he tapped to Palforma. 'You're doing much better than the last time I saw you.'

'I am,' Palforma agreed. 'I apologize if I hurt you or anyone else when I was first brought on board. I didn't understand what was going on around me.'

Jerif swayed his body slightly to demonstrate his curiosity about something. 'But you seemed to be calm for Zia. Are you familiar with humans?'

Remembering her conversation with Manto about Talins keeping humans as slaves, Zia watched Palforma with interest as he answered. 'I'm familiar with humans. They're so much smaller and weaker than us that they need to be protected. I reacted instinctively.'

Ignoring the part where he called her a wimp, she touched his arm to get his attention. 'No one blames you. You were injured and reacting on instinct.'

Her attention was drawn back to the Nimon as Jerif tugged at his antenna anxiously.

'Did you need to talk to me about something?' she asked him.

He moved a little closer to their table. 'I've already auctioned the shuttle and once we deliver it on Yarnetta, I'll have your part transferred to your account. Minus the ship's percentage, of course.'

'Of course. Thank you for taking care of that while I was busy.' After she thanked Jerif, she waited. He could have messaged that to her through the ship's system, so he must need to tell her something else—something he didn't want anyone to overhear or read on the ship's communal displays.

'The captain is displeased.'

That simple statement told her a lot and made her careful about what she said next. 'I'm sad to hear the captain is unhappy.'

Jerif continued, 'I heard he was unhappy enough to request aid from the Mineral Miner.'

The Mineral Miner was Red Ore's sister ship, owned by the same Nimon family. The captains of both vessels rarely called for help from the other unless there was danger.

Or someone wanted petty revenge.

Jerif's warning was clear enough. Their captain was so upset over losing the profit he might have made off the Talin that he asked for assistance from someone else, even though it would probably cost him. After having a few days to stew over what had happened during the shuttle salvage, he was feeling vengeful. He might even think he could still figure out some way to extort money from Palforma.

'That's unfortunate,' Zia answered neutrally.

Jerif waved his antennae in such a way that it could either denote a farewell or sadness. 'It seems the Talin's pants have some holes in them. It probably happened when he was causing so much destruction in your cabin. You might want to disembark the moment we dock so you can reach the markets before they close.'

Jerif was telling her in no uncertain terms to get off the ship with Palforma the moment they could or risk the captain's wrath when the Mineral Miner joined them in port. The captain must have decided that the damage to her cabin was enough to claim Palforma as payment.

At least she didn't need to debate with herself anymore about this job versus keeping Palforma. She probably wouldn't get her last paycheck, but at least she'd have the funds from the shuttle along with everything she'd saved up.

'Shopping sounds like a good idea,' she agreed. She needed to get her things packed and ready to leave the ship the moment they docked. Although Palforma had remained quiet and still during their conversation, she could tell he'd paid close attention. When she stood, he followed her lead and rose to his feet as well. Jerif flinched back slightly as the Talin towered over him.

'I'm peaceful,' he reminded the Nimon as he moved out from around the table and then paused. When he added the next statement, she got the feeling he understood at least some, if not all, the subtext to her and Jerif's conversation. 'I'm harmless and peaceful until I'm not, and then I'm the last thing you will ever see.'

She expected Jerif to be intimidated by the Talin's bloodthirsty statement, but he tapped his palps together in a sign of thanks.

'Good,' the Nimon declared. 'Then you two can look out for each other.'

CHAPTER 8

The closest market area to the station on Yarnetta was intensely crowded. Most of Yarnetta was that way. As a major trading hub in this sector, Yarnetta was the place to go for anything, especially if you wanted to buy it used. Red Ore had an exclusive contract with a Yarnetta scrapyard, so Zia had been here at least once a month for the last three years, which meant she knew her way around.

She navigated the crowded thoroughfare with ease, heading straight for the shop she wanted. Of course, it helped to have Palforma behind her intimidating everyone out of her way. He also insisted on carrying her duffle. It was sad that after working on Red Ore for so many years, all her possessions could fit into that one duffle. All her tools belonged to Red Ore and she had never been one to spend money on fancy clothes or shiny trinkets when she had new implants to save for and family to send funds to.

Although today she might splurge on the most recent season of the Ugarian soap opera Jerif introduced her to. But first Palforma needed some clothing, and then they needed to talk about where they were going next. That conversation could be done over drinks at one of the nicer cantinas.

After the satisfaction she got from watching him eat back on the ship, she was eager to provide him with more things, even if it was only a colorful beverage at a cheap bar.

Would that constitute a date? Her mom and dad described how humans used to date back on Old Earth, and this seemed similar, touring a communal area and then consuming libations in appropriate settings. Suddenly she felt a little giddy and had to share.

Stopping dead despite the foot traffic all around them, she smiled up at Palforma. 'We're on a date.'

Her eye registered a sharp, rhythmic sound as Palforma tapped. 'Date?'

'It's when a male and female are interested in each other,' she explained. 'They do activities together, like eating or drinking. Or seeing interesting things.'

He seemed to understand the significance because he tensed slightly. 'You're interested in me? Romantic mate interest?'

Her giddiness dissipated. What if she was reading this all wrong? What if Palforma saw her as a friend, not a potential lover or life partner?

'It doesn't have to be intimate interest,' she amended quickly. 'It could be friend interest. Colleague interest even. We are both knowledgeable and experienced space-farers, so we have that in common.'

At least she thought he was experienced, but she didn't know for sure. She really didn't know much about him at all. What if he had a wife and kids back home? Suddenly, she felt a little sick to her stomach.

'Never mind,' she said as she looked around for a clothing store that might carry something in his size. 'It was stupid of me. You couldn't possibly be interested in me anyway. And your spouse is probably worried about you and—'

Palforma crowded her space in the middle of the corridor, ignoring the angry looks they got from the passing crowd.

'I have no one like that in my life. No one. I've been alone. Lonely. Starved. And now you are in my life. A banquet. A feast. Don't take back your interest. I want to date. I'll accept any attention you want to show me,' he tapped fluidly. His quick command of the tapping language was impressive. Few integrated with their INT this seamlessly. But his beautiful use of Norka paled compared to what his words made her feel.

Her heart soared.

She'd always been bold. Why change now? She spoke her mind. 'I like you, Palforma. I haven't known you for long, but I really like you.'

'Good,' Palforma replied. 'Because I can't imagine life without you.'

Giddy with happiness, she pointed to a nearby shop. 'Let me buy you clothes and a few other things, and then we can plan our next move.'

Emboldened, she reached out to tangle her hand in his and led him to their first destination with a spring in her step. She might have lost a job, but she'd gained a sweet, handsome giant. She was sure she got the better end of that trade.

Palforma was content to let Zia lead him around the market. The area around the port was nothing but shops and eateries catering to a large variety of creatures. He wasn't sure if he'd ever seen so many difference species in one place before.

With Zia in charge, he soon found himself in a clothing shop. Without pause she led him to a section where the items might fit him, but he was dubious. When the first thing she pulled off a rack was a long-sleeved, multi-pocketed coverall, Palforma backed away a little.

'Most of us don't wear things that cover our upper half,' he explained and then turned to show her his back. He gently rattled the armored back plates that ran down his spine, trying to keep it quiet. The last thing he wanted to do was startle any of the shoppers around them.

If he wanted to, he could make a war rattle with his back plates loud enough to shake things on the shelf next to him. As with any Talin, he also used them to express dozens of different emotions. It felt odd to realize that she couldn't hear his rattles or his rumbles. It wasn't a bad feeling, only a strange one.

Turning back around, he saw understanding on her face. 'Do you guys ever wear anything on your top half?'

'Some shirts are specially designed so they won't get caught on our back plates, but I've never worn them. Some Talins wear long shirts because it's part of their profession, like healers. But if you don't need it to denote occupation, no one bothers wearing one.'

Zia grinned up at him. 'It's good to finally know how you were making all that sound my implants kept registering. I wondered what was making your chest vibrate.'

As she placed her palm on his chest, he sounded a soothing rumble. When he let go to tap, her hand stayed on his chest.

'The vibration you feel is coming from the soundbox in my chest. The sound I'm making right now is one we use to soothe or show affection to someone close to us.' He changed the rhythm of the rumble a little. 'This one means I'm sorrowful.'

Taking a small step back, Zia lifted her hand away from his chest to talk. 'I wish I could program my implants to recognize each sound, but they're old and weren't even the top of the line when *my parents* first bought them. They can be set up to recognize individual voices, but not sounds.'

A surprised rattle of worry come out of him. 'If your implants are old, do they cause you pain?'

She made a negligent gesture. 'They don't hurt, but they are limited compared to the ones *on the market* now. Well, I guess we could have bought nicer ones when I was a kid, but we couldn't afford them. It's not a big deal. These have worked well over the years. And I'm lucky. I'm sure most kids in my situation wouldn't have been able to get any implants at all. My entire community pitched in. That's why it's taking me so long

to save up enough to get new implants. I send funds back to my
family to help the community.'

Palforma was impressed. 'I've heard of human families
helping each other, but never an entire human community.' From
the stories a few wild caught humans told, many human colonies
were as brutal to each other as other species were to them.

'They are really great. I haven't been back to see them in
five years, but I get updates every few months,' she said with a
gentle smile. It took a moment for his INT to catch up and
translate year to solar and month to a fraction of a solar. Then he
marveled at how long his little human had been on her own
without the loving support of a family, colony, or even a close
friend. The Nimon back on Red Ore had been helpful, but he
could tell their friendship had been nothing more than surface.

'I'm going to get you new implants,' he told her, thrilled
to give her this.

Instead of becoming as excited as him, her expression
turned slightly sad. 'That's sweet of you, but don't worry about
that right now. Before anything else, we need to figure out our
next step.'

That's when he realized she thought he was completely
without funds.

'I can pay for them,' he insisted, and she raised an
eyebrow at him. He'd seen that look before. It expressed
disbelief, and he almost rumbled out a laugh. He could make all
kinds of claims, but without an Identification Cube he couldn't
prove anything. It didn't matter, he'd prove himself when they
got to a reputable Talin station. Everything would change when
he had an Ident and could gain access to Talin technology and
healers.

She gave him an affectionate smile. 'You're a sweet guy,
but let's focus on getting you some new clothes first.'

Turning to a rack of clothes, she pulled out several pairs
of pants. They weren't in the Talin style. Instead of bunching
just below the knee, these pants went all the way to the floor and,
like Zia's coveralls, had many pockets. He was getting the
feeling his little human liked pockets.

Since a quick glance around the store showed nothing
made in a Talin style, he let her lead him to a changing booth

where he tried on the pants she picked. The material felt thick enough to handle some rough wear, so despite the odd feeling of having fabric cover his entire legs, he approved.

'This will work,' he told her, expecting that to be the end of it. But then she picked out three more pairs to buy. 'I don't need those.'

'Clothes get dirty or damaged,' she countered after setting them down on a convenient table. 'I have four changes of coveralls. You should have four pairs of pants. Now, what type of shoes do you normally wear?'

He could tell by her expression his little human had made up her mind, and she wouldn't be dissuaded. Nothing in the shop was expensive, so he gave in to her and told himself he'd have ample opportunity to buy her all kinds of soft clothes once he had access to his funds again.

At least he could keep her from buying shoes. 'Talins don't wear anything on our feet unless we are going into battle or need to be outfitted to work in space.'

She stared at his feet. 'Yeah, you got some tough-looking skin there. I can see how you wouldn't require shoes.' Raising her gaze to his face, she asked, 'Do you need anything else?'

'All I really want is a replacement Ident Cube, but we can't get that anywhere but a Talin station or colony.'

She made a slight face. 'I take it that's where you want to go from here?'

He was surprised that was even a question. 'I need an Ident.'

She sighed out a breath. 'Let me get these, and then we'll find a place to sit and talk about our next step.'

Even though she didn't seem eager to talk about traveling to a Talin station, he adored the way she said *our next step. Our*. Not *yours* but *ours*. He'd never liked that word so much as now.

'Yes, we need to go to a restaurant because we are on a date,' he reminded her, and that made her huff out her soundless laugh.

He tossed the old ripped and stained pants into a recycler as she paid for the new clothes and handed them to him to be tucked away in the duffle he carried. Then she led him unerringly to a brightly and lively cantina.

'It's a little expensive here,' she told him as she found them a small table to sit at. 'But they don't water down their drinks.' She pointed to where a square-shaped robotic server was wheeling between tables to deliver items. 'And all their servers are programmed to monitor, so no one gets drugged.'

She tapped the display on the table to bring it to life and scrolled through the menu. She selected an item and then looked up at him. 'What do you want?'

'You order for me,' he suggested.

Even when he'd had time off to explore, he rarely bothered visiting non-Talin stations or colonies while in the military. He had wholly believed what his parents had said about the uselessness of pleasurable pursuits. He'd spent all his down time either training or studying.

But that mindset changed after they rejected him. With their dismissal of him, he felt free to question all the beliefs they'd instilled. The more he lived among the Talins and humans on Kalor, the more he understood that life was to be enjoyed. That meant if his little human wanted to indulge in frivolous drinks inside this loud and colorful place, he would sit and enjoy one with her.

Her expression was one of concentration as she scrolled through the list. Finally selecting one for him, she sent their order off and looked up at him, her expression slightly anxious.

'I hope you like it, but don't feel obligated to drink it.'

He sounded a soothing rumble. 'I'm sure I'll enjoy it.'

The drinks were quick to arrive. Hers came in a tall, narrow glass, brightly colored and decorated with long pieces of decorative frippery hanging off of it. With one finger she tugged at a long fringe and the entire drink changed color. She took a sip, shook her head, and then tugged at a different fringe. The liquid inside changed color again, and this time when she sipped, she nodded in approval.

'It can be a lot of different flavors depending on what colors you pick,' she told him and then pointed to the multi-colored fringe. 'It's fun to play around, but if you're not careful, you can get stuck with something really horrible. Now try yours!'

His drink came in a glass mug and wasn't colorful or decorated. Zia watched him closely as he picked it up and took a cautious sip. He expected it to be disgustingly sweet or overly powerful, but instead, it had a slightly briny flavor with a hint of spice.

He set it down and looked up to find her watching him intensely. 'I like this.'

She huffed out a laugh. 'I surprised you. Didn't I!'

'Did you guess I would like this or did you read this would be a suitable drink for a Talin on the menu?'

'The menu has nothing about Talins,' she said with a hint of pride. 'It was an educated guess. You ate everything on your plate back at Red Ore, but you really liked the spiced nako bean and fermented sal mix the best. You ate that first and fastest. That told me a lot about your tastes, so I figured you'd like this drink.'

'Your careful observations humble me,' he told her honestly.

He was used to being the ever-vigilant one, always looking after the humans on Kalor. It was the Talins' responsibly to care for the human pets around them. The Talins made sure the humans ate, slept, and saw the healer for even minor issues. When a human bonded with a Talin, they often wanted to make that Talin happy, but he couldn't think of a single human who cared enough to make such a meticulous study of him.

Few ever wanted to spend time with him, let alone bond.

Zia took another sip of her beverage, the colorful liquid staining her lips blue. Setting it down, she leaned forward a little as she tapped. 'Don't be humble. Be pleased. I don't have much to offer, but I take care of the ones I care about. This all means I'm coming to care about you.'

He wished she could hear his rumble of happiness. 'I'm pleased.'

She took a deep breath as she continued. 'I think this drink choice also proves I'm getting to know you quickly. I'm sure we could work well together. Even if things don't work out romantically between us, I'd like us to stick together.' She huffed out one of her laughs. 'Heck, I don't even know if Talin and human biology is compatible, so I might be expecting something that couldn't happen anyway.'

'We're compatible,' he was quick to assure her. 'I know Talins and humans who have bonded.' He paused for a second before deciding to share a deadly secret with her. 'It's important you never tell anyone this, but our monarch's son Searin is bonded to a human, and they have a child together.'

Zia looked fascinated. 'Humans are universal breeders, so I'm not surprised you guys are compatible. But which part is a secret? The bonded to a human thing or the having a kid part?'

'All of it,' he explained. 'According to Talin law, we aren't supposed to scent-bond with anyone. It's considered a weakness. Without scent-bonding, our females can't get pregnant, so we're all grown in artificial wombs and raised in a cresh.'

'Cresh? I've never seen that gesture used before. It's translating to school, but that doesn't seem correct.'

'They're much more than schools. Creshes are facilities specifically designed and staffed to raise and educate children. We don't live with our families until we're old enough to start learning and working with our family or clan.'

Zia's expression turned sad. 'That sounds like a cold place to raise a child.'

'It can be,' he agreed. 'It was all I knew until I lived on Kalor and saw how the young there are raised.'

'I'd never be separated from my kid.' The steely determination on her face told Palforma that her words were not idle.

An image of Zia nursing their child appeared in his head with such vivid detail that he went still. They would both be so beautiful.

'Now that I've got the background, finish explaining what so wrong about this Searon person being with a human,' Zia urged.

'Prime Son Searin not only scent-bonded but let his human get pregnant with a hybrid child. If it's discovered, the Apogee Assembly could call for him to be removed from the monarch's lineage and probably even sentence him to death.

Although he would die anyway if he had to be separated from Sora so the death sentence would only be a formality. If we're separated from our scent-bonded partners for too long, we die. It's called Ending and I've been told it's painful in the extreme.'

A horrified expression appeared on Zia's face. 'Not that I know anyone who would care, but I promise I won't tell a soul.'

'I know you won't.' All this talk of bonding was making the scent glands in his cheeks ache. He wanted to hold her and rub his bonding oil all over her hair. But they were in public and he never knew who was watching. He'd have to wait until they had some privacy. Absently, he rubbed one and then the other to ease the discomfort.

Her next question wasn't one he expected at all. 'Is it true that you guys only keep humans as slaves?'

Dismayed at the idea that Zia would think Talins were abusing humans, he was quick to deny her question. 'Absolutely not! While slavery isn't outlawed among us, no Talin keeps slaves. It's considered a barbaric practice.'

'That's good. Someone told me you guys hunted down and enslaved humans.'

Who had told her that? He knew he was prevaricating a little by not mentioning that all humans had the status of pet the moment they entered into any Talin-controlled area, but he didn't want to muddy the issue. Slaves were poor souls who were often worked to death. Pets were cherished and spoiled. The difference was an important one to all Talins. Even most Traditionalists, the conservative political faction, saw human pets as precious.

Although none of that meant humans didn't end up ill-treated among the Talins, but the Committee for Pet Welfare worked hard to protect humans from abusive owners, and the law favored the side of the committee in any dispute. Nowhere in the universe were there laws specifically protecting humans like there were among the Talin.

Once he had her safe among his people, he would explain it all to her. She might be a little mad at first, but he would make her understand it was better for her in the long run. With that thought in mind, he met her gaze boldly as he tapped.

'I don't enjoy being without access to my funds, and I want to tell those on Kalor that I'm alive and well. They're probably worried about me. That means I need to at least visit a Talin station or colony so I can get a new Ident and use a comm array. Then we can plan from there.'

'I was told to stay out of Talin-controlled space,' she explained. 'But you wouldn't lie to me about the slavery thing, so I guess we could make our first stop the closest Talin station. I know it can be hard when you don't have an Ident or personalized information square.'

'Thank you, Zia. This is important to me.'

She paused for a moment, and then her expression hardened. 'I'm trusting you. Don't break that trust. It won't go well for you.'

He blinked a few times at her forceful comment. That almost seemed like something Lakin would say. But while Lakin's threats meant she would mess up sensors or disable ships, Zia's words felt much more dangerous.

Insight hit him. Sitting across from him was a human who would kill to protect herself or someone she loved.

That revelation made him blurt out the next thought that entered his head. 'You're perfect.'

CHAPTER 9

Zia led Palforma through the second-rate transport, scanning each door for their names on the cabin display. When she found their room, the biolock un-clicked at her touch and the door slid open. She tried hard not to grimace at the space they'd be using for the next few days.

Leading him in, she turned around in the cramped space to face him. 'I'm sorry it's so small, but it's only for a few days.'

Palforma took in the room as he tapped. 'It's fine.' Then his eyes zeroed in on the single bunk. His gaze swept back to her. 'We're sharing a bed?'

She felt her face get hot, and she dropped her eyes for a moment. She could have gotten a cabin with two bunks, but she didn't want to sleep separately from Palforma. Now she wondered if she was being presumptuous. What if he had been all about holding and cuddling because he'd been injured? He might not want to do any of that now that he felt better. Was she acting like a sexual predator, expecting Palforma to share a bed with her because she paid for the ticket?

Guilt slammed into her, making her chest feel tight.

'We don't have to! I should have asked you before I booked the room. I could check to see if there's another room. This transport was filling up fast, so we might be stuck with this one. And this was the only transport that would stop at a Talin station. There isn't much traffic to Talin areas from Yarnetta.' Looking around the room, she pointed to a chair. 'I can sleep there. I've slept in worse places. Or the floor. I could sleep on the floor…'

Palforma gathered her hands in a gentle grip to stop her from talking. When she met his eyes, he let go and spoke. 'I want to share a bed with you, but I don't want you to feel forced. I can sleep on the floor.'

Her left eye registered a rumble from him, but she wasn't sure if it was a sound of worry, interest, or dismay. She really wished she could program his different rumbles and rattles into her implant.

He was being so kind that she needed to be honest with him. 'I picked this cabin on purpose. I wanted an excuse to sleep next to you. And maybe…' She couldn't bring herself to finish as another wave of embarrassment and guilt hit her.

'And maybe what?' Palforma urged. Her left eye was still registering that he was rumbling, and she felt the urge to wrap her arms around him and rest her face against his chest so she could feel those rumbles.

'Zia?' he used the Old Earth sign language gesture for her name she taught him on their way to the market on Yarnetta.

It was a simple Z-motion with the first finger and then pointing up and with a quick move. It combined the letter Z with one of the Old Earth signs for spaceship. Her parents said she was fascinated by ships the moment she was born, so that name sign started early and stuck.

Although all the Old Earth sign languages were effectively dead languages, her parents got a few vids and scanned books on the topic. They gathered enough information that everyone could communicate until they could save up enough for the implants and the tapping language downloads. But she kept her name sign because it always reminded her of the best part of growing up—the unwavering support and love of her family.

Watching Palforma make the longer name sign, instead of the faster tap, which meant *human female,* that everyone else used, made her heart beat faster. It was a stupidly small thing that meant the world to her.

'Zia?' he repeated the gesture, and she couldn't contain herself any longer. Dropping the small bag of snacks she'd been carrying, she jumped on him. He caught her easily, his arms going under her ass to help support her weight as she wrapped her legs around his waist and her arms around his neck.

Then she kissed him.

Palforma had watched other humans lip press each other. He'd also witnessed humans lip press with their Talins, but he had never experienced it before, at least not in the sexual way Zia was showing him.

He opened his mouth to her and was rewarded when her tongue swept into his mouth. Desire flooded his body so quickly he felt a moment of dizziness. As they kissed, Zia's little hands held onto the back of his neck. He'd never confessed it, but the flesh hidden under his neck plates was highly sensitive—even erogenous. Although he could barely feel her touch over the plates, he was desperate to feel those nimble little fingers slide between the plates and stroke the skin underneath.

Then she pulled her mouth away from his and wiggled to be set down. Disappointment filled him at the thought that she didn't want to take their encounter any further. But the moment she was standing on her feet, she met his gaze boldly.

She was frowning slightly as she tapped. 'This transport is stopping at Oglin station no matter what, so you don't need to do anything for me to get back to your people.'

Palforma felt a little confused. 'I know we're going to Oglin.'

Zia's brows furrowed. 'Right. It's just that I don't want you to think you have to service me or anything. You know, as payment or something. Being sexually compatible species is one thing, but I don't want to make you do anything you don't want to do. Consent is important to me.'

Palforma's mind went blank for a moment. Zia was worried about forcing him to rut? She was fearful that he felt obligated to her instead of desirous? She couldn't possibly know how much he craved everything about her.

'I don't feel forced,' he tapped quickly and then dropped to his knees in front of her. 'I want anything you're willing to grant me. You might not believe me, but my life is yours.'

A delighted grin curved her lips, and she huffed out a laugh as if privy to an inside joke. 'That statement might be truer than you think,' she stated mysteriously. Before he could ask about it, she continued. 'I want it. I mean, I want intimacy with you. If you want it, I want it.' The skin of her face darkened, something humans did sometimes when they were feeling powerful emotions.

'I want,' he said simply and bowed his head so the plates on the back of his neck separated. The edges of those plates was duller than the ones that ran down his back and didn't have attached muscles to move them so they couldn't be clattered together to make sound. It was a position of extreme vulnerability and a request for acceptance. She couldn't know how significant this postion was, but when he rolled his eyes up to see her face, her smile was gentle and her eyes soft.

Dropping his gaze to the floor, he tapped blindly. 'Touch me, please.'

When one of her hands slid down the back of his head to the separated plates, he froze, even holding his breath. Gentle fingers slipped between the plates and the tips of her fingers stroked the skin there. Pleasure zinged through his body, making him jerk a little, and a loud rumble of desire filled the room.

To his disappointment, she withdrew her fingers too soon. She started tapping the moment he looked up. 'Do this if I do anything you don't like,' she instructed and then pressed separated fingers into his arm, almost like she was trying to cage a small animal with her hand. 'I'll do the same.'

He tapped eagerly. 'Yes, that is a very good idea. But now will you touch me again?' He knew his pleading rumble

was lost on her, but he couldn't stop the sound from coming out
of him. He dropped his head forward to separate the plates
before she could even reply. Without hesitation, she slid her
fingers in again, rubbing his flesh and making his entire body
shake with pleasure.

Then it hit him. He was going to mate with a human. He
was finally going to touch and be touched. It was something he'd
always hoped for but never expected. He probably wasn't worthy
of this, but he was going to accept it anyway!

CHAPTER 10

Zia couldn't know what kind of havoc she was wreaking on him with her little fingers probing between his neck plates. Blood rushed to his mating shaft, making it rigid and causing the flesh pouch to grow uncomfortably tight. He needed to get his pants off and let his mating shaft emerge from the pouch before it became painful.

Unlike Talin-style pants where the fabric was gathered tightly at the waist with only one closure, these pants had multiple closures that each needed to be undone to get them off. Trying to undo them blindly while Zia's fingers were causing such an intense reaction was impossible.

Feeling like a green youth unable to decide on a direction to go, Palforma remained still under her touch. He ignored the discomfort and tried to control his body that wanted to shake as her touch got bolder.

When her fingers withdrew, he almost collapsed on the floor. Her small hand under his chin urged him to look up. 'You liked that,' she said, her eyes wide and her pupils dilated with budding passion.

Taking a deep breath, he caught the scent of her desire. 'I like everything you do to me,' he told her.

Her expression turned slightly hesitant. 'I want to touch you more.'

Instead of tapping out his answer, he grabbed her hands and put them over his swollen and aching scent glands in his cheeks. Then he dropped his hands away so she could do as she pleased. She rubbed her palms slightly, and then her mouth made a little O of surprise as she brought her hands to her nose and smelled.

'Vanilla,' she tapped with one hand while she kept the other one close to her nose. 'I love this smell. I knew you were producing it, but now I see how.'

'It's my bonding oil.' He felt a trickle of oil roll down his face. Most Talins would be embarrassed by that, but he wasn't. Why would such a blatant display of affection for his female bother her? His opinion was reinforced when she moved to capture the droplet and rubbed it between her thumb and finger.

Then she opened her mouth and ran the tip of her tongue over her finger. Watching that sent too much blood to his mating shaft and too quickly that he felt dizzy for a moment.

'I need… I need…' even with tapping, he couldn't get the words out. Lust was short-circuiting his brain.

'You want to rub it all over me. Don't you?' she asked. An electric current of need zapped through him at the images her words invoked.

'Need!'

With only a few effortless motions, she unzipped the front of her coveralls, pulled her arms out, and let them drop to her hips. 'Touch all you want,' she invited.

Palforma couldn't hold himself back. Rattling with aggression and rumbling with lust, he rose to his feet at the same time he snatched her up. Within a stride he was at the bed, setting her down and in rapid progression had her boots off and then the coveralls. She wore more clothing over her sex and breasts.

She peeled off the garment over her breasts as he hooked his fingers in the scrap of fabric at her hip and dragged it down her legs. And then she was gloriously naked before him.

He feasted his eyes on the sight of his perfect human. She was perfectly round from her lovely breasts to the swell of her hips. Her smooth, dark-tanned skin called to be touched and covered in his bonding oil.

Giving in to the impulse, he kneeled on the bed and brought his face to her flesh. Starting at her shoulder, he rubbed his cheeks on her skin. He didn't know his body could produce so much bonding oil, but as he moved his face down her torso, he left a glistening trail of it. He felt her inhale sharply. When he looked up, her expression was blissful, not disturbed. With one hand he rubbed the oil into her skin as he kept rubbing his cheeks on her.

Down her sides. Across her soft belly from hip to hip. Then up and across her breasts. As his face passed over her nipples, she shivered. Drawing back, he noticed her voluptuous breasts moving a little with every breath and her nipples tightening made his mouth water.

Although he'd never had a sexual partner, Talin or human, he'd read and watched all the educational material produced by the Committee for Pet Welfare. He'd also accidentally happened on a pair of human lovers enjoying a tryst in Commandant Holian's garden back on Kalor. They hadn't seen him and he'd given himself permission to watch under the guise of wanting to be able to please a partner if he was ever so blessed.

All of that meant he latched on to one nipple with his mouth while rolling the other gently between a thumb and finger. The bonding oil on her skin made her taste different. She didn't taste entirely like him or her, but a heady combination of both.

That taste made his mating shaft fully emerge from his flesh pouch and press painfully against the confines of his pants. Rising up, he clumsily ripped off his pants, not even bothering with trying to undo the closures. He had a few other pairs she'd insisted on buying him, and these were being sacrificed for a good cause.

With the pants gone and his position kneeling over her, Zia had a front row view to his engorged shaft. He froze, waiting to see how she would react. If she rejected him, he would withdraw, but it would hurt.

She lay immobile for a moment, her eyes wide and focused on his throbbing cock and seed sack. Sitting up, she took him in her small hands and stroked down his length, making him shudder. Her touch was delicate and tender but profound. It was the first time he'd ever been touched so intimately and he couldn't help the way his hips moved a little to thrust into her hands.

Looking up, she met his eyes and brought one hand up between them to talk. 'I want to taste you.'

He wasn't sure, but his eyes might have crossed.

In answer he curled a hand behind her head and urged her mouth toward his shaft. When her soft lips closed over the head of his erection, all the air he'd been holding in his lungs whooshed out and he was forced to close his eyes from the intensity.

He almost came right there.

"B-b-b-beauty Zia! K-k-kind Zia. Zia. Zia." Her name fell from his lips as his brain filled with the feel of her mouth on him and the smell of her in his nose. As she worked him further into her mouth, the scent of her lust because more prevalent. This sexual act was making her more aroused. He would have to return the favor and see if it affected him the same way.

Considering how much he loved the taste of her skin, he couldn't imagine he wouldn't adore the taste of her sweet sex.

She pulled her mouth off of him to lick up the side of his shaft and then down the other side. She nuzzled her face against his seed sack and brought her hand up to grip his shaft and slowly pump up and down.

He was so close that when she nipped at the sensitive skin of his sack, he almost finished. But no, not yet!

All his research told him that human females could come several times during sexual congress, and he wanted to make sure she had so much pleasure she would want to do this again.

He gently tugged her away from his sex and urged her to lie back. When she resisted him a little, he almost let go, but then noticed the gleam in her eye and the smirk on her face. When he forced the issue with a bit, she gave under the pressure and the scent of her arousal spiked again.

She liked this. Oh, his sweet little human was a delight.

Holding both wrists together, he forced them over her head as he swung a leg over to straddle her body. She tugged at her hands, but only halfheartedly as she stretched up her head. He lowered his lips to her and they lip pressed while his thick, throbbing shaft rested on her belly.

When she started undulating her hips with need, he broke off the current lip press so he could start lip pressing all over her skin. When he got to her breasts, he almost stopped to worship them some more, but he had a goal in mind.

Letting go of her wrists, he braced his body with his hands on the bed and then used one knee to part her legs. Settling himself between her thighs with his feet dangling off the end of the bunk, he regarded the soft curls that hid her sex from sight. Gently, he ran a finger between her feminine folds, parting them and revealing her glistening flesh. Her scent filled the air and he leaned closer to pull her into his lungs.

When he put his mouth down to lick the length of her sex, she gasped, and her thighs tightened around his head. They pressed on his scent glands, making pleasure shock through him as the taste of her on his tongue made his shaft throb.

Careful of his teeth, he settled his mouth on that little nub of nerves and teased it with his lips and tongue. She screamed softly. Her entire body went stiff and then shuddered violently as she pressed her hips up, forcing herself hard against him.

It belatedly occurred to him as he stimulated her, that she must have orgasmed. It shouldn't have happened this fast. It was probably a sign that it had been a long time since she was pleasured. Humans needed to be pleasured regularly or it could have detrimental effects on them both mentally and physically.

When he rolled his eyes up, he saw her chest heaving as she panted. Her fingers were dancing in the air.

'Palforma! So good. Oh good god! Please! So good!'

Or maybe she was very aroused by him. That thought delighted him.

Full of a sense of importance and happiness, he ignored his own throbbing shaft. He kept sucking and licking at her until her hand pushed at his head and her hips pulled back to get away from his touch. Her skin was covered in a light coating of sweat, and she was still panting. Her legs fell open around him and her hands fell to the sides of the bunk.

Worried that he might overstimulate her, he stopped licking and sucking, but he didn't reposition. He made himself comfortable between her legs, thrilling in her scent. His bonding oil was thick on the insides of her thighs, so he started rubbing it into her skin.

When it started trickling down his cheek again, he gathered it up and eyed her slick sex. Gently he pushed an oil coated finger inside of her, ready to withdraw the moment she objected.

He felt her stiffen a little and was about to stop when she bent one leg at the knee and pushed harder against his hand. As she forced his finger into her silken heat, he hissed out a breath.

Not only did the feel of her soft flesh make arousal pound through him, but the smell of his bonding oil mixed with her intimate slickness was feverishly pleasuring.

He eased a second finger into her, excited by the way her body gave to him. He knew he could fit inside of her. He'd seen plenty of evidence that other Talin-human couples managed just fine, but he marveled at how tight she felt around his fingers. What would it be like to sink his shaft into her velvety depths?

Suddenly, she was pulling away from him and sitting up. Her little hand closed around his wrist and urged him onto his knees between her legs.

'I need you inside me!' she demanded.

He didn't ask if she was sure, and he didn't hesitate. Pushing her back down, he uncurled his body and eased himself into position. Although he knew she had a will of iron and a strong spirit, her body was still tiny and fragile. The last thing he wanted to do was hurt her because he was too clumsy or eager.

Zia must not have appreciated his caution because she slapped a hand against his arm above his quills. 'Palforma, hurry! I need you! Now!'

She tapped something after the "now" that didn't register with his INT, but it didn't matter. Her demands and urgency were translating just fine. *Get moving or else.*

Pressing the blunt tip of his shaft to her entrance, he slowly slid into her. The heat and pressure around his shaft were intense enough to make his spine stiffen and pull him up straight. His back plates started making noise without conscious thought, and his soundbox was rumbling so loudly with pleasure it was making his whole body vibrate.

Zia liked those vibrations.

'Yes, that. That!' she said as she rolled her hips up and urged him to sink further into her depths.

Grabbing her hips with his hands, he held her still as he pushed in until his seed sack settled up against the globes of her backside. Under him, she moaned. Her hands had dropped to the bunk and were grasping the bedding. Her knuckles were white from tension as her breathing quickened again.

Raising one hand, she ordered him without opening her eyes. 'Move!'

Because he couldn't remain still either, he eased himself out and back again. He set up a slow rhythm, torturing them both. He wasn't sure how much longer he could last, and then she flexed and wrapped her legs around his waist. That hold allowed her to force him into a faster pace.

Next time, he would make her obey him and slow down. He would draw this out for marks. He would spend an entire sleeping cycle pleasuring her between bouts of sleep. But right now, he couldn't wait any longer. Letting go of her hips, he braced his hands on the bunk on either side of her. His claws sank into the mattress as he pistoned his hips into her.

She opened her mouth in a silent scream and arched hard against him. She tightened around him and convulsed as she climaxed. As if that gave his body permission, he followed her off that cliff into bliss.

Roaring, he released his seed inside of her, knowing that nothing would ever be the same again.

CHAPTER 11

Zia awoke slowly, feeling more content than she had in…well, ever really. She had her back to Palforma and his warm body was wrapped around her. He was vibrating against her as the implant in her left eye let her know a soft, rhythmic sound was coming from behind her.

He was purring.

A glance over her shoulder revealed that his eyes were closed and his mouth was slightly open to reveal a hint of his sharp teeth, which had been amazingly gentle as he had sucked and nibbled on her.

Palforma wasn't just purring, he was purring in his sleep. That made her feel all warm and gooey inside. The last time she'd had a lover had been over a year ago. A Doliman had crewed on Red Ore for a few months before he decided he didn't like working with Nimons and left. Because humans and Doliman were compatible, they'd shared a bunk a few times. It had been nice, but nothing spectacular.

Honestly, that's how all sex had been in the past. Pleasant at best.

But not with Palforma. With him she'd come so hard she was pretty sure she'd blacked out there for a second or two. And she'd never come twice in one session. That had been a fabulous surprise.

She really hoped they worked out because she was getting very attached. She might even love him already.

Was this too fast? A few days together and one round of exceptional sex and she was smitten? Did that make her pathetic or decisive?

Eh, she hated trying to analyze her feelings. Why bother worrying that she was falling in love too fast? Better to enjoy what she had and live in the moment. Especially if the moment was opening his eyes to find her looking at him and the vibration against her back got more intense.

Turning her head to face forward and dropping it back down to rest on Palforma's arm, she snuggled backward and took in a deep breath as he nuzzled her hair with his cheek. The smell of vanilla filled the air.

Lifting his arm from around her waist, he clumsily tapped with one hand. 'Hungry?'

'No. You?'

'No hungry. Happy. Content. Flawless.'

One hand tapping came with a limited vocab, but the use of flawless made her smile. He was probably looking for the word *perfect* and came out with *flawless* instead, which couldn't have been more appropriate. This moment was flawless.

Palforma dropped his arm back down to wrap around her. Unlike most others, he didn't seem to mind her silence. Others might chatter to fill the quiet, as if stillness demanded noise. Her right eye would fill with scrolling of their pointless words, making her irritable. Sometimes she wondered if others thought that if they talked enough, she might respond in a like manner and verbalize her words. They couldn't have been more wrong.

When she was young, before the implants, her family pushed her to learn to talk. They reasoned that her voice still worked even if she couldn't hear, so she should try to be vocal. They would sit with her for hours, having her make sound after sound until she got somewhat close to a proper word. Then they would have her repeat the word over and over again.

She hated it and no one understood her when she would try and say her words to them, so she stopped. Well-meaning, her parents tried to force her with the threat of punishment—no extra food beyond the basics. She went a step further and stop eating altogether.

At first they thought hunger would make her capitulate, but at that point everyone, including Zia, found out how stubborn she could be. When she fainted from hunger after a few days of refusing food, it was clear that no one could force Zia to do anything she didn't want to do. Her parents never tested her willpower again.

Like her, Palforma didn't mind the quiet. He was content to let the space around them stay empty except for his purring. But she liked the feel of his purring. That noise she didn't mind at all.

Suddenly she wanted to know more about her Talin. Untangling herself from his arms, she sat up and arranged a few pillows behind her and then leaned back. A few tugs had Palforma lying between her spread legs with his head on her belly. The hard plating on his head felt smooth against her skin and she absently rubbed gentle fingers over the damaged plates on his right side. In this position they could "talk" and still cuddle.

'What was your life like before?' she asked simply. She figured that kind of open-ended question would give him the freedom to share whatever he was comfortable with.

'I grew up on Talarian. That's our homeworld,' he started and she settled back to take in his life story. 'Our society organizes into clans. Each clan is made up of many families. My clan was known for producing warriors. War heroes.'

'And that's how you got hurt?' she asked and then ran her palm over his old injury.

'Yes. That's why I can't talk well. The healers were impressed I gained any speech back at all. They were sure I would wake up with no reasoning skills. After I could function again and no longer needed the supervision of the healers, I tried to go home.'

He stopped, and she gave him the time to figure out what he was going to say next. She kept stroking his head but now lengthened the strokes so her fingers also flowed over his cheeks. A little bit of his oil got on her hands and she rubbed it on her thighs before returning her hands to him.

Taking in a sharp breath, he turned his face so he could nuzzle the skin of her tummy. She could feel the bonding oil dampening the skin of her belly as he nestled a little more against her. The scent of vanilla filled her nose, and she was pretty sure the scent comforted them both.

He told her about taking a round to the head and being thought dead. Lying there helpless while he listened to Talin soldiers and civilians being tortured to death. All of it horrified her and made her want to wrap him up in a protective blanket and make sure no one hurt him again.

When he told her about waking up under the care of healers, she knew better than to think the story or pain was done.

'After it was over, I struggled. Struggled to cope with what had happened to me and the other Talins. I struggled so much I requested to leave the military, even though they wanted me to continue to serve *and* help with weapons testing where my lack of speech wouldn't be an issue.'

That was interesting to her. 'They would let you go at your request?'

'Unlike other species, all our military personnel are free to leave at any time. Serving is considered an honor and only the best are allowed to enter the military. At my request, I was released from my obligation with honor and the funds commensurate with my sacrifice. But my family wasn't pleased.'

Wasn't pleased could cover a lot of ground. Anger welled in Zia. 'Were they mean to you?'

That question made Palforma pause before continuing. 'Mean isn't a word Talins use. We do things that are logical or not. Advantageous or not. Honorable or not. Being mean or malicious isn't supposed to be part of the equation.'

'I'll be the judge of that,' Zia countered. 'What did your parents do?'

'They told me to leave and removed my name from the family registry. I'm Palforma of no family or clan. I'm a Talin without a lineage.'

Zia's heart broke for Palforma. He'd stopped purring as he tapped, and his body had become tense. 'But why would they do that?'

'If I was a corpse, they could have performed a mourning ceremony. Invited all the families of the clan and even had members of the Apogee Assembly there. But I didn't die.'

'Not dying is a good thing!' Zia protested, her outrage showing in her big movements.

'That would have been fine if I continued my military career. But I didn't. I left and became nothing but retired Palforma. Not Commandant Palforma. Not Planetary General Palforma. Not Interdisciplinary Coordinator Palforma. None of those would have been possible because of the long-term damage I sustained, but my parents weren't swayed. To them, I'd failed. To them, I was being selfish.'

'Are you kidding me?' Zia's motion to make the word *kidding* was so large and animated that she almost smacked Palforma in his nose. Reining in her anger, she tapped again. 'Your parents were the selfish ones. Your life shouldn't be about what you can do for everyone. Your life should be about contentedness and kindness.'

'Contentedness and kindness? Those aren't indicators of life goals I've heard before. And what about happiness? A few of the humans I've met talk about happiness.'

'Happiness is nice, but it comes and goes. Being content allows you to be happy,' Zia explained. 'Being content also helps to keep you from being unhappy. It's a solid but gentle middle ground that creates a platform for positive emotions to flourish and makes it hard for negative emotions to get a toehold. When you find your contentment, the most important thing is to help others find their own contentment. That's where the kindness comes in. The humans I grew up around after my parents moved lived by this philosophy. None of us ever had much, but we all made sure no one starved. And there was always laughter. It was a good place. If there'd been any job opportunities there, I wouldn't have left.'

'I like that philosophy. It allows one to act honorably but doesn't require proof of bravery or worth like achieving a high rank or earning Mattil medals.'

'Well, you're with me now, so let's go for contentedness,' Zia encourages. 'How long ago did all this happen?'

'Almost four solars, perhaps five or six of your years,' Palforma answered. 'I didn't know where to go, but then Commandant Holian offered me a home on his colony.' Then Palforma started talking more rapidly, as if excited. 'Kalor is a green planet with a lot of natural beauty. I have a home there. Actually, I have two homes. One is hidden in the side of a mountain and a good place to go if the colony is ever attacked. The other is a house I built myself of stone. Dalt has a nicer garden, but my house is much better. Better than any of the soldiers that live in the forest. I'd like to show you.'

Zia didn't like the idea of going so deep into Talin territory. Tiptoeing to the edge of Talin-controlled space by visiting Oglin station was worrisome enough, even with Palforma's reassurances that she wouldn't suddenly find herself a slave. But as uneasy as she felt, she couldn't bring herself to refuse him outright.

'Let's do business on Oglin and then decide about Kalor,' she offered.

'Certainly,' Palforma agreed. 'Visiting Oglin station first is top priory. I need an Ident and something might prove to you the goodwill of other Talins.'

'That sounds mysterious,' Zia teased. 'If the Talins there are like you, I don't need any more convincing.'

With his chest vibrating, Palforma reached down and stroked the top of her foot where it was resting next to his hip. They needed to get up and use the cleaning facility and explore the many diversions on the ship. Zia got the feeling Palforma hadn't experienced much outside of his life with the military, and she was eager to show him things he might enjoy.

Still, she didn't move. Lazily, she let her head drop back on the pillow and took in a deep breath of their combined scents.

She wasn't sure how long they stayed like that when a thought suddenly occurred to her. Raising her head, she asked, 'What's the worst insult you can call another Talin?'

'Calling a Talin a *self-centered disgrace to their family and clan* is probably the worst thing you can say,' Palforma answered with lazy motions. 'That's a dire insult. To tell someone they think only of themselves and not the Talin people, their clan, or their family. That they don't act for the benefit of the whole. Why do you ask?'

'Just in case I ever meet your parents, I want to know the best way to offend them.'

Palforma's chest vibrated as he rolled over and nuzzled his face into her skin. She was pretty sure he was laughing.

CHAPTER 12

Tickets for this transport had been cheap, which was one of the reasons Zia had splurged on one of the nicer rooms. It was also why the transport had filled so quickly. But where the ship lost funds by offering low-priced accommodations, it made up for it with its gambling and recreational area. At the center of the ship a large space was devoted to separating passengers from their funds in as many ways as possible.

One side of this communal area featured small theaters that offered live shows with a variety of acts at a modest cost. Tables and machines were set up for gambling in all kinds of games of chance where you could be pitted against other passengers or the house. All along the other side of the area were kiosks and restaurants offering almost any kind of food or drink anyone could want. The food wasn't cheap, but the drinks were. In fact, many of the establishments offered unlimited drinks of any type for free with a meal.

Most seasoned travelers knew better than to get taken in with cheap or free drinks and shiny gambling tables, but plenty of individuals were probably bored after serving out a contract on a ship or station and had funds to burn on anything pleasurable. The more sensible travelers bought reasonably priced meals, enjoyed a drink or two, and saw a show. They didn't go near the gambling.

Interestingly, this transport had something she'd only seen one other time on these types of vessels. At the center of the communal area was an oblong pit taking up about a quarter of the space with stadium seating all around it. In the pit was a kind of obstacle course, which was empty of participants at the moment. Above the pit hovered a massive holo-billboard that announced the countdown to the next race as well as who had entered so far along with their stats and betting percentages. Two places were still open for passengers to enter the race.

Looking down at the obstacles, she shuddered at how many sharp objects were included in the course. The participants better have tough skin or be very fast because they risked being skewered on at least one obstacle.

While Zia might shy away from even watching one of the races held in that pit, Palforma looked intrigued. 'What is that?'

Turning to face him, she explained, 'It's a type of race that anyone on the ship can enter. You pay an entry fee that goes into a pot and the winner of the race gets the pot and a percentage of the bets.' She pointed to the holo-billboard. 'Anyone on the ship is allowed to bet on the outcome of the race, including if someone ends up dead. You can see that right now one of the Tomaris is the favorite to win, and the Lomo has some bets that he'll die during the race or at least be critically injured.'

Palforma stared at the board for a bit and then asked her another question. 'What's the number next to the name mean?'

'That's how much that individual will get if they win. The numbers differ depending on the point spread.' She pointed to the Lomo. 'His number is big because the point spread is so biased against him winning.'

'Have you watched these before?'

'A few times,' she admitted. 'It can be exciting. But not on a course this extreme. This one includes death percentages, but none of the races I've watched really had that kind of risk. This course looks…' She couldn't even finish as her gaze swept back down to the course. Wait, was that a booby trap? How could anyone be crazy enough to sign up?

'I want to race.'

At first, she thought he must have used the wrong gestures. The motion for *race* was very similar to the motion for *leave*. But then he pointed to the holo-billboard and tapped again, leaving no doubt of what he wanted.

'Will you pay so I can enter the race? When I win, I'll be able to pay you back.'

'*No!*' Although the gesture to denote a negative response was a small one, she made it large to demonstrate how upset she was at the thought of him participating in anything to do with that pit.

They were standing next to the railing that would lead to the seating area round the pit. Out of the way of foot traffic, when he knelt down in front of her, no one even took notice. As crowded as the ship was around them, they might as well have been all alone. Leaning forward, he nuzzled his face between her breasts. Without thinking about it, she wrapped her arms around his head.

They'd been holed up in their room for several days now. Making love, sleeping, and ordering from the limited menu the ship staff would deliver to the rooms. Because they only had about two days left until they reached Oglin station, Zia pushed for them to get cleaned up and explore the ship. She wanted to show Palforma a good time and maybe even buy him something to remember their first trip together.

The last thing she expected was for him to want to join a dangerous race. Looking down at him, she struggled not to frown. Those who glanced at him probably thought he was acting submissive by being on his knees in a traditional begging position. They couldn't have been more wrong. Palforma wasn't being subservient. He was placating.

He pulled back a little so he could speak. 'Please? I know you're concerned for me, but nothing in that pit worries me. Let me join the race.'

'Why?' Fear for him made her hands a little shaky. She wouldn't be able to deny him this, but maybe she could talk him out of it. 'Why would you want to put yourself in such danger?

Let's go eat and watch a few shows. The Vinar acrobats put on an amazing act.'

Palforma wasn't swayed. 'I need the funds. It will be several more rotations before I have access to my personal funds, and I need some right now.'

'I can lend you—' Her left eye registered a loud, rhythmic sound making her stop. It must be Palforma rattling his back plates.

'I don't want to borrow funds. I want to earn them. Let me do this. It's important to me.' Put like that, she couldn't refuse him.

'Fine,' she agreed, glowering down at him. 'But if you get hurt, I'll never forgive you!'

He was still on his knees when she turned on her heels and stomped off. She was only a few strides away when Palforma appeared at her side. He didn't take her hand or touch her, which was a good thing because she was spitting mad.

Without even looking over at him, she found the nearest betting terminal and entered Palforma into the race. After she paid, she turned and pointed to the terminal so he could press his palm on the display. It recorded his bio-sig and requested information on his height, weight, and profession. As she watched him enter his information, she took note that all he entered into the occupation spot was *retired*.

When he finished, the terminal chewed on the information for a moment, and then Palforma's name and stats showed up on the holo-billboard. Betting and percentages went crazy for a little while. When it settled down enough for the holo-billboard to display Palforma's chances of winning, the betting pattern put him in the lower third of the pack.

That told her the crowd didn't have a lot of confidence that Palforma could win.

Dread pooled in her belly. Touching Palforma's arm to get his attention, she rapidly tapped. 'This is a bad idea. These races are brutal even without a spikey, booby-trapped course. Let me withdraw you. Please? I don't care about the funds. I don't want to put you in danger.'

'I'll be fine,' he promised. 'Will you watch?'

She was torn between wanting to see what happened and fearful she was about to witness the male she cared so much about die a violent, unnecessary death. 'Do you want me to?'

'Yes,' he answered without hesitation.

'Fine, I'll watch. But if you die, your ghost better find me so I can tell you how mad I am at you.'

Without another word, he picked her up and cradled her against this chest. The move was unexpected, so she startled and flailed a little as he strode down the aisle between seating sections. He set her down in a seat right in front of the railing.

Remaining bent over, he rubbed a cheek against the top of her head, filling the air around her with the scent of vanilla. She'd gotten so used to being covered in his bonding oil that it felt odd when her hair wasn't shiny and slick from it.

When he was finished, he straightened up. 'You'll watch me from here. I'll win and you will see how capable I am. You'll see how worthy I am.'

Before she could say anything, he turned and loped off to join the others in the hidden starting area. Fear spiked through her. He wasn't doing this for the funds, or at least not only for the funds. He thought he wasn't worthy. That she thought less of him.

She wanted to chase after him and tell him all the ways he was better than anyone else. Foremost because she was sure now that she loved him more than she'd ever loved anyone but her parents and siblings. She'd thought she was falling in love with him before, but now she knew for sure.

Dazed, she stood up and thought about running him down, but it was too late. As she stood, he disappeared into the area under the stands. She couldn't get access to him unless she entered the race, and now all ten spots were filled.

With horror she realized the tenth entry was a V'mil, one of the largest and fiercest species out there. The V'mil shot to the top of the board, eclipsing all the other entries and enlarging the death stat number for all the other contestants.

If Palforma survived this, she was going to kill him!

As he entered the waiting area, Palforma realized he was the last one there. Nine other racers were already milling around, stretching, flexing, and mostly trying to intimidate each other. Two officials walked around the room holding stunners and scowling at the racers—a clear warning not to start anything before the race began.

Trying to be unobtrusive, Palforma took a spot against a far wall and watched the racers interact. Although the many Tomaris were working hard to appear threatening, and a V'mil was standing dead center of the room growling, the quiet Meelton lounging against the opposite wall caught Palforma's attention.

Like him, the Meelton was carefully observing the others. Palforma wondered if the Meelton had already noticed the V'mil was moving stiffly, indicating a pain in his spine. Or that one of the Tomaris had twitchy eyes, probably because of a drug addiction. Although he was sure everyone was betting on either one of the six Tomaris or the V'mil to win, Palforma believed the only one in this room who would prove to be a problem was this Meelton.

As if sensing his eyes on him, the Meelton raised his gaze to meet Palforma's. Probably weighing slightly less than him, the Meelton was about the same height and equipped with some effective natural weapons, including stingers jutting out from his spine that could inject an efficient neuro toxin. The toxin wouldn't kill anyone in the room, but it would make them uncoordinated and probably render them unable to finish the race, except for the V'mil who wasn't susceptible.

He wouldn't know until they started, but Palforma hoped he could use the V'mil to inhibit the progress of the Meelton. He would have to be quick on his feet and adaptable once everything started, but that was something he was good at. Even Dalt, the fastest fighter he'd ever seen, had complimented

Palforma in the past for his quick thinking during combat situations.

When the officials began herding them into start boxes, he was surprised he wasn't put next to the V'mil. As he glanced down the row of boxes that all resembled small cages, he realized what they were doing. They were alternating the racers so the weakest and strongest were mixed. That put the Lomo, the racer with the lowest stats, next to the one with the highest stats, the V'mil. He thought this was done to ensure an injury early on and make it more exciting for the spectators. It was smart because the swiftest one here would be the Lomo, and Palforma would bet anything that the guy's strategy was all about speed and avoiding confrontation. If the Lomo didn't make a clean getaway the moment the gates opened, he had little chance of winning.

Or staying alive.

Above them the announcer's voice filled the air as he reminded everyone who was racing and their current stats. Then he built up the tension with a quick rundown of each species' strengths, making the V'mil sound almost unstoppable.

A thrill went through Palforma at the warning buzzer signaling the race was about to start. All the cages moved forward on tracks so the stands could see the racers. The V'mil roared and banged on his gate, making the Lomo next to him squeak and change color with fear.

The second buzzer sounded and Palforma crouched, digging his clawed toes into the cage floor. He focused on finding the part of himself that was calm and ready. That place where time slowed down and he could take in everything going on around him without being overwhelmed. He could move without having to think and react without weighing options.

The third buzzer sounded, and the gates flung open with a clang. With one stride, he cleared the gate. In the middle of the second stride a Tomari barreled into him, sending both of them into the V'mil's back.

In fact, a Tomari had attacked each racer while one of them ran off to complete the course. Palforma realized he'd severely miscalculated. All six Tomaris in the race were working together so one of them could run unimpeded, and they'd split the winnings. He'd thought the Meelton had been the major threat. He hadn't expected a conspiracy.

As the V'mil's massive, spiked tail rose to come crashing down on his head, Palforma regretted asking Zia to watch. She wasn't going to be happy about this.

CHAPTER 13

Heart in her throat, Zia watched one of the Tomaris leave the gate only to deliberately barrel into Palforma, pushing the large Talin into the massive V'mil. The moment the V'mil roared with rage, the Tomari backed away, leaving Palforma to his fate.

When four of the six Tomaris stayed behind to waylay the other racers and only two of them took off to complete the course she understood that there was a conspiracy in play and Palforma was about to get very hurt.

Next to her two Marooks had been engaged in a lively conversation ever since the first warning buzzer had sounded. Their conversation only got louder as the race started.

"Oh, he's a dead one now."

"Naw, those Talins are tough ones. You'll see."

She wanted to slap the Marooks. Wanted to reprimand them and explain that they were talking about a living, breathing person, not some hunk of meat. But her entire attention was on the race and she couldn't be bothered to even slide the Marooks a dirty look.

As she watched the V'mil's thick-spiked tail rise up, she cursed herself for giving in to Palforma. She knew how dangerous these races were. If Palforma survived this, she was going to tie him hand and foot in their cabin and not let him out until they docked.

Expecting to watch her lover die a horrible death by bludgeoning, she sucked in a sharp breath when Palforma pivoted with the grace of a dancer to avoid the deadly tail, and then with surgical accuracy he unleashed his claws and slashed them across the base of the tail. The thick appendage went limp, and the V'mil cried out in pain. Stumbling back, the creature grabbed his tail up and hugged it to his chest, rocking slightly on his feet as blood dripped from the deep gashes.

When the race had started, everyone in the now crowded stands had been on their feet, shouting and cheering. But the moment Palforma hurt the V'mil, her left eye registered almost complete silence around her. Turning her head, she noted the stunned faces of the other spectators.

One of the Marooks next to her was waving a tentacle with excitement. "See, I told you the Talin would make it. I knew I was right to bet on him."

Silently, she agreed with that Marook. Pride in Palforma made her stand tall and want to declare to everyone around her that this Talin was hers. And as soon as he worked everything out with his people, they'd go find jobs together and eventually she'd drag him back home to meet her family and…

"…that was only one player. And he still has all the obstacles to make it through and the two Tomaris ahead of him to contend with. Your win is not guaranteed," the Marook told his companion, interrupting her thoughts.

Thankfully, the second Marook countered that objection before Zia felt the need to smack his friend around.

"You can already see he is gaining ground. It's unlikely he will fail, and I will win and you will owe me so much!"

The Marooks continued to banter as Palforma reached the first obstacle on the course. It was a tall, smooth wall with spikes jutting from the top in all directions. He didn't even pause as he got close. With one powerful leap, he got his fingers over the edge and hauled himself up, moving gingerly across the top to keep from cutting himself on those sharp, dagger like barbs.

The two Tomaris ahead of him were just clearing the second obstacle as Palforma landed on the ground past the first one. He sprinted to the second obstacle. This one consisted of narrow beams crossing over a large pit of tar. She knew from watching other races that if Palforma landed in the tar, he wouldn't drown, but one of the race staff would need to come pull him out. And it would take hours to get all the tar off him.

She expected him to slow down to traverse it. But, as with the wall, Palforma didn't slow down.

With one perfectly placed foot at the starting pad to one of the beams, he leaped halfway across the pit. Zia held her breath as his second foot landed perfectly on the beam, and his momentum carried him the rest of the way over the pit to land both feet on the other side. He was forced to take a few stumbling steps after the landing but soon regained his balance and was sprinting off again to chase down the Tomaris.

Zia could picture this male at war. Wearing armor and carrying deadly weapons, he must have been a sight to behold. He would've been a fierce fighter and loyal beyond measure.

How could his parents have cast him aside like they did? It was incomprehensible. But he had her now, and she'd make sure he knew he was loved and adored.

That was assuming he survived this damn race!

Although Palforma had speed and skill on them, the Tomaris stayed one step ahead on the course because they were helping each other. Except for the part of the stands full of Tomaris, most of the audience was booing at them and shouting insults. While this kind of collusion wasn't strictly against the rules, it was frowned upon and none of the Tomaris in the race would ever be allowed to enter another competition on this ship or any of her sister ships. But none of that mattered if they hurt her Talin.

As she watched, one of the Tomaris glanced back at Palforma, frowned, and then said something to his partner. They were planning something, and she vowed that if they injured Palforma, she'd hunt them down and make them pay. She still had the punch-stick, and she'd learned all kinds of ways to make weapons over the years. She might belong to one of the smallest species in the universe, but that didn't make her helpless.

"This should be entertaining," the hateful Marook commented. "I've watched those rings dump a lot of players over the years."

He won't get dumped, Zia thought as she leaned over the rail to see better.

She watched Palforma grab the first set of rings for the third obstacle. Under him was a catch net designed to trap whoever fell into it, so if a participant lost hold of the rings, they would need to wait for someone to release them from the net.

To make it more difficult, the rings were attached to ratchets that would raise and lower each one without rhyme or reason. A competitor could be stretched out, about to grab a ring, and have it yanked out of reach. They could also find themselves suddenly pulled up or dropped, and only a strong grip would keep them from falling into the net.

Both Tomaris managed to make it through but only barely. At one moment Zia was sure one of them would end up in the net, but the other one grabbed his leg and pulled him onto the platform at the end of the obstacle before he completely lost his grip on the rapidly rising ring. The edges of the ring were lined with spikes, so if you fell when you were starting or finishing, you would face major injuries or possible death.

This was by far the most dangerous part of the race.

Despite the Tomaris cheating, Palforma was gaining on them, and he was now the crowd favorite. One section had even started chanting his name. He was so focused she didn't think he realized he was being encouraged by the spectators. Palforma's concentration on the race was absolute.

Unlike all the obstacles he'd faced so far, Palforma paused at this one to watch the rings move. After studying them for several moments, he leaped and grabbed one. She didn't know how he did it, but he must have figured out the timing because as he got hold of it, he seemed prepared for the ring to fly into the air. Palforma used the upward momentum to launch himself at a ring that was stationary. No sooner had he gotten his hand on the stationary ring than it dropped fast, but he was already reaching out for a ring going up and again used the upward motion to jump to another stationary ring.

With unstopping, fluid movements, he crossed the obstacle so quickly that the Tomaris didn't even have time to reach the next one before Palforma was running at them. One Tomari turned to face Palforma as the other one scampered away.

"See! Didn't I tell you that Talins are unmatched!" the Marook crowed to his companion, his voice registering at a loud volume in her left eye.

His friend was more subdued when he answered but still sure of himself. "Even if the Talin gets past the Tomari, the other one still has a good head start. He isn't going to win. Your bet was foolish. And look, the Tomari facing him down has a weapon!"

Zia had been so focused on Palforma she didn't notice the edged weapon the Tomari was carrying until that last comment scrolled across her eye. The weapon meant the Tomari was now disqualified, but that didn't matter if all he wanted was for his teammate to win.

Dirty, rotten cowards! she screamed in her head as fear for Palforma made her heartbeat wildly and adrenaline flooded her system. She looked around for a way to get down to the pit. It was too far for her to drop over the railing. The only way down was either from the winner's platform at the far end that stood up even with the audience, or to take the narrow staircase down to the starting cages.

A glance told her the staircase wasn't an option, as two guards were stationed there to keep eager spectators from going down into the pit. She would need to climb onto the winner's platform and then make her way from there to Palforma.

A loud shout from the Marook that bet on Palforma made her pause and sweep her gaze back down to the pit.

"I proclaim that this Talin has no equal!" the Marook shouted as he banged the single hooked claw at the end of his tentacle on the seat in front of him. The creature in that seat cast him a nasty look but then turned back to watch the race.

Zia agreed with the Marook. Palforma had no equal! She missed how he'd done it, but not only did Palforma remain uninjured, but the cheating Tomari was pinned to a support beam with his own weapon through his shoulder. The Tomari cried out for help, tried to pull the knife out, and then passed out cold.

It was a satisfying sight to see. Served the bastard right!

Palforma and the last racer were at the final obstacle, which was a long, smooth, and steep incline leading to the winner's platform. At unpredictable intervals, parts of the incline would shake and shift. Sometimes it would become even more vertical or curling over the racer like a cresting wave and then snapping back into place to launch the racer off.

The Tomari was only a few paces ahead of Palforma but both of them were struggling to maintain their footing on the slick ramp. A booming sound registered in Zia's left eye at the same time the entire ramp bucked violently. Zia held her breath as both the Tomari and Palforma went flying.

The two of them landed back on the ramp so close to each other that their shoulders brushed. They were quick to gain their feet, but instead of climbing to the platform, the Tomari turned to Palforma and aimed a kick at his head.

Palforma was about to start scaling the ramp when the Tomari lashed out. With a speed Zia would have said was impossible before this, Palforma caught the Tomari's foot and flung his opponent over his shoulder. The Tomari cried out as he landed and then slid the rest of the way down the ramp. He scrambled to his feet at the bottom. Launching himself back up the ramp, he tried to catch up, his face enraged.

Palforma ignored the Tomari now that he was no longer in the way. Her Talin bounded up the ramp, dropping to all fours for the top third of the steep climb. The ramp undulated under him but Palforma braced and then lunged, making it to the platform just at the entire ramp waved, crested, and fell away sending the Tomari plunging to the pit floor. Landing in a heap, the Tomari didn't try to get up again. She could see he was blinking and breathing, but he knew he'd lost.

The crowd went wild around her and the implant in her right eye gave her the warning dots that told her the implants had dialed down their sensitivity because too much noise was coming from too many angles to register.

Leaning over slightly and panting from exertion, Palforma swept the stands for her. Their eyes met. She waved her arms in the air wildly and jumped around, trying to tell him how impressed she was.

One of the race officials stepped onto the platform from the seating area and presented Palforma with an information square. That square would have all the winnings and also a certificate of accomplishment that might buy them dinner at one of the restaurants. The square looked tiny in Palforma's big hand as her Talin accepted it and then shoved in unceremoniously into a pocket. The officials were asking him things, but when Palforma tapped out a response, they looked confused. Those who worked in the eateries and shops would have Norka programed into their INT, but probably not these individuals who were higher up on the pay scale.

When it was obvious the officials couldn't understand him, Palforma turned to leave. Instead of taking the roundabout way that would walk him around the end of the platform to wave at the audience, he hopped over the short rail between the winner's platform and the arena seats. When he loped off, the official watching him go looked equal parts confused and annoyed. They were probably used to winners wanting to crow and strut around after winning, but not her Talin.

He covered the distance between them quickly, ignoring all the well-wishers along with those booing him because their favorite lost to him.

The moment he got to her, he started tapping. 'I'm going to take you on a date now!' He used her created motion for date instead of the Norka words that literally translated to *a meeting of individuals*. It made his words feel more intimate and meaningful to her.

'Yes,' she agreed. Later she'd lecture him about never putting himself in that kind of danger again. But for now, he was alive and jovial, and he wanted her to be happy with him. She could do that. 'Let's go on a date.'

'I'm going to buy you any food you want.' He was so excited he almost clipped another passenger who was trying to edge by them.

Not surprisingly the passenger didn't growl or curse at Palforma. He didn't even give Palforma a dirty look. Instead he moved quickly to avoid Palforma's arm and then scampered back the way he'd come to take the long away around and get out of the arena seating. Zia felt bad for the innocent passenger but also amused. Everyone was going to give Palforma a wide berth now that he'd won that very rigged race. It wasn't every day you saw someone go up against a V'mil and a troop of Tomaris and come out of the encounter without a scratch.

But Palforma wasn't done telling her what he wanted to do with the winnings. 'And we're going to buy you nicer clothes. Soft things for you to wear.'

Her heart melted at his enthusiasm. 'I don't need any clothes. But if you want to go shopping, we can. We can do anything you want to do.'

'No, not what I want,' he argued. 'Now that I have funds, we're going to do whatever you want. We'll feed you, clothe you, and upgrade the cabin if you like. I can do all of that now!'

Blinking up at him, it took her brain a moment to figure out what those words meant. 'You did that all, *the whole race,* for me? So you could buy me things?'

'Of course. What would you like to do first?'

She took one deep breath and held it. Then another. By the third she was calm enough. 'Funds are great, but no amount of funds would be enough if something happened to you. I love you, you spikey moron!'

Had she really just done that? Proclaimed her love? Basically she'd done the equivalent of shouting it out.

Worse, did Palforma even understand what that meant? Saying you loved someone was a big deal to her. Outside of her family, she'd never said it anyone. Ever!

They stood there not talking while he blinked at her for several quiet seconds, making her desperately wish she could call back the words.

Then he grabbed her up in his arms and cradled her close to his chest. She felt his cheek rub against the top of her head as vanilla filled her nose.

"Me second," he stuttered out, his breath warm against her oil-soaked scalp as his words scrolled across her right eye. "Scent-love you. F-f-forever Zia's. Yours al-al-always."

CHAPTER 14

With her hair saturated with his bonding oil and the smell of vanilla strong in her nose, Palforma carried her away from the pit and to the nearest shops. Because this vessel was geared toward the frivolous, an entire row of shops were full of mostly useless but eye-catching baubles.

Palforma carried her into the largest clothing shop on the row, but he didn't set her down right away. He swept his gaze around the place before striding for a section near the back corner. When Palforma set her down, they were next to several tailoring machines, and their displays were rotating through images of the various items anyone could order.

'You need better clothes,' he stated then pointed to the machine.

'I guess I could use another set of coveralls,' she allowed.

Palforma made a negative gesture and then leaned over and started tapping on the machine's display. She watched as he searched through several menus and then finally settled on an item. She blinked, surprised when the item's image filled the screen. To her it looked like a cross between a coat and a dress. It reached all the way to the floor, with long sleeves and a high neck, and she didn't see any fastenings down the center. Instead it had old-fashioned ties so the garment overlapped in the front and was tied at the hip on each side, one tie on the inside and one on the outside.

Palforma looked over at her. 'What is your favorite color?'

No one had ever asked her that question before, so it took her a moment to come up with an answer. 'Silver, I guess.'

He turned his attention back to the screen and pressed a few more options. The fabric of the garment in the image changed from a soft amber to a lovely deep blue with white trim and wide, ornate, silver embroidery in a stylized pattern down the sleeves.

'They don't have anything that's all silver, but do you like this one?' he asked.

Instead of saying yes because she loved what she saw on the screen, she responded with the practicality she'd learned to live by. 'I don't need a coat.'

'You get cold. I see it,' Palforma responded. 'You tuck your hands in your pockets and bounce on your toes to help warm yourself.'

'You're observant,' she said at the same time realizing she'd gotten so used to always being in mild discomfort that she'd stopped noticing when she was cold.

'I am,' Palforma agreed, and a soft rhythmic pattern registered in her left eye. 'I'd like to get you this omnie, and I think it would look good with your bright eyes. Would you step close so the machine can measure you?'

She glanced at the small print at the bottom of the display and grimaced. 'It's awfully expensive. I'm sure we could find a cheaper option in there.'

'Zia, let me do this.'

She gave in with a shrug. 'If you want to waste your winnings on me, fine.'

'This isn't a waste,' Palforma argued. 'This is important. You should be comfortable and dressed in something nice.'

A look down at her coveralls reminded her that this pair had seen better days. She'd patched several spots with fabric-fix to cover holes, and one sleeve had multiple stains from when she had to reach that arm deep into a reverb socket to replace a broken part.

Palforma rubbed a bit of her stained sleeve between his fingers and then let it go to talk. 'This is practical but old. We can start with getting you a warm omnie and then move onto other items.'

'This omnie-coat thing is enough,' she countered.

Palforma didn't respond. Instead he made a few small changes to the garment on the screen and then held up the information square with his winnings to pay. The display flashed a countdown on the screen as it got started on the coat.

With some time to wait while the machine worked, Palforma looked down at her feet. 'You need slippers.'

No, that was a hard line for her. 'I wear boots. Human feet are easily hurt and these boots are made of duron, which is the same stuff they make landing pads out of. They're the most expensive item I own, and I will not be replacing them until they're completely worn out.'

'Duron? Really?' Palforma commented as he crouched down to get a closer look at her feet. 'The slippers I want to get you will have duron soles.'

'Everything except the closures on these boots are duron,' Zia countered. 'It doesn't get more protective than that.'

'Very true. The armor we're issued is mostly made up of duron. I found it to be effective.'

'Same here,' Zia agreed, feeling a strange camaraderie form with Palforma over protective gear. 'Those slippers are cute, but they won't keep my feet safe. It took me half a year to save up for these boots, and they've kept my feet from getting injured or even crushed a couple of times.'

'No slippers then. But what about one of these?' Palforma asked as he pointed to a dress displayed on the wall. Like with the omnie, the wraparound garment tied at both hips. Those kinds of outfits were so common they were sold almost everywhere.

'No!' her gesture was big to note her adamant refusal. 'Forget it. I'm not wearing a dress. Ever.' Then she paused and added, 'Well, except on my wedding day. The dress I wear that day will be big and fluffy and everything.'

Palforma went perfectly still. 'Wedding day?'

'Getting married is a custom among humans. It's when two people decide to devote their lives to each other and cement it with a ceremony in front of friends and family,' she explained.

'I know what marriage is. We Talins have the same custom, but I didn't realize humans got married also. I know they can deeply bond to a partner, but I'd never heard they had any kind of formal celebration to denote pairing off.'

That answered one question for her; when she eventually asked Palforma to marry her, he'd understand what she meant. 'Well, we do, and it's important to us. Humans, I mean. So keep that in mind.'

'I will.' The gestures he used to make those words struck her as solemn. Hmmm, she hoped she wasn't making him nervous with talk of marriage and permanence. Maybe it was time to lighten the mood.

'Why are we only looking for clothing for me? You need some new pants! That race left you with more holes than fabric,' she teased. Although it was an exaggeration, Palforma did have a few rips in his pants from close encounters with sharp things during the race.

'You bought me four pairs back on Yarnetta. I can change when we get back to the room, he told her dismissively.

'Or we could get you a pair made here to replace these,' she countered. Before he could respond, the machine display flashed, and a small compartment opened. The smell of freshly cooled cloth binding gel hit her nose, making her want to sneeze. As she stepped back to let the smell dissipate, Palforma reached in and pulled out the omnie.

Her jaw nearly dropped at how beautiful it was. The image on the display hadn't done it justice at all. The silver embroidery shimmered under the bright lights of the shop and took her breath away. The white trim wasn't as eye catching as the embroidery, but helped to set off the cerulean blue of the fabric.

Her hands itched to touch it, but she hesitated. It looked too nice for her to wear over old, stained coveralls. Shaking it out, Palforma stepped behind her and held it up so she could slip into it. She wavered for a second but shoved her arms in.

The first thing she noticed was how soft and warm the garment was even before Palforma finished sliding it onto her shoulders. It felt self-heating, so it must have been infused with some kind of nanos. She had only one pair of socks made out of the stuff because it was pricy, but worth it. The nano-infused fabric was self-heating, self-drying, and self-cleaning.

She never imagined she'd be wearing an entire coat made out of the same tech. It was like being enveloped in a warm hug by some super soft and warm creature.

'This is nice!' she said as Palforma stepped in front of her so he could tie the omnie closed.

'I haven't met a human who didn't like omnies,' Palforma commented after he'd finished securing the last tie. He pointed to her left side. 'I had the machine make an alteration for you.'

Looking down, she frowned, trying to figure out what Palforma was talking about. Then she noticed a small imperfection in the fabric on the front and slightly below the tie on her left hip. She ran her fingers over it and realized it was a pocket as it opened under her touch. The tailoring machine had lined the opening of the pocket with magnetic nanos so there were no obvious closures. Using the nanos to secure the pocket closed meant it was almost invisible to the casual observer.

When she opened it by simply running her finger the length of the seam, it revealed a pocket large enough to store her small information square and a few other odds and ends. The voluminous fabric of the omnie would hide all but the most bulbous items she put in there.

Closing the pocket, she looked up at Palforma, making a show of hugging herself before talking. 'This thing is wonderful. I might never take it off again!'

'I can buy you more,' he urged. 'In any color or pattern you want.'

She grabbed his arm before he could move back to the machine. 'That's too much to carry around,' she argued.

She couldn't think of a single job she could or would do wearing this beautiful garment. After they got jobs and she went back to work, this omnie would be carefully folded and stowed in her room or equipment locker. She wouldn't risk getting it ripped or stained.

'We can get more later when we pick a permanent domicile,' Palforma allowed.

'Good,' she said with a smile. 'If you won't let me buy you another pair of pants, we're done shopping for now. I'm hungry.'

Tangling her hand with his, she led him off to the food court section of the communal area. Most of the places were kiosks, but a few had spots where people could sit down and order a meal. She picked one that had the widest assortment of food offerings. The place was small so it only had only a few tables, but one of them was empty so she and Palforma headed to it.

They both studied the menu pictured on the table display, and Palforma expressed disappointment at the lack of Talin foods.

'The kiosk three shops down offers Nimon food,' she offered. 'You stomached that well, so we could go there instead.'

'Do you want Nimon food?'

She made a face as she answered. 'Want? No. But I can eat it, of course. I don't want you to go hungry because we picked a place that didn't carry anything you can eat.'

He dismissed her concerns. 'I can eat anything here, but I was hoping to have you try some Talin food. Humans can eat some of the dishes, and they seem to like them.'

Oh, he wanted to share some of his culture with her. That was sweet and understandable. 'We're heading to a Talin station,' she reminded him. 'I promise to try everything you ask me to at least once.'

'Yes, that's true. Thank you.' Mollified, he went back to perusing the menu and picked a few items.

They ordered the food and Palforma insisted on paying. Once they were done selecting everything, he pushed his chair back and reached for her. In short order she found herself seated sideways on his lap snuggled against his chest.

Vanilla filled the air as he rubbed a cheek against the top of her head. She relaxed against him, enjoying everything about this moment. It didn't get much better than this. They were safe, about to be fed, and had enough funds to know they were safe from taking dangerous jobs.

But the most important thing about this moment to her was that she wasn't alone anymore. Until Palforma she hadn't realized how lonely she'd been. And from what he'd said, he'd suffered from the same loneliness as her.

It made the romantic side of her smile to think they were meant to be. Destined to meet. It was fanciful but enjoyable to contemplate.

The food arrived, and she moved to get off his lap, but he stopped her. 'Would you let me feed you?'

At first she was mildly insulted. Feed her? Like a child?

But then again, this might be a Talin thing. They might show love and affection by feeding each other, so she nodded and let him pick up a bite to offer her. He was gentle and didn't try to give her too much at once. It helped that the food she ordered came prepared in pieces small enough for a human mouth.

He alternated between feeding her and then himself. They didn't bother with conversation. They didn't need to. Feeding and being fed filled an instinctual part in both of them.

Quietly and contentedly, they lost themselves in the moment.

Much later, after they got back to the cabin and bedded down for their rest period, Zia realized this was the first time she'd felt a kind of bone-deep peace. No fear for the future. No worry about finding another job. No anxiety about proving herself to everyone she met. She'd dealt with all of those things back when she was alone, but she wasn't alone any longer. She and Palforma were together now, and she was sure they could take on the universe together.

CHAPTER 15

As he and Zia waited in line to enter Oglin station, a bad feeling built in Palforma's chest—a feeling that this could all go wrong.

The first issue he was going to have to contend with was collars. Human pets wore collars. All humans living among the Talin were pets. Therefore Zia should be wearing a collar.

He knew beyond a shadow of a doubt that trying to put a collar on Zia wouldn't work. Besides, he had no desire to force a collar on his clever and self-sufficient human. But the lack of collar made her an anomaly among the pet humans and had the potential to draw unwelcome attention. He hoped a simple medical excuse would appease everyone, but a lack of collar wasn't the only issue.

If she drew too much attention and conversation from the surrounding Talins, Zia might figure out what he'd failed to mention to her, and his little human would be livid. He could only hope the ancestors were on his side because a lot was going to need to go right for everything to happen how he hoped it would.

There were so many unknowns here. If getting Zia through Oglin station without her finding out the truth was a military mission, no commander would approve it.

On the positive side, Oglin was still under construction, so no pets should be here at all. Keeping Zia from seeing other humans wearing collars would be the best way to skirt the issue of human pets and ownership among Talins.

The line shifted forward and a bolt of fear went through him. Ancestors help him, he was about to lead Zia onto a station where she was automatically considered property, and he hadn't warned her.

If everything blew up in his face, at least she wouldn't be able to run. The transport they'd come on had left almost as soon as the two of them got off. They'd been the only ones scheduled for this stop, and no one was scheduled to board. The only other transports on the schedule for the next few rotations were Talin-owned and heading deeper into Talin-controlled space.

If things went wrong, she'd have little recourse. Part of him was glad to note that she wouldn't be able to get away from him. But a bigger part of him knew their relationship would be shattered if she no longer trusted him.

Nerves made him twitch a little when a worker dropped a heavy tool on the metal bay floor not too far from him. The other workers teased the clumsy Talin, but it was all Palforma could do to keep his rattle of anxiety to himself.

What had he been thinking? Why hadn't he told her?

No, he knew why he didn't tell her. He was desperate to get her here to see a Talin healer, and if she knew about humans being pets, she wouldn't have come. Humans were fragile creatures, prone to all kinds of diseases and physical defects that could kill them without warning. Even if he'd tricked her, it was worth it for her to see a healer.

He remembered clearly when Maka suddenly cried out in pain and fainted in his arms. She'd been visiting him at his home, deep in the Kalor forest. Holding her dead weight to his chest, he'd run hard through the forest with no regard for the toll the trip took on his body. Forging a shorter path to Holian's compound, he used the treacherous dry riverbed full of shale to cut the distance in half. The shale ripped apart his feet, and he was bleeding heavily by the time he'd stepped into the infirmary with Maka in his arms.

But he was too late.

The healers tried to comfort him by saying it wasn't his fault. They told him that no one could have known she had an irregularity in the blood vessels in her head. No one could have moved fast enough to save her.

Still, he felt like it had been his fault.

Many of the other soldiers in the forest and the humans in the compound seemed to blame him. She'd been the only one willing to visit him in the forest. When she died, the other humans had refused to be near him, even within the safe confines of Holian's compound.

What happened to Maka put a deep fear in him that human bodies were prone to expire. They were full of biological faults waiting to go wrong. Every second Zia wasn't seen by a healer was a moment she could die from some unseen medical condition. If Maka had been scanned more regularly, the healers might have found the irregularity and fixed it. He needed Zia to get a thorough physical. He needed to know he'd done everything in his power to keep her safe, even from her own fallible human genetics.

If Zia died, his life was over.

He needed her to be healthy. He needed to know nothing was wrong with her that could suddenly take her away from him. This need to have her see the healers overrode everything else. Even the fear of making Zia furious with him.

Talin healers were better than any medic, doctor, or med-staff she could see anywhere else. They had to study human anatomy as much as Talin anatomy, and he'd even heard one of the Verde clan healers worked on this station. That clan was well-known for making careful studies of human welfare and health. Zia would be in good hands.

Hopefully he could get her checked out at medical and registered without her seeing another human or anyone asking too many questions about where she came from. If anyone asked why she wasn't wearing a collar, he could claim she suffered from Choker Syndrome. It usually happened when a human had a bad experience with a collar and panicked if forced to wear one. He'd only ever read about it, but everyone reading the standard-issued literature on taking care of human pets would be familiar with it.

This could work. He would make it work.

He'd get a new Ident Cube and access to his funds. Zia would be seen by the healers and receive whatever medical assistance she needed. Maybe they could even improve her implants. Then he would book them on a transport to Kalor. Once on Kalor, he'd explain everything in a way that wouldn't upset her.

As the line shuffled forward, he watched several Talins staring at Zia. At least she was wearing the omnie. Because it fell to the floor and was long sleeved, it hid the fact that she was wearing coveralls and boots. If other Talins saw the coveralls, they'd be incensed at a human pet dressed in such rough fabric. They would hate that she was wearing clothes meant for laborers. Looking down, he winced because he could see her boots peeking out from the hem of the omnie. No one would like seeing her wearing those either.

Despite his internal pep talk, dread build in his chest.

The omnie wasn't cutting it. Her lack of a collar was drawing attention, and a few worried or confused rumbles. Her implants wouldn't be able to interpret the rumbles, but he could.

Eyeing the Talin in front of them who kept casting looks over his shoulder, Palforma drew Zia close to his side. So far she hadn't noticed the looks. Part of that was probably because she was used to being stared at, as humans were rare wherever they went. The other part was that she was too busy taking in the station that was still under construction.

Catching his attention, she pointed to a spot high on the wall to their right. 'What are they planning to do there?'

Looking up to where she pointed, he saw a partially built standard weapon defense system commonly used in docking bays on Talin stations. 'It will be a system to track and kill if anyone thinks they can invade the station through there,' he explained.

Several Talin were openly staring at the two of them now as they talked. One of them was sounding a soft, aggressive rattle along with a rumble of interest. The aggression was for Palforma and the interest for Zia. He couldn't let that go unanswered.

Flashing teeth, Palforma straightened to his full height and fixed his gaze on the male. He'd been told by others that he had an intimidating presence due to more than just his size since he exuded strength and conviction. He tried to focus all of that into his glare.

"Mine," he barked at the Talin, who jumped slightly and turned away as if suddenly interested in examining a shuttle having repair work done on it.

Casting a wary eye around, he tucked Zia half behind him. He could hear her laughing huff as she wiggled out and stood slightly in front of him.

Her expression was unconcerned. 'Don't worry, I'm not going to leave you for anyone else. You're the only tall, spikey guy I want.'

He knew she was trying to be humorous, but it only made him feel worse for not telling her about her new pet classification. She thought others might want to seduce her. She didn't realize that they wanted to own her. She was blithely unaware of the status she had acquired the moment she stepped on Oglin station.

'That's good because you're the only human I want,' he responded. Then he paused for a second before adding, 'If anyone becomes aggressive, get behind me.'

She didn't appear concerned. 'Sure thing, big guy. I saw your skills in the pit. I don't mind letting you be in charge of the fighting.' At that point, she finally seemed to notice quite a few Talins were watching her. Her expression turned concerned. 'Am I doing something wrong or weird?'

He chose his words carefully. 'Their interest is because they want to meet you.' There, that sounded innocent enough.

A female behind him made an inquisitive rumble. When he turned to look, she pointed to Zia. "Does she have Choker Syndrome?" When Palforma sounded a rumble of agreement, the female Talin's rumbling turned soothing as she addressed Zia. "You're a very pretty human, but you need to make sure you don't wander away from your owner or someone might steal you. Both of you need to be very careful."

That was all it took to undo all his wishful thinking. He was an idiot for thinking he could make this work.

Eyes narrowed with suspicion, Zia turned to him and started tapping rapidly, her movements sharp from agitation. 'Owner? Why would she think I'm owned? You said Talins don't have slaves.'

'We don't,' he answered. The line moved forward so he urged her to keep up. She walked but didn't take her eyes off him.

'Owned, Palforma. The woman behind you said owned. No alternate meanings scrolled next to that word. No idiom or slang. That word means one thing, property. Why would she say that if you guys don't have slaves?'

Before he could answer, they were at the gate to get from the bay into the station. The Talin posted there sounded a cheerful rumble when he saw Zia. "Oh, hello sweet one! I have a treat for you if your master says it's okay."

He pulled a sweet from his pouch and Palforma recognized it as the candy many Talins bought specially for humans. He held it up to show Palforma and sounded a questioning rumble. It was a way of asking permission.

Palforma sounded a rumble of assent as he looked down at Zia. Her expression had gone from suspicious to sly as her eyes jumped from Palforma's face to the guard's hand. The earlier doubt was giving way to amusement. Slaves weren't offered candy by strangers. The way Talins treated human pets might throw her off enough for this plan to still work.

'She didn't mean you were a slave,' he said. 'But now's not the time. I'll explain everything once we leave the station. For now, go along with everything. Please?'

'I want the explanation the moment we are alone,' she warned him. 'I'm not waiting until we leave the station.'

He accepted the compromise because they wouldn't be alone until after she was seen at medical. 'Very well. But would you please accept the male's offering? Talins think all humans like sweets, and it would make the guard happy if you took it.'

Her expression softened as she looked at the guard. He'd lowered his hand so Zia could reach the candy. She took it, popped it in her mouth and sucked on it. 'Thanks.'

Even though she couldn't hear his confused rattle, it was obvious to her that this Talin's INT didn't have Norka programmed in when he didn't respond to her. Without hesitation she pulled out a small information square from the pocket of her omnie. She typed and then showed it to the guard. The guard rumbled out a laugh as he read what she wrote out loud.

"Thanks for the candy, but he is my Talin, not my owner." The others in the line around them sounded rumbles of amusement along with the guard.

Despite the fact they were holding up the line, no one got upset or demanded they hurry. That didn't surprise Palforma. When it came to humans, most Talins had an abundance of patience and a willingness to indulge.

Looking up at Palforma, the guard sounded a rumble of envy. "That's adorable. Has she scent-bonded to you then? That must be so nice to have such an attached human. A member of my clan has a human that's the same way."

Palforma hesitated. Even at the best of times, it was difficult to get his words out, and right now he was so tense he couldn't imagine he'd be able to get a single syllable out without putting his weakness on display to everyone.

"Palforma?" They all turned at the loud voice to see a Talin striding toward the gate from one of the areas under construction further inside the station.

The Talin was as big as Palforma with almost his entire left side covered in burn scars. That same side was also missing quills, and the hand only had three fingers. He'd sustained almost no damage to his head, so he retained both eyes, but it looked like the healers hadn't been able to save the keratin plating on his left shoulder, neck, or chest. His stride wasn't perfectly fluid as he moved, probably indicating some deep muscle damage to that side even though he didn't have any burn scars on his legs.

Even without the scars, Palforma would recognize this Talin.

Palforma hadn't seen Tamerin since the accident that ended his military career. They'd both started their recovery in the same place, but Palforma had been transferred away long before Tamerin was healed enough to leave. After his parents had disowned him, Palforma had feared trying to contact any other families in his clan. But by the sound of Tamerin's welcoming rumble, he shouldn't have been so wary.

It was good to see this male walking without pain. As cousins of the same age, Tamerin and Palforma had entered the military at the same time and done early training together before separating to different branches. They'd also both been badly wounded and retired around the same time although they'd been stationed in different systems.

While Palforma disappeared to Kalor to be alone and lick his wounds, it looked like Tamerin had found employment as a civilian building space stations.

"It is good to see you looking so well," Tamerin said as he drew to a stop next to them at the gate.

"You t-t-t-too, T-t-tamerin. Cousin," Palforma stuttered out as he tapped an explanation to Zia. 'This is a good male who was badly wounded. He is family and dear to me. Please be kind to him.'

Remembering the way even some medical personnel shied away from the deformed Talin while he was recovering, Palforma hoped Zia wouldn't flinch from Tamerin's appearance.

Far from acting fearful or disgusted, her expression was open and welcoming. 'I won't hurt his feelings. I promise.'

Looking at the Talin stationed at the gate, Tamerin sounded an impatient rattle. "Let them pass through, Sominan, this is my cousin Palforma and his human. I can vouch for them." He pointed to the growing line. "Others need to get on with their day, and the line is backing up."

"You be a good little human and stick close to your Talin," Sominan told Zia with an indulgent rumble of affection. Then he sounded a slightly disgruntled rattle as he looked to Palforma and waved them through. "You watch her. This place isn't done yet and she could get hurt by accident."

Then he said something under his breath about the station not being fit for humans before looking at the Talin behind him in line. He didn't even bother checking the readout from the scanner as they passed under it.

"Next," he barked out as Palforma and Zia stepped away from the gate to stand with Tamerin.

"This way," Tamerin said as he turned to lead them. "Let me take you some place less crowded."

He took them to a small temporary office filled with all kinds of tech. A glance around the room told Palforma that Tamerin was likely involved in the installation of internal station security. Then Tamerin surprised him by looking at Zia and tapping with an almost equally fluid grace.

'Hello, as this one mentioned, I'm his cousin. I won't come near you if I make you uncomfortable.'

A delighted expression covered Zia's face. 'You tap!'

"I worked on a Norka station for a solar, so learning their language was important,' he explained.

Boldly, Zia stepped up to Tamerin and gave him a little bow. 'It's nice to meet you, Cousin Tamerin. If you're family to my Palforma, you're family to me.'

Palforma listened to his cousin rumble out a sound of affection at Zia's declaration and his own heart beat a little faster. That was twice now she'd declared to strangers how important he was to her. He filed away these moments to hold close to his heart and remember later.

'And if anything ever happens, you can always come to me,' Tamerin offered, casting a meaningful glance at him. Palforma understood that it was an offer to both protect them and to help keep Zia safe from being stolen by other Talins. With his cousin's help, Palforma felt he might have a chance of getting through this without either making Zia angry or running afoul of the station authorities.

It wasn't until this moment that he realized he had no way to prove ownership of Zia. No transfer of ownership or slave auction paperwork. Nothing. She could be stolen and he would have a difficult time proving she belonged to him over anyone else.

Cold fear ran through him. Not that he'd let anyone take and keep her, even if he had to resort to stealing her back. But it could be traumatizing for Zia to be taken away and end up owned by a Talin who didn't understand. They might even try to train her before he got her back.

That wouldn't end well for either Zia or the Talin who thought her actions could be curbed.

'I trust you to guard my back always, Tamerin,' Palforma answered, and Tamerin sounded a satisfied rumble.

'But what are you doing here?' Tamerin asked. 'This station is off the beaten path, nowhere near Kalor at all. And it's barely fit for Talins, let alone fragile humans.'

'Don't worry about me. I'm tougher than I look, and I know how to keep clear of construction sectors,' Zia answered, her expression unconcerned.

'I'm sure you're very tough,' Tamerin said with an indulgent rumble. It's a very good thing Zia couldn't pick up on rumbles, or she'd probably take exception because that rumble was the kind you used with children. Then Tamerin shifted his gaze to Palforma. 'Last I heard you were never going to leave Kalor again. Now you're way out here and you have a human. Is she from Holian's collection?'

Palforma watched Zia stiffen. Her hands came up to start asking questions and demand answers. Desperate to derail this conversation, he said the most shocking thing he could think of.

'Zia saved my life,' Palforma stated boldly.

Tamerin sounded a shocked rattle. 'What?'

'Zia is freeborn,' Palforma explained quickly. 'She worked on a metal trawler called Red Ore. I can't divulge why, but I was injured and trapped in an inoperable shuttle they salvaged. She kept me calm and got me medical attention. It cost her that job. But she loves me and agreed to come with me to the closest Talin station *from* Yarnetta.'

'She agreed?' It was more a statement than a question, as if Tamerin was trying to work out what Palforma wasn't telling him. Then he sounded a rattle of worry, his eyes bouncing between Zia and Palforma. It was well-known that wild-caught humans found it difficult to adjust to life as pets. Except for Lakin's family, Palforma hadn't heard of any free-born humans willingly accepting collars. Most wild-born humans were bought at slave auctions or kidnapped when Talin mercenaries ran across them on a station or planet.

'He needs a new Ident,' Zia told Tamerin, unaware of all the history and information that was probably bouncing around in Tamerin's head. 'I have funds to get us started again, but he was insistent that he needed funds too. He even ran this race on the transport we were on so he could pay for things.' She cast Palforma an indulgent smile. 'He didn't have to, but I wouldn't want to be without the ability to pay for things even temporarily, so I understand.'

'You paid for Palforma?' Tamerin said, as he sounded an incredulous rattle. Even unable to hear the nuanced rattle, it was clear that Zia understood the meaning. However, she didn't take offense.

Her expression was sincere as she spoke. 'I know you've probably heard that humans are dumb and untrustworthy because of what happened to our homeworld. But I promise you, we are capable of skilled labor and are hard workers. Red Ore didn't pay me as much as the Nimon crew, but I made a good living.'

Stepping over to Palforma, she nudged him playfully with her shoulder before she started talking again. 'Palforma and I haven't talked about where we will go from here, but I know I can get a good position on another ship that will agree to hire him also. Even if they don't, I can take care of him. You don't need to worry about your cousin.'

Tamerin didn't respond right away. He was too busy staring at Zia while he continued to sound a rattle of disbelief. Palforma could understand his incredulity because Talins weren't taught to see humans as able to live on their own. He'd been privileged to interact with the humans on Kalor and had even meet a few especially talented humans like Nalia and Lakin. To Tamerin, Zia's claims were inconceivable.

'I… uh, good?' Tamerin finally said as he sounded a confused rattle and cast a glance at Palforma. 'That's kind of you?'

If he wasn't so tense, Palforma would have sounded a rumble of laughter at Tamerin's bewilderment. For the moment it looked like the crisis with Zia had been averted. Tamerin was going along with what she was saying, even if he didn't comprehend how this little human could have had a job and funds all her own. But his cousin wanted Zia to be content, so to that end he accepted everything she said at face value and simply addressed Palforma next.

'I can help with the new Ident,' he offered. 'I play gav with the one who updates and issues new Idents for lost or damaged ones. I can ask him to put your request at the front of the queue as a favor to me. I could have it within a few marks.'

Palforma sounded a rumble of gratitude. 'That's generous of you. Getting the replacement Ident is important, but I want Zia to visit the healers too.'

Tamerin sounded a concerned rumble at the same time Zia sent Palforma a confused look.

'Why do I need to see the healers?' she asked. 'I feel fine. If anyone should get checked out, it's you.'

'Then we both should go to the healers,' Palforma countered, already prepared for that argument. Then he looked to Tamerin. 'Afterward the three of us can enjoy a meal together, yes?'

'It would be my honor to prepare a meal for us all to share,' Tamerin said with an excited rattle. 'And you both can stay in my cabin. It was meant to be shared by a crew of four, but we lack workers right now, so I have it to myself. A meal and a nice place to sleep will be a good reward for after you've finished with the healers.'

'That sounds nice. Let's skip visiting the healers and head straight to Tamerin's cabin,' Zia suggested.

'Why wouldn't you want to visit our healers?' Tamerin asked quickly. 'We have a prestigious Verde clan healer here. You won't find better unless you go all the way to Talarian.'

'I guess it couldn't hurt,' she agreed, but her expression wasn't thrilled. 'But if I have to put up with seeing a healer, the dinner better be amazing.'

Tamerin rumbled out a laugh. 'I'll do my best.' Digging around the mess on a nearby table he unearthed a battered information square and handed it to Palforma. 'Give me your Ident details, and I'll put the paperwork in to get you issued a new one.'

Palforma took the square, entered his information, and handed it back. Tamerin examined what Palforma had entered, typed a few things, and then tucked it into the pouch on his belt.

'Right, that's in the queue. It should be done before you're even finished with the healers.'

Unclipping his Ident, he tapped at it, read something, and then secured it back on his belt. 'I've finished my duties for this cycle so I'm free to escort you up to medical. Then I'll go see about collecting your Ident. After you two are done, I'll collect you and we can enjoy a meal and conversation back in my cabin.'

Having Tamerin with him made Palforma feel like he had an ally. A buffer to keep Zia separated from other Talins. A little of the tension in his shoulders relaxed as he sounded a rumble of gratitude. 'Thank you, cousin. That would be most welcome and kind.'

With that Tamerin led them out of the room and they were off to face the next hurdle.

CHAPTER 16

Zia wasn't a fan of Oglin station. She didn't like how the Talins around them looked at her. She also didn't like how they reached out to touch her, only stopped by Palforma brushing away their hands and making that loud noise with his back plates. And she really didn't like the way a small group of Talins even started following them.

She liked Tamerin and was thankful he was with them. It didn't take long for him and Palforma to realize she was getting more attention that she was comfortable receiving, even if the hands weren't getting through to touch her. Without even needing to consult with each other, Tamerin took the front and Palforma the back. She walked between them, partially protected from curious gazes and unwelcome hands by their imposing bulk.

It helped make her feel more secure, but it also weirded her out. What was with these Talins? She'd never interacted with any species that not only recognized humans but also seemed to be happy to see one. Most other species who had any knowledge of humans and human history expressed a combination of pity and disgust because humans didn't have a home planet or any kind of unifying government.

"Would you like a sweet, little female?" a Talin asked as she tried to thrust a piece of candy at Zia. Palforma knocked her hand away, causing the candy to go flying. The Talin gasped and looked up at Palforma. "That was unnecessary. It was only one sweet treat. Why would you deny her that?"

Tamerin answered for Palforma. "Some humans shouldn't have too much sugar; you should know that, Dorienil. Do you think you're the only Talin on this station who wants to give her sweets? I saw Sominan give her a treat at the bay gate already. Before that I don't know how many offered them to her. Palforma is simply guarding his human against acts done without thought."

Zia watched as Dorienil drew back as if she'd been struck. Although Tamerin's words seemed mild to her, it was obvious he'd delivered a serious reprimand. If her implants were to be believed, this Talin was making some loud sounds as she took a step back and met Palforma's gaze. Her body was stiff, and her hands were curled into tight fists.

A small crowd had gathered, and her implants told her they were all staying silent as they watched the drama play out.

"I declare sincere regret for my careless deeds," Dorienil announced, her eyes moving back and forth between Palforma and Tamerin. Zia could tell she was debating about something, and then she fumbled with her pouch and started to drop to her knees. Both Tamerin and Palforma reacted quickly to keep her from sinking down. Tamerin held his hand out, and Palforma physically grabbed her arm and kept her on her feet.

"No," Palforma said, that one word full of stress. "No n-need."

Tamerin spoke also. "Your offense wasn't so dreadful that it requires that kind of apology. Stand tall, Dorienil. All Palforma and I would wish is that you act with more caution when seeing a human." His body language softened as he said the next words. "You aren't alone. Most of us have similar impulses."

Dorienil made some kind of rhythmic sound and addressed Tamerin. "Yes, of course. I won't act so poorly ever again." With that she turned and hurried away.

Tamerin and Palforma didn't even watch her go but went back to making their way with her between them. But Zia was confused and slightly shaken. What had Dorienil been about to do when Palforma and Tamerin stopped her? And why did Talins keep trying to give her candy? It was all very odd.

At this point she was so discomforted she would have liked to insist they go straight to Tamerin's cabin and hang out until it was time to leave, but she knew Palforma wouldn't be happy about that. Although she was perfectly healthy, it seemed important to him that she get checked out. As long as they checked him over too, she was willing to get poked and prodded.

Gah, she hated seeing healers, doctors, or medics. They all loved to ask personal questions, and every medication she'd ever taken left a nasty aftertaste in her mouth.

Ignoring her misgivings, she examined the Talins around her as they walked. After that incident with Dorienil, everyone else kept their distance but still watched them. Zia tried to ignore their inquisitive gazes and focused on taking in details.

Talin clothing was surprisingly uniform. It was apparent quickly that this species favored only wearing pants that were gathered at the waist and just below the knee. And none of them had pockets. How could they live without pockets? It was mind boggling for Zia.

Instead of nice practical pockets on their pants, everyone wore decorative belts with Ident Cubes handing off of one hip and a pouch on the other. The Idents were all basically the same, but the belts and pouches differed greatly. Some belts were plain and serviceable while others were covered in elaborate designs. A few even sported gems. The same went for the pouches. There didn't seem to be any uniformity as far as size and appearance.

Tamerin would be taking care of getting Palforma a new Ident Cube, but she wanted to make sure her Talin got a few sets of Talin-style pants and a nice belt and pouch. He would be much more comfortable if he could wear the kind of outfit he was accustomed to. She thought about what type of belt and pouch Palforma might like.

Nothing with gems, that would be too much for her practical Talin. But maybe one of the ones with a nice design. Maybe she could even get her name engraved on it somewhere. She liked that idea. Her mother and father both had matching necklaces with their names written on them in one of the Old Earth languages. She could dig up the symbols for her name in that same language and have it etched on the belt. To everyone else it would look like a random bit of decoration, but she would know that her name was on Palforma, marking the big Talin as hers.

Palforma interrupted her musings by drawing her to a halt in a narrow section of the corridor. They were away from the more crowded areas now and blessedly free of spectators.

Although his immobile face didn't betray any emotion, she could tell by his body language that he was worried about something. She worried that dealing with a crowd of Talins had stressed Palforma out more than she realized. When Palforma came to a halt, Tamerin came to a stop and watched them. When Palforma sounded one of his rhythmic sounds, Tamerin turned his back so they could have a conversation in private.

'What's wrong, Palforma?'

Palforma bought his hands up to tap but then hesitated, his hands holding still in the air between them. She waited patiently for him to figure out what he wanted to say. She knew from experience that nothing was worse than others being inpatient while you searched for the words.

When his hands started moving, it was to say something she didn't expect. 'They will say things. You need to ignore them. They might treat you like a child or a pet. Try not to let it bother you. It's a thing Talins do with humans, so don't take offense. You and I know how capable and smart you are. That you're the equal to any Talin. But they won't see it and might say… things.'

This reminded her of the first few months she worked on Red Ore, when all the Nimons expected her to be emotional, bothersome, and dramatic. Maybe Talins had heard the same thing about humans as the Nimons had. Back in his office Tamerin had been shocked she had enough funds to take care of her and Palforma, so they must all think humans were idiots.

Well, humans did destroy their own homeworld, and it would be many thousands of years before it was fit to inhabit again. Like the Nimons, most species assumed humans were too dumb to live. She prided herself on proving every wrongheaded, preconceived notion as false.

'Don't worry. I'm hard to piss off,' she offered him with a smile, but that didn't placate him. If anything, he seemed more agitated. Her left eye was registering a rhythmic sound that was on the loud side.

'Do you remember when the man at the gate called me your master?'

She rolled her eyes. 'Considering it only happened a little while ago, of course I do.'

'Everyone on this station will assume the same thing. Don't bother correcting them. They won't believe you. It would better if you could just ignore it. We'll finish here and leave, and then it can just be the two of us again.'

She wasn't an idiot, and the way she was being treated was odd and informative.

'I hate to tell you this, Palforma,' she stated wryly. 'But no one around here is subtle. I already figured out that everyone around here thinks you own me, even if you keep telling me your species doesn't keep slaves. Fess up. What aren't you telling me?'

'It's nothing you should be concerned about, but I don't want you to get angry or upset because other Talins don't understand what we have.' He paused for a moment, and she could tell he was debating what to say next. 'To them our relationship is wrong. They would think I was being inappropriate and predatory.'

'Then I'll just set them straight,' Zia argued. 'Explain that I instigated—'

'No!' Palforma was quick to respond. 'It would be better to not say anything at all. Let them examine you and answer the medical questions. If they ask about me simply say I treat you well. That's all they need to know.'

She didn't like the idea of being a dirty little secret, but she reminded herself that a lot of social and political dynamics were at play that she didn't entirely understand. She was glad he didn't seem interested in hanging out in Talin-controlled space for long.

'Right, you guys aren't allowed to love or anything,' she answered, feeling grumpy. 'Let's forget this and go straight to Tamerin's cabin. We can hang out there until it's time to leave.'

'We aren't leaving until the healers see you,' Palforma announced stubbornly. 'But I need you to promise me that you'll ignore anything they say outside of their professional duty. And not answer any questions about our relationship. Please?'

The *please* got her. As he tapped it, he slumped his shoulders and lowered his head a little. To other Talins, it might mean something else, but to her it felt like he was acknowledging her as the decision-maker. That if she pushed, he would relent and they could leave on the next available transport.

She had never been treated with as much respect by someone who wasn't another human. It made her weak, and she nodded her head. 'Okay, I promise not to get pissed.' Then she quickly added. 'Unless it's warranted! This isn't a free pass. I won't be abused.'

Several loud rhythmic sounds came from Palforma. She thought it might be a combination of relief and his soothing purr. 'You'll be treated kindly,' he assured her.

'Fine. Let's get this over with.'

"Has she been sick?" That was the Talin in the dark green tunic. She was pretty sure he was the head healer or something, and everyone in the light green tunics were either assistants or healers in training.

"Sick?"

The healer made an impatient gesture as he pointed at her head. "Her mane is short. Was she sick, and it fell out or you needed to crop it short to help care for her? There aren't many reasons a human would have short hair."

Of all the things Zia had expected the healers to be concerned with, her hair wasn't even on the list. But they'd started asking the oddest questions the moment the two of them had walked in and were swarmed by staff.

Tamerin had left them at the door to medical, saying he would be back to see how things were going later. Now that she'd witnessed firsthand how pushy these healers were, she could understand why Tamerin didn't want to go inside.

The Talin in the dark green had taken over, ordering tests and urging her to sit on an elevated bed that would be narrow if she was the size of a Talin, but it was roomy for her. Others wearing the light green took painless samples of her blood and hair before rushing off to perform tests.

Up until now, the healer had been entirely focused on her, only looking to Palforma to ask questions. They hadn't even asked Palforma if he needed attention. She didn't like it, but she wouldn't say anything unless it looked like Palforma wouldn't get seen. No reason to raise a fuss before it was necessary. They might want to get her out of the way first and then deal with Palforma next.

She did everything they asked, opened her mouth, moved her fingers, and held still for the head scanner. But then they'd tried to get her to take off her clothes and she'd adamantly refused. Palforma backed her up with a simple no. The healer reluctantly dropped it, but Zia could tell he wasn't happy about it and was probably going to press the issue later.

And now the healer was focused on her hair.

"She like short. She cut," Palforma told the healer. Tamerin had warned them that no one in medical had downloaded Norka, so Palforma had been answering all their questions so far with yes or no answers. This was the first time he'd given more than a one-word reply.

The healer reared back and regarded Palforma. "You let her cut her hair? That's not a good idea."

"Cut before me. Before us." As he talked, Palforma stepped closer to where she was sitting and tangled his hand with hers. She gripped him tightly, trying to be reassuring. He was as tense as she was. Maybe even more, and he wasn't even on the exam table.

The healer typed something into a display on the wall near the head of the bed. "Are you trying to tell me that you only recently acquired this human?"

As she'd promised Palforma, Zia ignored the healer's verbiage.

"Yes. Recent. Came here to check for hurt. Check for problems."

Using one hand she talked to him in the simpler form of Norka. 'I'm fine. *You* need to be checked out. You're the one with the head injury. Tell him that.'

The healer stopped entering information into the display to watch her talk. "What is she doing?"

"No hear. No speech. Norka instead," Palforma explained as he made the single hand motion for the Norka Tapping Language.

"She can't hear?" His question was more of an outraged declaration. Why would he be so upset that she couldn't hear? It wasn't like she couldn't function perfectly fine.

'What's his problem?' she tried to ask, but Palforma wasn't looking at her. His entire focus was on trying to communicate with the Healer.

"She smart. Much clever. Put in," Palforma instructed the healer, tapping his head where the INT was located under the skin. "You t-t-talk also."

"You make no sense," the healer said, taking a step back. "What is wrong with you? I thought you were taciturn, but it's more than that. Isn't it?"

She got angry at the healer's words. Shouldn't someone who's been trained to help others be more sympathetic?

Zia tugged at Palforma's hand to get his attention. 'We should go.'

To her relief, Palforma agreed. 'Maybe we could try healers somewhere else.'

Or nowhere else, Zia thought but kept it to herself. When she moved to get off the table, Palforma easily lifted her off. No sooner was she standing on her own two feet than the healer was objecting.

"What are you doing? You don't think I can let you leave. Do you?" As he talked the healer pressed something on the wall display. "I haven't finished checking her over. I don't know the reason for her hearing loss. And she hasn't been decontaminated yet. But most of all, I have serious misgivings about you owning this human. You will remain here until this is sorted out."

Decontaminated? What did they think, that she was harboring lice? She made a rude gesture brought over from Old Earth. These guys wouldn't understand it, but it made her feel a little better.

"No. Leaving," Palforma informed him tersely. Her eye was registering rhythmic sounds coming from all around her, so it wasn't only Palforma making noise. She didn't like this. Didn't like how the healer talked to Palforma or treated her. She tugged at his pants, trying to convey that she was more than happy to depart.

But they didn't even get a chance to take a step toward the door.

"You're not leaving, at least not with this human," the healer announced. "You're free to leave at any time, but this human will remain here until I'm satisfied that she's both healthy and has an owner up to the task of caregiving."

As much as she hated the healer's language, she wasn't above playing the part if it got the two of the out of medical without incident. They'd left her bag in Tamerin's office, so all she had was her small information square. But it was in the hidden pocket of the omnie, trapped between her and Palforma. She tried to lean a little away so she could dig it out, but Palforma reached around and wrapped an arm around her, holding her tightly to his side.

"She mine. Stay mine. No take! Mine!"

The healer looked at her and then up to Palforma. "Do you have any intelligence or reasoning skills at all?"

Zia didn't need to have working ears to "hear" the disgust in the healer's words. She went from worried to furious in zero seconds flat. Instead of trying to get herself free to get to the information square, she now wanted to be free so she could hit him. She still had the punch-stick in an arm pocket. She was going to get it out and—

"Even now you hurt her!" the healer announced and pointed to where Zia was trying to jerk herself out of Palforma's hold. She froze and shook her head at the healer. Palforma's grip wasn't tight enough to hurt. He was simply tense and didn't want to let go of her. Honestly, he was saving the healer's life.

'Let me at him!' she tapped with one hand to Palforma. 'I'll make him understand that he can't talk to you like that!'

But that's when everything turned to chaos.

Before Palforma could answer her, station security swarmed the room.

"Ah, you're here, good," the healer said then pointed at Palforma. "Remove him. I need to assess this human without him trying to intimidate her or take her away. Be careful. She's tiny even for a human. I think he might be abusing her, so use as much force with him as you need."

Zia was caught out for a moment, gaping at how rapidly this simple situation had escalated. For a species that prided itself on emotional control and clinical thinking, they sure liked to jump to conclusions.

Between the heavily armored station security and the medical staff, enough intense sounds ricocheted around the room for her implants to shut down the feed for all background noises. On one hand it was good because it meant fewer things were showing up in her left eye to confuse her. The problem was that now she wouldn't get any warning if someone tried to sneak up on her. The implants wouldn't start registering nonword noise until there was no loud background noise for several consecutive minutes.

Judging by the body language of both the medical staff and the security personnel, this whole situation could get extremely bad fast. Not only did she want out of here, but she wanted to get Palforma away from these small-minded Talins who questioned his intelligence. Assholes!

Angry, Zia fumbled with her clothing as she moved behind Palforma. The heavy omnie was making it impossible to get to the sleeve pocket of her coveralls. She would need to untie and shed the whole garment to get to the weapons, and she didn't want to take the time to do that.

"No right to t-t-take!" Palforma warned them. "We leave. You no t-t-take!" Peering around him, she could see that Palforma's quills were up, and his claws were out. She knew from watching him during the obstacle race that he could make good on a threat of physical violence. It was worrisome that security was wearing armor, but they weren't carrying much in the way of weapons and nothing that could kill Palforma.

Before the guard could respond to the healer's statements, someone grabbed her from behind. Twisting her head, she found herself in the arms of one of the light green clad Talins who had appeared from a half-open door she hadn't noticed before.

She struggled in the Talin's hold, trying to get loose. It was useless. His grip was strong as he moved fast, back-pedaling through the partially open door. Palforma turned and roared. He was about to advance on them when the security detail started moving. They converged on Palforma all at once, not giving him a chance to move away or even surrender.

No! they were going to hurt him! They were being so much more brutal than the situation called for, and despite Palforma's intense skill level, he was struggling to defend against so many in such tight confines.

Fear made her fight. She bit, clawed, and kicked, trying to get free. The sound of battle wasn't registering in her left eye, but the voices talking around her scrolled across her right eye as she was surrounded by Talins in green.

"She must be scared."

"Try not to hurt her."

"I'm trying but she's surprisingly strong."

"Hold her still so I can do this."

"If I hold any harder, I might hurt her."

Then one of them was pressing something against the skin of her neck. She got the sensation of heat for a brief moment, and then her brain started moving sluggishly.

Her body went lax and her head lolled to the side. The Talin holding her changed his grip so her head was supported on his shoulder. The position reminded her of how a human parent would hold a baby.

He rubbed a hand up and down her back as he talked. "You're safe. No one will hurt you ever again."

The Talin holding her shifted slightly, and she could see a little of the battle raging through the partially open door. Palforma looked like he was winning. Several bodies lay on the ground either not moving or not moving very much.

Then the healer was there, blocking her view. "Get that door shut so we can implement the fail safe."

Fail safe? That sounded bad. She wanted to get free and join Palforma so they could fight their way off the station. She ordered her body to move, but all it did was twitch a little.

"Easy, little one. Don't fight the drugs. Close your eyes and sleep. You're going to be well taken care of. I promise. No one will hurt you ever again."

Helplessly she watched one of the staff tap a display and recognized one of the emblems that popped up on the screen. It took her a moment because her brain was moving so slow, but then it came to her. It was a shorthand symbol for sealing a room so you could fill the space with medicated vapor. The system was used on a lot of stations as a noncombative way to subdue an unruly group.

That could only mean thing. They were gassing the room! The medication should be harmless, simply putting everyone to sleep. but there was always a chance someone might react badly and suffer damage or even death.

Fear for Palforma and her own helplessness made tears form in her eyes. And then whatever they gave her took full effect and her mind went offline.

CHAPTER 17

Palforma paced. He'd been doing the same thing for the last three marks. After they flooded the room and knocked him and station security out cold, he woke up alone in this cage. He hadn't seen anyone yet.

So, he paced. And growled. And rattled.

Alone with his thoughts, fear, regret, and fury warred for supremacy. He should've listened to Zia and turned around and left. He was so eager to have Talin healers assess her that he ignored how they would react to his own deficits. It should have occurred to him that they would think the worst. After all, his own family rejected him, so why would the healers be kind?

Anger, an emotion he was normally good at controlling, raged inside him. The pacing wasn't helping. He could picture the glimpse he'd gotten of Zia's face framed by the partially open door. Her lids were half closed from the drugs they'd given her, and tears had leaked from her eyes.

He'd put his human in a position of helplessness. She might never forgive him.

That thought snapped the last fragile thread that was holding his raw emotions in check. With a roar he raked his claws down the walls, leaving deep grooves in the thick metal. One claw stuck deep enough it got caught, and he didn't even pause as it ripped away from his hand. He tore apart the fold-down bunk, shredding the thin mattress and then ripping the thing out of the wall and using it to bang on the cage door.

The bunk was made of a lightweight material, and he quickly reduced it to nothing more than crumbled bits of metal. Bleeding from one hand and panting, he stared at the door. All his effort hadn't even dented it. All he'd done was deprive himself of a place to sleep.

And now that he'd spent his rage, only fear and regret were left.

Nalia, Derani's human, was stolen from Derani the first time they went on a Talin station, and Nalia had even known and acknowledged her status as a pet and could easily verbalize and identify her owner. Derani had been a well-spoken Talin of a respected clan and family. Even with all that, they ended up having issues.

Considering that, why did he think he could get away with visiting this station and deceiving Zia?

Sounds outside his cell made him hurry to the door to peer out the lone window trying to see who was in the hall. He recognized Tamerin, but two other Talins accompanied his cousin that he'd never seen before. They all walked straight to his cell.

Knowing what they would want, he backed up into the small circle drawn on the floor even before one of the men called out the instruction. When the light flashed indicating he was in the designated space, he heard the door unluck and the men came in.

Tamerin didn't bother looking at the mess, but the other two Talins made sounds of disgust as they took in the destroyed room.

His cousin pointed to the blood dripping from Palforma's hand. "You're bleeding. How badly are you hurt?"

'It's nothing,' Palforma tapped. 'Where is Zia?'

One of the strangers stepped forward. "I'm Station Director Glormun. When you were questioned about your pet, you lost control and attacked a healer and station security personnel. I looked into your record and noticed you were badly wounded and suffered long-term effects. While that might explain your actions, it doesn't excuse them. I'm saddened you are here, but I won't be swayed by anything but a reasonable response."

Palforma sounded an angry rattle as he pinned the man with his gaze. "Ac-c-c-c-cused me of h-h-hurt. Said h-h-hurt Zia. Never!" Frustrated by his damaged brain, Palforma roared out the last word.

Glormun and Tamerin didn't move, but the third man flinched away. Palforma turned his attention to Tamerin. 'Can you explain to them that Zia's mine. And that I didn't hurt her?'

"I explained all of that," Tamerin said out loud as he slid his gaze at the man who flinched and then back at Palforma. It was a clear message that this male was someone significant. "I dug up the vids of her coming through the gate from the bay with you. They clearly show her clinging to you."

'So they believe I own her?' As Palforma tapped, Tamerin spoke his words out loud for the benefit of the other two males.

The station director answered. "Everyone acknowledges that you own the human Zia."

'Then I can pay for damages and leave?' He knew it wouldn't be that simple, but he had to try.

"There's still the matter of abuse," the third man said.

Palforma sounded a rattle of frustration and looked to Tamerin. 'Did you explain that she was born deaf and she was wild caught? She won't react the way most humans among us will. Did you tell them I'd never abuse her or any human?'

Tamerin sounded a soothing rumble. "By the time I was called back to medical, the healers had already discovered the state of her ears and noticed how old her implants were. The original implants have been replaced with new ones of a higher quality. Right now she's asleep, but she should be waking soon with only a little discomfort from the procedure. The healers also noted a few things that are only found on wild-caught humans, so there's no question that Zia is new to captivity. I told them you would never hurt a human. I told them to ask her once she woke up." Tamerin sounded a rumble of regret. "But I've been told her words might not hold much weight in what happens to her."

'What happens to her? There should be no question about what happens to her. She's mine. They give her back to me and let us leave. I was unjustly accused and then attacked. I acted out of defense, and a review of the security vids from the room will show you that.'

"I'm afraid not," Tamerin answered. "The question now isn't about ownership or abuse. It's whether you're fit to own a human. Committee Citizen Lotyaum is here to assess if she will be given back to you or reallocated to a different owner."

Cold dread filled Palforma. He had no doubt that if Zia was given to another Talin she would do everything possible to escape. She might even get hurt.

"Scent-b-b-bond," Palforma stuttered out quickly as he rubbed a bloody hand on his cheek over one of his swollen scent glands. "Hurt Zia if away. If part-t-ted. No part."

Even before he finished trying to get the words out, he started tapping to Tamerin. 'You can't let them take her away. She already scent-bonded with me. Make them understand that she even told me she loves me. You know how important that is for humans. Love is significant. Being away from her beloved owner might make her anxious and upset. Everyone knows humans are so fragile they can die from excess emotions.'

Zia would hate him saying something like that, but he needed them to believe her health would be in peril if they weren't together.

After Tamerin told the men what Palforma said, Lotyaum stepped forward. "Don't concern yourself. We have medications that can mitigate her discomfort if she has scent-bonded to you." He sounded a rumble of humor. "And human love isn't like scent-bonding between Talin couples, or the way humans love each other. I'm sure she won't die or even suffer overmuch from your absence. It's been my experience that humans are quick to fall in and out of love. It's one of their many charms. You should be more concerned about whether the station director will press charges against you or not."

"They attac-c-c-ked f-f-first," Palforma protested as he met Glormun's eyes. "Healer thought wrong. Wrong contusion—concussion—conclusion! Wrong belief."

When he heard a rumble of pity sound from Lotyaum, he almost lost his temper again. He hadn't heard that rumble for a while, but all the times he heard it after he was injured was enough to last him a lifetime.

It was the last sound he heard his parents make before they told him that he was a disappointment to the clan.

Taking a small step sideways to put himself between Lotyaum and Palforma, Tamerin gave a calming rumble. "Getting emotional won't help anyone right now."

When he met Tamerin's gaze, his cousin moved his head slightly. That was all it took for him to remind Palforma that if he attacked Lotyaum, he would never get Zia back.

"I'm g-g-g-good Talin. G-g-g-good owner."

Lotyaum sounded a loud rumble of disbelief. "By the look of this room I have a hard time believing you're in control of yourself."

Before Palforma could respond, Tamerin stepped up to the committee citizen, looming over the smaller Talin. "Palforma was a highly decorated soldier. By the time he retired he had collected five Mattil medals. Five! Do you realize how rare it is even to achieve one or two? How dare you treat him with such disrespect."

Lotyaum shrank back from Tamerin, rattling out a startled sound. "You're being unnecessarily aggressive, Tamerin."

Surprisingly, Glormun responded in defense of Tamerin. "I think he's displaying an appropriate amount of aggression for his cousin and fellow warrior. You, Lotyaum, need to remember that our wealth and expansion into this sector was paid for with the blood of our bravest."

Lotyaum became silent and still for a moment as he realized he had no allies in the room. Stepping to the side and putting himself in the doorway to the room, he addressed them.

"I apologize if I've caused offense," he said at Glormun, purposely avoiding Tamerin and Palforma's gazes. "But I have a duty I take very seriously. Humans are so few that owning one is a privilege that should go to those that can provide the best home and care. We can't afford to lose even one, especially one in her prime breeding years."

"Then you couldn't do better than Palforma," Tamerin interjected. "Our clan brought the first humans to Talarian three hundred years ago. We were the ones who first started the trend and even helped other clans rescue humans from Orlok mining outposts after the Talin-Orlok war. Both he and I were raised around humans. How could anyone be more fit to own Zia?"

"Your loyalty to your cousin is commendable," Lotyaum said with an annoyed rattle. "But I'm afraid your clan's legacy doesn't help with the basic fact that Palforma could be emotionally unstable and a threat to the human."

Palforma wanted to roar. He wanted to sink his claws into Lotyaum and throw him across the room. But as long as the circle he was standing in was lit up, stepping outside would mean getting hit with an energy weapon that would knock him out.

"You have no evidence that Palforma would be a bad owner," Tamerin argued.

Glormun spoke up. "I believe it would be important for you to note, Committee Citizen Lotyaum, that Palforma isn't alone. As it's been pointed out, he is part of a clan famous for their humans. Perhaps you should contact his parents or sibling and see what their opinions are. One of them could even agree to be co-owner to Zia. That would give Zia the option of going to another Talin if she felt scared."

Considering Palforma had been disowned by his parents and his sibling was dead, Glormun's suggestion wasn't helpful at all.

Avoiding the topic of parents, Tamerin was quick to speak up. "His sister died in battle. But I could stand as that family member. We are cousins and in the same clan."

"While I don't doubt your sincerity, you work here. Until the work is complete, humans aren't allowed to reside on this station," Glormun announced. "You know that as well as anyone."

"Then I could—"

Glormun sounded a rattle of impatience. "No, Tamerin, it will need to be his parents or a separation, and then Zia is reallocated. Now, I have other things I need to see to, and this situation has already wasted enough of my time."

Swinging his gaze to Lotyaum, Glormun sounded a rattle of assent often used when superiors were giving orders. "Contact his family, give him the assessment test, and then come to me with your conclusion." With that he turned on his heels and strode out of the room.

Lotyaum was quick to follow him. "Of course, Station Direction Glormun. But if you could just spare a moment to listen to my proposal about the communal area…"

Their voices faded as they moved down the hall. A male wearing a station security unforms popped his head into the room. "You'll need to leave now, Tamerin."

Before he could turn to leave, Palforma tapped quickly. 'Don't let them give Zia away. She won't understand. She'll fight. She could get hurt. If you need to, run away with her. You can have all my funds.'

'I already know there is no way I will talk her into leaving without you,' Tamerin answered as the guard warned him again that it was time to leave. 'But don't lose hope yet. I'll see what I can do.'

And then Tamerin was gone, the cell door was shut, and the circle under his feet went dark. He was left alone except for the mess he'd created of the cell. How fucking poetic.

CHAPTER 18

The first thing Zia was aware of as she woke up was a foul taste in her mouth. The familiar taste of Medication Mouth was bad enough to tell her she'd received numerous medications recently. Although it wasn't an issue for anyone else in her family, some strange chemistry in her body caused her to have a horrible aftertaste linger on her tongue after being given any kind of medicine. Ugh, she hated that taste and knew from experience it wouldn't go away with simple mouth cleansers. Nope, she was stuck with it until the medication was entirely out of her system

On top of having Medication Mouth, her brain felt sluggish and her body heavy. Should she try to open her eyes, or go back to sleep? The second option sounded better, especially considering the pounding headache behind her eyes. Had she taken a bunch of medication for a headache and it didn't work?

No, that couldn't be right. Pain relief drugs wouldn't make her this groggy.

Then memories came flooding back to her, and the pain took a back seat to the adrenaline that flooded her system. Her eyes flew open and she sat bolt upright, frantically taking in the room around her. She was in medical, still wearing her omnie with the coveralls under it. Except, for some weird reason, her boots had been replaced by the same kind of soft, warm slippers Palforma tried to talk her into wearing.

They had to have given her multiple medications to cause this level of Medication Mouth, not only the stuff they drugged her with to knock her out while Palforma was fighting. Cautiously she moved her limbs around but nothing felt sore or tender, so they didn't do any procedures. Had they dosed her repeatedly to keep her asleep?

The action of the medical staff and then waking up like this felt both alarming and bizarre. What the hell was going on?

Then a display on the wall over her head dinged, and that one sound made her realize they had done a procedure on her. They replaced her implants.

Before she could explore that any further, the door to the room opened and several familiar Talins walked in. One was the healer she'd met earlier, and the other was Tamerin. She was so relieved to see him that she swung around and let her legs dangle off the side of the bed.

'Where's Palforma? Was he hurt? Why did they call the guards? I want to leave. Could you find my boots?'

Before he could answer any of her questions, script she'd never seen before scrolled across her left eye.

Rumble of relief.

Followed quickly by:

Rumble of amusement.

Several years ago she'd watched an educational vid on the advanced implants she wanted to buy, and one of the sales points was that the implants could be programed to interpret the emotions or intentions behind sounds. It looked like the ones they'd put in her had that same feature. Not only was her implant telling her the meaning of the Tamerin sounds, but a 3-D arrow blipped in both her eyes pointing to him to indicate where the sound originated.

Damn, this was amazing! Even better than the implants she was saving up for.

'Palforma's safe, but he's in the brig. It's too much to explain. For now, I need you to stay calm and cooperate with the healers. I'll remain with you if that would make you feel safer and keep you calm.'

She wanted to ask Tamerin more, but then the healer was at her side.

Rumble to soothe.

With that came a 3-D arrow pointing to the healer. She couldn't wait to see what these implants could do in a room full of noise.

"You're awake and alert. That's good. Tamerin explained that you use Norka. All the staff and I have downloaded the language into our INTs. We might not be as fluent as you, but we should be able to get by."

Ah, now she realized why Tamerin was being circumspect with his answers, the Healer could "hear" their conversation. She would need to be patient and wait until they were alone to talk.

'You gave me new implants,' she commented to the healer.

"You noticed? Excellent. We're going to need to run some tests to verify they've fully integrated, and when your ownership is settled, you'll need to make regular check-ins with a healer. I know you can't stay here on Oglin, but I've put myself in the Reallocation queue to request ownership of you anyway. I'm from the Verde clan after all, and we're the most knowledgeable of humans of all the medical clans. And my contract with the station is at will, so I can leave at any time. I could take you home to Talarian. My family has a large and well-maintained compound with plenty of green areas for you to enjoy. And of course, we have indoor enclosures instead of the barbaric outdoor ones. If you're reallocated to me, you won't need to live in the elements or suffer in any way."

Zia went perfectly still at the healer's little speech. Reallocation queue? It was one thing to go along with the illusion that Palforma owned her, but no way would she let some random Talin cart her off to a planet she'd have little chance to escape from.

Fear hit her. She wanted out of this room. She wanted to find Palforma. But most of all she wanted both of them off this station.

Despite what her instincts wanted, she knew immediate action wasn't a good idea. Not only was the healer here, but several others had come into the room. It wouldn't take much effort for them to drug her again and then she might wake up anywhere, including the Talin homeworld.

Nope, no panicking allowed, she told herself firmly. She needed to keep her head and wait for the right opportunity.

As she listened to the healer tell her about the implants, she subtly searched her person. Some of the fear eased when she felt the small, hard mass of the punch-stick in her sleeve pocket. Not only had they let her keep her clothes, but they hadn't searched her for weapons either.

"…so you need to tell me if you're in any pain," the healer continued, and when she subconsciously went to nod her head, she made a horrifying discovery.

A collar was around her throat.

All thoughts of staying cool, calm, and collected went out the window. She reacted on pure instinct as she put both hands to the collar and started pulling. The back of it dug into her neck and the edges bit into her fingers as she tried to pry it open with her bare hands

Rattle of surprise.

Rumble of worry.

Rattle of anger.

She didn't pay attention to where her implants indicated the sounds were coming from. She was too busy panicking at having a piece of metal locked around her throat.

Talin hands closed over hers, trying to stop her. She bit one of them. Her teeth didn't do any damage to the thick skin, but the hand pulled away anyway.

Rattle of outrage. "She's out of control. She tried to bite me! Only the young try to bite."

"She's panicking. She knows me. Move out of the way. Let me get to her!" Then Tamerin was there, filling her vision.

Rumble to soothe.

"Zia, stop," he ordered. He grabbed her head in both hands to force her eyes to meet his. He ignored her hits and kept repeating her name. "Zia, this isn't helping you or Palforma. He's trapped right now, and you need to be calm to help him."

That managed to get through her terror. She stopped thrashing to regard Tamerin. 'Get this off me,' she demanded and then tugged at the collar. 'Get this off me right now!'

Rumble of regret.

"It has to stay on," he said. Leaning in close, he put his forehead to hers and whispered. "It needs to stay on for now. They know you're wild-caught, and the Choker Syndrome excuse won't work. I've already tried. If they think you really have Choker Syndrome they'll drug you again, but they won't take if off until they've tried a few different medications. You can't do much if your mind is dulled from drugs."

Bad. Very bad. It took everything in her to ignore the band around her throat and drop her hands into her lap.

Rumble of relief.

Rumble to soothe.

Tamerin straightened and let go of her head to regard the others in the room. Zia stayed seated on the table as Tamerin addressed everyone.

"She's wild-caught and you put a collar on her while she was drugged? What were you thinking?" Tamerin roared out, his loud voice registering in her right eye with a volume meter next to it that gave her degree context and then offered a shorthand that basically said *volume high*. Oh, that was a nice feature.

Rattle of embarrassment. "You're correct. I should've listened to you earlier and waited until she was awake and aware. That would be a startling thing for a wild-caught human," the healer said. "Everything turned chaotic so quickly when she was first brought in that we weren't able to get a history on her, and I was afraid she might be absconded with if we didn't get a collar on her right away."

The healer stepped sideways a little so he could meet Zia's gaze. "Do you need medication? I can make it so you're not afraid."

Worried he might do just that, she jumped off the table and put herself right behind Tamerin. Sticking her hand out from behind him, she tapped, 'No! Stay away from me!'

Rumbles of amusement, all persons.

Rattle of concern, source unseen.

"Do you think you can get her calmed down enough to let us finish checking her?" Those words were almost a whisper judging by the meter, but her implants picked them up easily. Her hearing wasn't just better than the average human anymore. It might be better than most species. These implants were top of the line with everything she couldn't have ever afforded on her own.

She was still pissed at these Talins for putting a collar on her, but giving her this kind of gift might help her toward forgiveness.

Might.

"It would go a long way to ease her if she and I were the only ones in the room. She's very bonded to Palforma and that might allow her to trust me enough to convince her to behave," Tamerin told the healer as he wrapped an arm behind himself to pin her in place against his back. Probably because she'd jerked at his use of the word behave.

Behave? They put a damn collar on her and then got upset because she reacted badly? Let her put a collar on one of them and see how they like it.

His arm kept her from being able to draw back her arm very far, but she was still proud of the small punch she delivered to the left side of his lower back. She probably hurt her knuckles more than doing any damage to Tamerin, but at least she could tell by his slight flinch that he knew she was pissed.

Good, because she was livid! But hey, it was better than the earlier panic. Fury was almost always better than fear in her book.

And once she found Palforma, she was going to hug him really tightly and then yell at him for bringing them here. And he was going to need to do some major groveling before she forgave him.

"…call me back in when you've managed to calm her. If you're not capable of that, we'll be forced to sedate her. I'd rather not, but we need to finish the exam and recheck her implants. We can't do that if she fights us or keeps reacting badly to the collar."

Catching the end of the healer's words to Tamerin made her tense up, ready to fight. Tamerin's arm kept her pinned, and she could feel the vibrations of his rumbling.

Rumble to soothe.

She almost punched him again. Some rumbling wasn't going to convince her to let go of her anger.

"I understand. Thank you for your gift of time and skill," Tamerin said to the healer. "Given a little time, I'm sure I can move her into a more submissive mindset."

"Certainly." With that, the healer left.

The moment the door shut behind them Tamerin let go of her.

Backing away, she fumbled with her omnie. She probably bruised herself from forcing the sleeve up so high, but she managed get the punch-stick out of the coveralls' sleeve pocket. Aware of the vid captures in the room, she did all of that while still behind Tamerin and then held the weapon hidden in her hand, ready to use if he tried to grab her again. Scowling, she regarded Palforma's cousin suspiciously.

She could tap while holding the punch-stick because of long practice, so she didn't hesitate to start hurling orders at Tamerin.

'I want this fucking collar off, and I'm not letting any of them touch me. We're going to go get Palforma, and then we're leaving.'

Without replying Tamerin stepped to the side, forcing her to turn as he moved. She was surprised that he moved away from the door instead of toward it to block her from the exit. But then she realized he was placing himself so that he blocked both of them from the vid capture, making it safe to tap.

'I believe Palforma failed to tell you many things before bringing you here. I need you—' Tamerin began, but she interrupted him before he could continue.

'I've figured that out myself.' With her free hand she pointed to the collar. 'They put a slave collar on me. Palforma told me you guys don't have slaves, but now I'm wearing this. That means one thing. *He* lied to me! Outright lied!'

'Zia—'

'No! I'm a free-born human. Free-born! I have funds of my own. I'm not property. But with this thing around my neck, all of that is gone." She felt a strange manic humor rise up in her. '*I need you to pretend to go along with them, Zia.* That's what Palforma told me. *Ignore what they say.*' She made the gesture for the word "say" big to emphasize it. 'But now I'm trapped here. It wasn't words that I needed to be warned about. It was deeds!' She tugged brutally at the collar, ignoring the pain it caused. 'I will fight this to my dying day, Tamerin. To my last breath. No one gets to make me an owned thing. I'm not a slave!'

'We don't have slavery,' Tamerin began, and Zia was about ready to stick him with the punch-stick for saying something so inane. He must have read her intentions because he took a hasty step back. 'Let me explain, please. We don't have slaves, but we do have pets. Human pets.'

'If both slaves and pets wear collars, I don't see a difference between the two,' she retorted.

'The difference is significant,' he argued. 'Slaves are bought to be a value-added commodity. They are meant to toil for their owners. But pets don't labor. They don't work. Their only job is to be companions to Talins. To let us take care of them.'

She understood each individual word he was tapping, but when she put them all together it didn't make any sense to her. 'Why bother owning a person if they're not going to increase your wealth with labor or provide some kind of service? You're speaking nonsense!'

Rattle of frustration. Then he tapped, 'Zia, it's complicated.'

She barely kept hold of her temper at that. Pulling her lips back, she bared her teeth in a clear threat display. 'I won't be treated as though I lack intelligence.'

'It's not that I believe you can't understand. It's that it would take me too long to explain. For right now I need you to agree to stay calm *and* let the healer finish with you.'

'Why should I listen to you?'

Rumble to soothe.

He replied, 'Because I'm going to do my best to get Palforma out of the brig and you two back together. But I can't do that if you're misbehaving.'

That last word made her see red.

Misbehaving was something children did when they snuck around after bedtime. Telling her she needed to behave made her want to act without thought, but before she could even advance on him, Tamerin took a step forward and grabbed her wrist. He took away the punch-stick and then moved out of her personal space. He accomplished all of that with astounding speed and fluidity of movement.

He must have been a fine warrior, almost as good as Palforma.

Her eye registered his continued soothing rumbles that didn't stop even when he was disarming her. He tucked her weapon in his pouch and met her gaze again. They stared at each other in silence as she worked on getting her emotions back under control.

I'm responsible for my second thought and first action, she reminded herself. Repeating the familiar phrase in her head was like a calming mantra.

When she was a kid, she'd had a horrible temper. It had taken a lot of work for her to learn restraint and keep from acting before thinking. What had helped was when her dad sat her down and told her that she didn't have control over the first thing that popped into her head. That first spike of anger or frustration was going to happen no matter what she did. But after that, she had all the control. That's when they came up with a sentence to help her focus on not doing anything she would regret later.

After all these years of practice, Tamerin and these Talins had managed to make her lose her hard-won control. That's not an accomplishment they should be proud of.

Working on keeping her breathing regular, she lowered her chin a little and looked up at Tamerin through her messy hair.

'I'm only going to say this once, Tamerin, and I'm going to need you to take me very seriously. I'm giving you a single unit in Common time measurement to get me out of here and get Palforma free. After that I will do things.'

'I know you think you can escape—'

She cut him off with a sharp movement of her hand slicing across the space between them. 'I'm not talking only about escape. I'm talking about destruction. I won't be owned by anyone. Ever. Whatever title you might give humans, it won't be applied to me. If escape isn't an option, I'd rather be dead. If I'm going to die, I'm taking you all with me. I have the skills necessary to make this entire station nothing more than debris. Don't doubt me.'

She expected anger from Tamerin after her little speech. Or maybe disbelief after the way he'd easily disarmed her.

What she didn't expect was for her left eye to register *rumble of humor*.

'You're a good fit for Palforma,' Tamerin declared. 'When we were young everyone assumed he had a mild temperament because he was quiet. But he was never one to cross. He has a rage that once unleashed is difficult to cage until his revenge has been satisfied. You have that same rage in you, little human.'

That mollified her somewhat. 'Then we understand each other.'

'Yes, I think we do. Be calm and respectful to the healers, and I'll get the two of you off the station. You'll need to give me four marks because it's going to take some arranging.'

Her new implants shot up a quick formula to inform her that four marks translated roughly to a little over two units in Common time.

'I want assurance,' she said.

'Assurance?'

'The punch-stick.'

Rattle of rejection. 'I'm not comfortable with that. Think of something else.'

She eyed his person and then pointed to his belt. Unlike the other Talins, Tamerin was carrying a few tools that hung off his belt along with the standard pouch and Ident.

Without hesitation he unclipped a tool and handed it to her. 'It*'s* only a standard short-draw cutter,' he warned her. To him it might be a standard short-draw cutter, but to her it was much more than a simple tool. It was a quick way to make the station into a giant bomb. You didn't do her type of job for so many years and not know how to get around all the safety protocols that kept station stabilizers from igniting.

Or the grav system from combusting.

Or the unity drives from exploding.

She could do all kinds of terminal things to this station with a little time, access, and a standard short-draw cutter.

After taking it from him, she hooked it to a convenient loop on the waistband of her coveralls and then carefully tied the omnie shut so it didn't show. The bulky omnie easily hid the tool.

'Thank you, Tamerin. I'll be genuinely sorry if I have to kill you later.'

Rumble of humor. 'I'd regret that too, Zia.'

CHAPTER 19

When she agreed to give Tamerin four marks, she never expected it would be four marks of Talins constantly asking her questions. First the healer and his assistants—although she didn't mind so much because it was all about her implants. They even showed her how she could program them with hand, jaw, and eye movements.

And they kept handing her candy. She tried to refuse, but they acted as if she'd hurt their feelings, so she started accepting the sweets and sticking them in her pocket when no one was looking. That pocket was going to be a sticky mess when this was all over. Why did these Talins insist on unwrapping the candy before giving it to her? Did they think she'd eat the wrapper too?

Eventually the healers stopped asking her questions while scanning her over her clothes—because no way was she getting naked—and asking her to swallow harmless antivirals and anti-parasitics that she was dosed with years ago. But boosters wouldn't hurt her, so as long as they let her read the label, she took them without complaint.

She was even a good girl when they asked her to step into a pod designed to kill off any nonnative organisms from her skin and clothes. She rolled her eyes as she complied. Usually, only low-wage workers or slaves ended up in the worst conditions that needed this type of treatment. Where did these guys think she came from, some microbe infested Petri dish of a planet?

It was a relief when the med staff was done with her only to have the station director show up and start asking a lot of questions.

How did Palforma treat her?

Did he ever get angry and hit her?

Did he ever refuse her food as punishment?

Was she ever forced to sleep outside without proper shelter?

Had she ever been refused care when she was sick or injured?

Even though she was still frustrated with Palforma for bringing her here to begin with, she couldn't stand to have him maligned. She treated the station director as she would treat any authority figure she didn't trust. Her answers were short, truthful, and without elaboration or detail.

No, he never hit her.

He didn't get angry.

He took good care of her.

He fed her plenty of food and provided adequate accommodations.

She was at medical. Wasn't she? That should be proof enough that he wanted her to have the best medical care.

By the time she was done answering the station director's questions, she was disquieted by all these Talins. If the Talins thought of her as owned, they shouldn't care how Palforma treated her, only that he legally acquired her. But no one asked a single question about a bill of sale or acquisition providence. All the station director and the medical staff wanted to know was if she was happy.

She answered yes and the station director made note of it and left as abruptly as he'd arrived.

Unfortunately, that meant the medical staff descended on her again. But mostly they wanted to double-check her implants, which didn't require her input, so she sat and thought about the station director's last question. Was she happy?

Happy?

What a strange thing to ask her. Not even her parents or sibling ever asked her if she was happy. Happiness was the luxury of wealthy individuals who were part of a species with enough political power to keep them safe. Contentedness was the best she had ever expected out of life.

Despite her strong views on slavery, she was starting to realize the marked difference between a slave and a pet. She wasn't about to volunteer to keep a collar on if given the opportunity to get it off, but she had to admit that if this was the way Talins treated all the human pets, it wasn't that bad.

She knew plenty of humans who would jump at the chance to be in this position. They wouldn't resist the collar or loss of freedom. They would put up with a lot for regular access to food, safety, and basic comforts.

If Talins showed up to abduct most of the humans on Wimol Colony, ninety-nine percent of them wouldn't object if this was how they were treated. They would probably settle right into captivity among the Talins.

But she'd always been clever and quick to learn, and she'd managed to get good jobs despite being deaf and human. One of the girls she grew up with, Lasha, struggled with everything and was often reduced to tears by even the simplest task. The last she heard, Lasha entered into an indentured servant contract with a Leemron corporation as a manual laborer. It was a position barely better than a slave.

No one had heard from Lasha in years and most feared she'd passed away working under conditions too harsh for her to survive.

But among these Talins, Lasha wouldn't have had to accept such a dangerous and demeaning job. It sounded like a Talin owner would've taken care of everything for her.

And after one set of questions from the healers about rutting, she knew for a fact that the Talins didn't expect to get sex from their humans. She did remember Palforma mentioning that emotions like love and bonding were taboo, so sex must be also. She clammed up after the third question about her sexuality. If they thought she was too dumb to consent to sex with Palforma, all they'd get was her silence.

Intrusive, judgmental bastards.

They muttered something about wild-caught humans being less sexually liberated than their captivity-born counterparts and gave up that line of questioning.

After the station director left, the medical staff went over a few more things before they left her in peace. She thought she was done interacting with Talins for the moment, but she was wrong.

A Talin walked in with an air of self-importance and loomed over her reclined position. Everyone else had taken a seat when they'd needed to be next to her, but not this guy. That put her on the defensive right away.

"Hello, human Zia. My name's Committee Citizen Lotyaum, and I work for the Committee for Pet Welfare. I've been told that you can't speak because you were born deaf, but that you've been given implants so you can understand me."

'Yes.'

When her one-word answer was echoed in the room, she startled and followed the 3-D arrow in her vision to the vid capture mounted high on the wall. Lotyaum sounded a rumble of amusement.

"I've asked the staff to enable the security captures' interpret mode for Norka in this room," he explained. She was familiar with this tech but unhappy about it. Among those who tapped, using any kind of device outside an INT to interpret was considered rude. In an age where languages could be downloaded and learned so easily, what this Talin had done wasn't only lazy. It was insulting. As if she needed an electronic voice when her fingers could talk perfectly well for her.

She glanced over to a display that told her Tamerin had one mark left to get back to her. Taking a deep breath to rein in her temper, she reminded herself that she promised Tamerin she would wait. She was a human of her word, but she had a strong suspicion this committee guy was going to try her patience far more than the med staff or station director.

"Now, I don't have any sweets to give you, but I'm sure the staff here have already spoiled you. Not only are too many sweets bad for humans, but it's important that your kind have strict rules and discipline. You really can't be trusted to make good decisions. But don't worry, I'm here to look after you."

Rumble to soothe.

"I want to assure you that you won't be going back to Palforma. I know you might feel close to him because he can't talk either, but Talins with deficits such as his shouldn't be allowed to own a fragile human, especially one with special needs like you. I'll find you a wealthy family with a breeding male your age. Your eye color isn't optimal, but your dark skin and hair are lovely."

This guy managed to irritate her more with every sentence out of his mouth. Not only did Zia feel insulted, but she was upset on Palforma's behalf. Who did this privileged idiot think he was? Who maligned someone who was wounded in service to his species? And what was that about finding a breeding male?

All kinds of retorts and counter-insults jumped around in her head, but she clenched her hands together to keep any of them from getting out. Eyes narrowed, she glared at Lotyaum and waited for him to finish and leave.

For his own sake she hoped it would be before the mark was up. If he was still here when Tamerin ran out of time to get back, she was going to do something nasty to this guy. Maybe the short-draw saw to the vulnerable flesh under the plates on the back of his neck. Yes, that would be satisfying.

"We have a human reallocation queue here on the station, but I'm going to ship you back to Talarian, which is our homeworld. Far better individuals are in the queue there."

She didn't have any trouble reading between the lines. Back on his home planet were actually Talins willing to bribe him to get at her. He droned on about how she would travel in a specially designed box, and it wouldn't be bad because she would be drugged and surrounded with soft pillows.

She let him drone on while keeping track of the time. This Talin certainly liked to hear himself talk because he never once paused to ask her a question. He only stopped talking when the door opening interrupted him.

Tamerin was back, and from a look at the nearby display, she knew he'd cut it close.

"Greeting, Committee Citizen Lotyaum. I'm here to drop off something to comfort Zia while she waits for your decision." Tamerin held up what Zia could only describe as a light blue, furry pillow.

"Is that a sachie squeeze?" Lotyaum asked with an interested rumble.

"It is. I bought it a solar ago with the hope to give it to a human of my own someday. But I'd like to give it to Zia instead. I can always buy another one, and she could use the warmth and softness while she sleeps in an unfamiliar place."

"I don't have the budget to pay you for that when she's shipped to Talarian," Lotyaum warned him.

"No need, it's my pleasure to gift it to her," Tamerin assured Lotyaum as he stepped up to her bed and handed it to her. She took it gingerly, half expecting it to be hard and lumpy because of hidden tools or other items. But it was nothing but a warm, soft, and fluffy mass.

Actually, it was extremely soft and fluffy. She couldn't help herself, she hugged it to her chest and rubbed her cheek on it. It was so plush it must have been imbued with the souls of thousands of fuzzy creatures.

It grew pleasantly warm in her arms. It must also have the same nano tech as the omnie. Some day she wanted an entire bed made out of this tech.

"That was very kind of you, Senor Security Technician Tamerin," Lotyaum commented as they both watched her snuggle the pillow.

"My satisfaction comes from giving a human comfort. She might not be mine, but maybe someday someone else will show the same kindness to the human I will end up acquiring."

As Lotyaum and Tamerin exchanged a few pleasantries, she cuddled the pillow. It wasn't as comforting as hugging Palforma would be, but it was soothing. Even tough girls like her needed to snuggle something soft occasionally. Heck, this pillow was so awesome that she was sure a couple of humans she knew would rush to be Tamerin's pet just to get one.

An image of Lasha trying to be brave the day she left for her new job filtered through Zia's mind. She'd never had the resources to find Lasha and check on her, but maybe Tamerin could.

If Tamerin would be willing, he could help find Lasha. He would probably even agree to give Lasha the choice of returning to her family or staying among the Talins as a pet. Hmmm, it was worth thinking about.

Of course, that was assuming they all made it out of here alive because the gift of a plush pillow wouldn't make up for not fulfilling his promise to help her and Palforma leave together. She was totally serious when she'd threatened the station, and no way was she ending up on the Talin homeworld.

Tamerin's words to Lotyaum brought her out of her thoughts.

"The healer also told me he will be coming in soon to give her medications that will put her to sleep, so he asked that you come back at second mark tomorrow to finish your interview," Tamerin informed Lotyaum.

"Very well," Lotyaum responded as he looked down at her. "Rest well, Zia, and be assured your next owner will be an elite Talin with an impeccable reputation."

Over my dead body, she thought even as she gave a little nod and watched him leave. Without moving anything but her eyes, she slid her gaze to the security vid capture and then back to Tamerin. He sounded a reassuring rumble as he slid a small device out of his pouch, turned it on, and then handed it to her.

'It's a key coder,' he explained. Delighted she quickly made the device disappear up the sleeve of her omnie. Station security used key coders to check the algorithms that observed vid captures, but if set high enough it disrupted those same feeds.

His tapping wasn't turned into words by the vid capture in the room, telling them both the key coder was working.

'When I'm gone, turn it off, or they might get suspicious,' he continued.

'What's going on? How's Palforma?'

'The station director has decided to ship Palforma to his registered domicile planet, Kalor. As you must already have figured out, you're to be given to someone else.'

Her eyes narrowed and she scowled at him. 'Nope.'

'I know. I have a plan. By about seventh strike, only one staff member will be left in medical. Everyone else will be off shift. Strikes are—

'I know. *S*trikes are nighttime and marks are daytime measurements, which is dumb because marks and strikes are the same length. It's even dumber because if I'm referring to a unit of time instead of a specific time, they're called marks. Why you guys can't use Common time units for timekeeping I don't understand. But anyway, hurry up and tell me the plan,' she urged impatiently.

Rattle of surprise.

Rumble of amusement.

'I forgot for a moment you're Palforma's human, so you must be smart.'

'You got it backward,' she argued with a slight grin. 'He's my Talin, and I've got the paperwork to prove it. Now finish telling me what's going on before someone comes in here and drugs me.'

'I made that up to get Lotyaum to leave. You won't be drugged, as they wouldn't want to risk it after having to sedate you earlier. As I said, Palforma's being set home. I told the station director it would be best to send Palforma off as soon as possible, so he's booked to leave on a Talin transport a little after seventh strike. The moment it gets quiet enough, I need you to follow the map in there,' he points to the pillow, 'and I'll meet you. My plan is to get you and Palforma on the transport and long gone before anyone realizes you're missing.'

'Couldn't they simply contact the transport and tell them to detain us?'

'The captain owes me a favor. He's going to be unable to find any passenger named Palforma or human fitting your description on his ship. This is a busy station, and the station director pushed to open before it was finished. We're still figuring out a lot of issues, especially with security. They'll find that when the vid feeds are examined, it's impossible to figure out what order things were recorded. That happens sometimes when the algorithms watching the vid feeds aren't set up and programmed for the specific station. I'd warned him in the past that buying a generic algorithm was a bad idea.'

Zia nodded her head in admiration. 'That's an excellent plan. But what about you? I don't think I want you to get into trouble after we're gone.'

'Once they realize they can't find you anywhere, I'm sure the station director and Lotyaum will be too busy blaming each other to bother looking at me. After all, I only set up the systems I don't design or control them.'

Clever guy. 'Someday I'd like to sit down and have a round of drinks with you, Tamerin,' Zia offered.

'I would like that,' Tamerin agreed and then tapped the pillow in her lap. 'It's up to you to be on time. Otherwise I'm going to have to come up with a much more elaborate plan. I'm trusting you to make this work.'

She petted the pillow and then answered. 'I promise your faith in me is well-founded. Just in case we don't get a chance to talk later, I want to tell you about a human, a friend, who might be in trouble. Her name's Lasha and I want you to find her.'

Tamerin didn't even hesitate. 'I can do that; give me all the information you have.'

'Before I tell you anything, you need to promise me something,' she countered. 'You can't do to her what Palforma did to me. You have to explain everything and give her a choice.'

Rattle of agreement. 'I vow to explain everything and abide by her choice.'

'Good,' Zia said, satisfied that Tamerin would do as he promised. 'Here is what I know.'

CHAPTER 20

As they walked Tamerin remained silent. Palforma couldn't blame his cousin. After all, what was there to say? Tamerin was escorting Palforma onto the ship that would take him to Mondron Colony. From there Palforma was supposed to find his way to Kalor. He didn't bother fighting Tamerin's hold on his arm. There was no point. He was wearing so many restraints that his movements were limited, and the inhalant drugs they'd flooded his cell with were making him clumsy. His cousin had already saved him from falling to his knees several times, but Palforma couldn't bring himself to care.

"Easy, these steps are steep," Tamerin broke their silence to warn him as they stepped up onto the main entry deck of the transport. Palforma grunted and tried to make his legs work. It was more Tamerin's vigilance than Palforma's effort that got them on board the ship.

As they walked, other Talins watched them go by, occasionally sounding rattles of curiosity and talking with each other in hushed tones. Palforma couldn't be bothered to care what they were whispering among themselves. He was a dead man walking.

His life would probably end before this transport got even halfway to its destination, and he could see no way to escape it. He'd pleaded with Tamerin in the brig, begging him not to do this. Not to separate him from Zia. He couldn't tell his cousin that he scent-bonded to the human without everyone else finding out, so he tried to put it in terms of what was best for Zia. But everyone knew the truth; she might be upset, but she'd survive their separation probably with little to no physical issues.

He wouldn't.

Scent Collapse Disease, more commonly called *Ending*, happened to Talins who were separated from their scent-bonded partners for too long. It was a painful way to die, and even though they hadn't been apart for even two full rotations, he was already feeling the effects. His chest felt so tight it was hard to breathe, and his head hurt beyond a simple headache even before they'd drugged him.

Due to Ending, thousands of years ago a monarch declared scent-bonding as unnecessary and old fashioned. Because Talin women couldn't get pregnant outside of a scent-bond, that same monarch also encouraged Talins to start using artificial wombs. He even took it a step further and told his people to put their children in institutions called creshes so they could focus their efforts on expanding the might and reach of the Talin species. Using artificial wombs and creshes went from being rare to common, and within several generations laws were set in place to make live birth and scent-bonding illegal.

That meant Ending was one of the most shameful diseases a Talin could die of. The other being Fading, a disease caused when Talins fade away because they aren't scent-bonded. It's widely said that the root cause of both diseases was an inherent weakness in that Talin. He'd heard the same thing all his life:

No Talin should be a slave to the scent-bonding urge.

The outdated biological urge can be conquered through will power.

Good riddance to those who die of Fading or Ending because it only strengthens the species as a whole.

At least that's what everyone's expected to say and believe.

But even as much as Talins want to deny it, they crave touch and affection—enter humans. Human pets became the only avenue by which Talins could display or receive the softer emotions. Because humans were believed to be so fragile and needy, of course their Talin owners would be required to cuddle them, comfort them, and assure them that they were adored.

But Palforma knew the truth. He knew all about the worst-kept secret among the Talin. Humans weren't just an outlet for the softer emotions. They could be full scent-bonded partners for Talins. They were breeding compatible, and when bonding oil was absorbed into their scalps, it changed with that human's body chemistry. That allowed the Talin to scent-bond even if the human didn't have scent glands to create bonding oil.

He hadn't been lying to Zia when he told her one of the potential heirs to the throne was scent-bonded to his human pet, and they had a child together. It was true but a tightly controlled secret. To most Talins, Sora was perceived as a happy, spoiled pet, not a dedicated life partner to Prime Son Searin.

As Tamerin led him down a long hall, Palforma briefly debated about trying to contact Prime Son Searin and pleading his case. But even if he could get through to Searin, it would be foolish. The Prime Son couldn't risk advocating for some lowly retired soldier. It might draw the wrong attention, and he wouldn't put Sora or their child at risk—not when tensions were so high and the Traditionalists were so willing to be violent.

A wave of desolation slumped Palforma's shoulders as they came to a stop in front of a cabin door. After passing Palforma's new Ident over the door display, it slid open.

"I got you full accommodations," Tamerin explained as he helped Palforma step inside. Dismally Palforma noted that it was one of the more exclusive cabins, so at least he'd have a nice place to die. Maybe he should beg Tamerin for a weapon, something that would give him a quick, painless death.

With his hands bound to his waist, he couldn't tap, so he was forced to use his ungainly voice. "W-w-wasted money."

"I don't agree," Tamerin argued as he guided Palforma to sit on the edge of the bunk. With quick efficiency he locked

Palforma's restraints to one of the support beams at the head of the bunk. As part of the bulkhead, there was no way he'd be able to rip himself free before the timer of the restraints clicked to zero and released him.

He watched with dull eyes as Tamerin fussed with the settings on his restraints to make sure they were all set to the same time.

"These will release in two marks. Then you'll be able to move around. But I suggest you stay in the cabin for another few marks until you're sure the medication has worn off. That stuff can be insidious."

He stared at his bound hands as his cousin talked. He should say something to absolve Tamerin of the guilt he'd feel when he eventually found out Palforma died before he ever reached Kalor. But he couldn't get his words to work. He already felt dead inside.

He'd failed. Again.

Standing up straight, Tamerin carefully took off the large bag he caried over his shoulder. Unable to summon any curiosity, Palforma eyed the bag as Tamerin gently placed it on the floor just out of reach. It wasn't one of the bags he carried for Zia and himself when they got to Oglin station. Tamerin must have taken it on himself to pack all their things in a single, larger bag.

Poor Zia… mostly her things would be in that bag. He'd tell Tamerin to take it to her, but he knew they wouldn't let her have it. They'd want to give her a clean break from him. It was considered the best way to separate a scent-bonded human from their Talin.

Maybe he could dig her clothes out. If he's lucky they'll still have her scent clinging to them. It would be a small comfort, but the thought of having her smell in his nose made Palforma straighten up a little.

"I packed some things for you," Tamerin explained. "You'll want to go through them as soon as you're free. Some of the things in here are fragile, so handle it with care."

What could Tamerin have packed that required special handling? He couldn't think of anything important Tamerin would want to send with him—unless it was a weapon!

Did Tamerin decide to supply Palforma with armaments for this trip? Tamerin was a soldier after all. He'd know how uncomfortable Palforma would be with absolutely no weapons on him. Palforma might use such a generous act in a way Tamerin didn't intend.

"Careful," he agreed, relieved that he would have the means to end his own life when the pain became too much.

Tamerin sounded a rumble of satisfaction. "Good." He stepped to the door but then paused before exiting. Turning, he sounded a soft, sad rumble. "I wish things had gone differently, but I want you to know you've opened my eyes."

Palforma met his cousin's gaze and sounded a rattle of confusion. "Opened?"

"I'd heard rumors," Tamerin continued, dropping his eyes to the floor. "About humans and Talins. But before Zia I thought they were fanciful. But she loves you, as if you were another human. She was ready to fight for you. Protect you. She told me she'd be willing to destroy the station to get you back, and I believed her." He sounded a rumble of humor. "Well, I believed she wanted to, being capable is something entirely different."

"I-i-if said could. Then can," Palforma assured him, feeling a heartwarming pleasure fill his chest. His Zia wanted him back even after he caused all of this. But he still needed to warn Tamerin. "Be guarding. Guard station."

"I could see her being a very wrathful human," Tamerin agreed with another rumble of amusement. "She bit a healer on the hand."

Although Palforma was proud of his scrappy human, a worried rumble sounded from his chest. "Punish her?"

"Absolutely not. I was there and interceded," Tamerin assured him. "And the last time I talked to her in medical, she gave me a unapparelled gift."

Palforma sounded an inquisitive rattle. "Gift?"

Tamerin sounded a rattle of excitement. "I'm within several rotations of finishing my contract here. I intend to leave even if they offer me a generous renewal. I'm like you. I don't need the funds, but I like working. And now Zia's given me a mission that I intend to see through. I'll contact you about it once I've accomplished my task."

"Good luck," Palforma grunted and then felt the energy drain out of him. His head hurt and his chest felt tight. The drugs weren't the only cause of his suffering, so he knew his mind might clear, but the pain and lethargy wouldn't go away. He couldn't imagine what kind of assignment or task Zia bestowed on Tamerin. Even though his cousin wouldn't share the details, Palforma was happy to see the male as eager and enthusiastic as he was when they were young.

"I'll see you when I get back, Cousin," Tamerin declared as he stepped out the door. He shut it before Palforma could respond.

Scooting back on the bunk a little, he leaned his upper body against the wall and let his head thump back. Closing his eyes, he let his mind wander and tried to focus on memories of Zia instead of the steadily increasing pain in his head.

Before long the ship vibrated around him as it launched from the station. He lost all sense of time as he sat there and tried to submerge himself in memories. They were probably deep in one of the travel corridors before the timer on his restraints clicked, and suddenly he was free.

He didn't move at first. He wasn't woozy from the drugs, but he had no place to go. He felt the faint vibrations of the ship, but the cabin was expensive enough to have good insulation so no other noises came through.

Finally, curiosity go the better of him and despite the pain that nagged at him, he sat up and slid off the bed. On his knees next to the bag, he carefully opened it, expecting to find it full of Zia's things, his few pieces of clothing, and at least one weapon.

He was wrong.

At first he thought he must have been hallucinating, but as he opened the bag entirely, he was greeted with the sight of Zia curled up and asleep. She had a small breathing mask on her face and was clutching a sachie squeeze in her arms. She was still wearing the omnie he bought her with his race winnings, but her boots where gone, replaced with the more common slippers that human pets wore.

She didn't stir when he eased off the face mask or when he carefully tugged her free of the bag and gathered her in his arms. Leaning his back against the bunk behind him, he cradled her against his chest, his chestbox rumbling loudly and the scent glands in his cheeks overfull and weeping.

Without hesitation he started rubbing his cheeks against her head, soaking her hair with his bonding oil. Soon the air around him was full of not only the scent of his oil,but also the slightly changed scent of his oil reacting with her body chemistry.

Burying his nose in her hair, he breathed in deeply. As their combined scent hit him, the pain in his head vanished, and the muscles in his chest relaxed. He wasn't sure how long they stayed like that, but eventually Zia started to stir.

Sitting up straight, he laid her across his lap and watched her eyes flutter open and focus on his face. A warm and open smile formed as she came fully awake. She brought up her hands and yawned as she tapped with languid movements.

'I'm glad to see Tamerin was as good as his word. I would've hated to destroy the station after they gave me such nice implants,' she commented.

'He told you what he was doing?'

She rubbed her eyes with one hand and spoke with the other. 'Not all of it. But it looks like it worked."

After yawning and stretching again, she sat up. He watched as her brain fully woke up and he could tell the moment she remembered every detail of the recent past. Her eyes narrowed on him and her smile disappeared.

Before he could even begin apologizing to her and begging for forgiveness, she balled up one of her small hands into a fist and punched him in the nose.

CHAPTER 21

Zia was absolutely ecstatic to be back with Palforma, and by the looks of it, going somewhere on another transport. But that didn't mean she wasn't still pissed as hell at his deception.

'Pet!' she tapped with sharp movements. Then realizing she was still lounging on his lap, she scrambled off to sit on the floor in front of him.

'They put a collar on me.' She jabbed a finger at the collar. 'Look! Do you see it? Tamerin wouldn't take it off because he said it would raise too many questions if I was caught without it. He disabled the tracker in it, but still, this is all kinds of wrong!'

Rattle of anger.
Rumble of shame.

'I'm sorry. I should have told you what you were walking into—'

'You lied to my face, Palforma!' she raged. 'How can I ever trust you again?'

'It wasn't a lie. We don't keep slaves,' he tried but her scoffing expression told him that wasn't going to work.

'You deliberately misled me,' she argued. 'You told me Talins didn't keep slaves but then conveniently didn't mention the human pet situation.'

Rumble of shame, volume indication high.

'You're right. My only excuse was that I was afraid you wouldn't agree to go, and I desperately wanted you to have the best medical care and implants. My people study human anatomy as much as a Talin anatomy. I knew you'd be well-treated by our healers.'

'Collar!' she reminded him, her motion for collar so strong she almost smacked herself in the neck slightly above where the collar rested at the base of her throat.

She took a few deep breaths to calm herself down and then started again. Palforma remained respectively silent and attentive as she tapped.

'I appreciate that you wanted to give me something, but the only way I'm going to stay with you is if you see me as an equal. That means you tell me the truth, always. No matter how ugly or scary. We discuss it, together. You don't make decisions for me and hope it all works out. You might be able to do that with humans raised among you guys, but not me. I've been forced to fight my entire life. There's no way I could simply let you take over. I don't have the mindset to be a slave or pet.'

She paused for a second. She knew what she needed to tell him, but it broke her heart to say it. 'If you can't handle that, we need to part ways.'

Her words had a strong and immediate effect on Palforma.

Rumble of fear, volume indication high.

Rattle of aggression, volume indication extreme.

Extreme? What the hell did *extreme* mean? Then she saw the reflective display in the wall waver. He was making so much noise that the vibrations were disrupting the visuals in the display. Damn, they weren't kidding when the implants marked a sound as *extreme*.

"N-n-no!"

His hands were balled into fists, and she got the impression he was fighting the impulse to reach for her. When he started tapping, his movements were fast and jerky, as if too many words wanted to get out at the same time.

'Don't leave me! I'll do anything you want! We can leave Talin-controlled space. We can rent a domicile anywhere. Live where you wish. Do you have family? We could find a domicile big enough to accommodate all of them and us. I'll do whatever you want. Anything but don't leave me!'

Although hearing it felt good, Zia knew words were meaningless without any action to back them up. 'Can I assume we're on a transport heading for your homeworld?'

At her question, Palforma visibly calmed. 'No. We're on our way to Mondron Colony. From there I was to find a transport to take me to Kalor Colony, where I've been living since I retired from the military. But all of it is in Talin-controlled space.'

'Can we book passage on a transport out of Talin-controlled space from Mondron Colony?'

Palforma didn't even hesitate when he replied. 'Yes, absolutely. There are no mandates or restrictions attached to my Ident, the station director didn't want to press any formal charges against a war hero. I'm free to buy passage anywhere. You pick the destination and we will go.'

His words went a long way to making her feel better, but she was still angry. 'But until we're away from Talin-controlled space, I'm a fucking pet.'

Rumble to soothe.

'In name only, I promise you. On my life I swear.' He looked down at the bag Tamerin had put her in and reached out to drag it closer. Along with her bags, Tamerin had included a few other items. Rummaging around Palforma found her punch-stick along with a few other weapons. Palforma plucked one up and unsheathed it to reveal a large dagger. The hilt was etched with symbols she didn't recognize, but it looked formal, like something a warrior might wear to a special occasion.

He pressed the weapon into her hand and then covered her hand with his and guided the tip of the dagger to a strip of flesh where the plates of his neck met those of his shoulder. With his hand still over hers, he pressed until the very tip of the knife broke the skin.

Then he let go of her hand and spread his arms out to his side. Closing his eyes, he waited. She'd wanted proof of his repentance. She'd wanted more than words and he'd given that to her.

She knew in her heart this wasn't theater. This wasn't a show to appease her. His body language clearly told her he wasn't sure if she would do it or not. He was braced for her vengeance.

He was ready to die.

She didn't simply remove the dagger. She stayed there, poised. She contemplated what it would mean to thrust this blade into his flesh. Thought about how it would feel to take the life of someone she loved this much. Thought about what life would be like without Palforma.

If he was going to sincerely offer up his life to appease her, the least she could do was truly appreciate what his sacrifice would mean for both of them.

For the universe really because nothing would be right ever again if Palforma wasn't in her world.

She took a deep breath and heaved out a sigh as she moved the dagger from his neck. His entire body sagged, his breathing ragged. Setting the weapon aside, she urged him to look up with a finger under his chin. Once their eyes met she dropped her hand away to speak.

'I couldn't bear to live in a reality where you weren't part of it,' she explained. 'But from now on, we're partners. We're honest with each other. We tell the truth, even if we don't think the other person would like it very much.'

Rumble of agreement, volume high.

Rattle of joy, volume high.

'Yes,' Palforma agreed readily. 'I'll do whatever you ask.'

She pressed a finger to the lock of the collar. 'First things first, I want to be able to take this off.'

Without another word, Palforma reached up and gripped the collar on either side. She watched the muscles of his arms strain for a moment and then the collar was gone. Holding his hands up, he presented her with the collar broken in two, both the clasp and the hinge wrecked beyond repair.

She grinned. 'I can't say I'm not thrilled to see it ruined, but don't I need a collar to keep other Talins from staring at me and getting suspicious? And the healers said something about humans being stolen. I'm not interested in getting kidnapped because someone doesn't see a collar and thinks I'm free for the taking or easy prey.'

'I'll figure something out,' Palforma responded after tossing the pieces of collar into a corner. 'And no one will take you from me. And even if someone managed to kidnap you, I'm sure you'd make them regret it quickly.'

His faith in her abilities made her shoulders roll back and her spine straighten up. It was nice to be acknowledged as a possible threat. 'That's right. I would. So, I guess the plan is for me to pretend to be your dutiful pet. But once we get to Mondron Colony, you buy us tickets to the closest destination that isn't under Talin control.'

'Pretend only,' Palforma agreed readily. 'You and I would know the truth. And the moment we land I'll see about buying those tickets. I think Sormin station is the closest and it's under Nimon ownership and command.'

'Nimon works for me,' Zia agreed.

'In the meantime, I can buy you new clothes, tools, and anything you want. Do you want weapons? I can get you weapons and teach you how to use them.'

Zia had to fight a grin. 'Weapons and combat lessons?'
Rumble of joy.
Rattle of eagerness.
'We can start now if you want.'

'Maybe not right away,' she said casting a glance over at the discarded dagger. It was strange but despite the fact that, for all intents and purposes, she was property until she got away from Talin-controlled space, she felt surprisingly peaceful.

Almost absently, Zia became aware of how grubby she felt. She hadn't bathed in a while and thought she could even feel the last few days gathered on her skin. She wanted to take advantage of the private bathing facility attached to their room. Then maybe a nap. She still felt a little groggy from the sedation wafer Tamerin had given her.

But before all that she needed to touch and hold Palforma. She would never admit it, but she felt a little shaky from everything that had happened, including holding a dagger to his neck. He probably felt the same. They both could use some reassurance.

'You're forgiven,' she said. 'The slate is wiped clean. But if you ever try anything like that again I'm taking a zimmer-saw to you!'

Rumble of affection.

Rumble to soothe.

'Because you love me.'

She felt a soft smile curve her lips. 'Because I love you,' she agreed.

'You are the most important person in my life. You have my body, so by default, you have my heart too. From now on I breathe for you. I move, eat, and sleep for you.

She launched herself at him, wrapping her arms around his neck and holding tightly. He went stiff for a moment, and then his body relaxed and he wrapped his arms around her to return the embrace.

Rumble of adoration.

He started rubbing his cheek over the top of her head and the air filled with the scent of vanilla. She wasn't sure how long they stayed like that, but it felt like they were melding together. Hearts beating in rhythm, breathing in synch. Soon she wasn't even sure where she ended and he began.

She'd never understood before why her dad had told her that finding her mom had been like "finding his other half." But now she got it. Having Palforma in her life was as if she'd found a part of herself she didn't even know she'd been missing.

Zia could hear Palforma coming back into the room as she finished up in the cleansing chamber. Because Tamerin had been throwing her stuff into the bag he'd put her in, she had all her familiar skin cleaning products. But Tamerin had gone a step further and included a bunch of human-safe soaps and lotions. She'd been impressed because they were all top of the line and luxurious.

She'd never let herself splurge on any of these products and felt like a kid with new toys when she'd found them. She'd scooped them all up and sprinted into the cleansing unit. Now that she'd used them, she might need to at least make the lotion a regular thing in her life. The stuff was fabulous.

Unfortunately, Tamerin hadn't included her other pairs of coveralls. He probably hadn't recognized the garments and thought he was being helpful when he'd replaced them with several wraps. That meant she had to wear one of the ubiquitous wrap garments while her dirty coveralls went through the small clothing cleanser in the room.

She was mildly surprised to find that the wrap was both comfortable and not revealing like she'd expected it to be. But the lack of pockets would always be a deal breaker for her. Pockets weren't a luxury. They were a necessity.

She was untangling her hair with the beautiful, hand-carved comb Tamerin had packed when Palforma politely knocked on the cleansing room door.

Rumble of inquiry.

She really loved the additional programing on these new implants!

Pulling the comb free of her hair, she stepped over to the door display and keyed it open. Palforma stood tall, still wearing the pants she bought him, dirty and ripped from his fight in medical. Looking him over now, she could see he was the worse for wear and could probably use a turn in the cleansing unit and a new set of pants. And this time she'd buy him a set in the proper Talin style that he would probably prefer. She'd get him a belt and pouch, too.

Only when he thrust a package at her did she realize he had something in his hand. Setting the comb down, she accepted the package with both hands, although it was small enough to hold with one.

With his hands empty, he started tapping. 'I got you something. This is a Talin ship, so if we want to leave the room, you'll need to blend in. But this one doesn't lock anymore. You could take it off any time. It's the best I could do on this ship.'

Rattle of excitement.

Rumble of adoration.

Grinning, she opened the package to find a necklace made of a lot of glittering gems. Stunned, she went still, unable to take her eyes off the gift.

Very few people knew about Zia's deepest secret. She never spoke of it or even looked at certain items twice because intense longing might make her do something wasteful with her funds. But the truth was that Zia liked sparkly things.

No, *like* wasn't a strong enough verb. She *loved* sparkly things. She always had, even when she was young.

When she was a little girl, she would put the latching dock to the atmosphere regulator on her head and wear it like a crown. The cross hatching around the outside of the circular latching dock caught the light and looked vaguely like jewels. Her family would laugh and make her put it back, but her love of things that sparkled had an early start and never abated.

She owned exactly one gem and it was tucked safely away in a lockbox on Muki station. Every single jewel on this necklace was bigger than that one gem. The clasp of this necklace alone had more gems than she could have bought with all the funds she'd saved over the years. It boggled her mind how much Palforma must have paid for it, especially at a specialty kiosk on a transport instead of a crystals and precious metals section of a large station where prices could be compared and deals bartered.

Pulling it out of the box with shaking fingers, she dropped the container on the floor and lifted the necklace so it could catch the light. The gems sparkled, dazzling her with their shimmer.

Unlike human-style necklaces, the cluster of gems on the clasp were meant to weigh it down and keep the clasp in the front of the body instead of hidden at the back of the neck. Judging by the length, the clasp would sit at the hollow of her neck with all the jewels circling her throat at evenly spaced intervals of deep blue, vibrant green, sparkling topaz, and gleaming amber. The size of the gems ranged from as small as the tip of her pinky, to the largest one the size of her thumbnail. All of them were expertly cut and lacking any obvious flaws.

Hanging it off her forearm to free her hands, she looked up to him. 'How could you afford this.'

Rumble of confusion.

'I told you I had funds,' he reminded her and then pointed to the new Ident Tamerin must have gotten him.

'Are you…' She didn't even want to ask. It felt rude and wrong. Like she planned to exploit him. But she had to know. 'Are you rich?'

He stared at her, silent and still. She couldn't tell what he was thinking or feeling at all, and she wanted to call back the question. Then finally he made a sound.

Rumble of laughter, volume high.

'My heart, to most humans even the least wealthy among the Talins would be considered rich. None of you command much in the way of resources. This necklace wouldn't even register as a large purchase to most Talins. Because of my distinguished career, I was given a large settlement after I retired from the military. I also had family and clan money I was given for every solar I was in the military as well as bonuses when I achieved a higher rank or was given an award. All those funds have been sitting in my accounts for solars, untouched. I had no reason to bother with them until you.'

She blinked up at him and felt a little like her world had tilted on its axis.

Because she was the one insisting Palforma leave Talin society behind, she'd believed it would be her responsibly to support them or at least look after him until they could figure out a job situation. When he'd said he had funds, she'd assumed it meant he had a little bit stored away. She'd never entertained the notion he could be so wealthy.

Palforma kept talking as she wrapped her head around this new information. 'Remember I told you I could buy a domicile for us and your family. Did you think I was overstating my resources?'

She'd thought those promises were poetic license, a way for him to tell her he was willing to do as she asked no matter what kind of hovel they were forced to live in. But now she understood that Palforma wasn't exaggerating about purchasing domiciles for her and her family. He could do it.

And more importantly, he wanted to do it. He wanted to do anything to make her happy. His words hadn't been empty promises but assurances that could be backed by real wealth. She was struck by all the good his funds could do for the small human community her parents still lived in.

'If you don't like it you don't have to wear it. We don't even need to leave the cabin, so worrying about a collar is a moot point.' He was tapping fast now, probably worried she wasn't happy with his gift. 'We can order food to be brought to us, like we did on the other transport. If we need anything that can't be brought to the room, I can run out to fetch it.'

Rattle of concern. 'Tell me what you want and I'll do it.'

Realizing she'd been silent too long, she thrust the necklace back at him. 'Put it on me,' she demanded.

Palforma didn't hesitate as he thumbed the clasp to open it and then draped it around her neck. The click of the clasp registered in her left eye as he brought the ends together at the hollow of her neck.

'The Sai gems match your eyes,' he told her.

Rumble of happiness.

Rattle of pride.

Running her fingers over the stones, she grinned up at him, no longer worried about showing teeth. 'It's perfect.'

'And you can take it off any time you wish. I had the seller disable the locking feature of the clasp so you or anyone could remove it.'

'Wait, this clasp could lock?'

'Yes, but I had the seller disable that,' Palforma assured her.

Incredulity hit her. 'No, that's not it. I meant to ask; this necklace was meant for a pet? To lock around a human's throat? Something this expensive was specifically designed to be worn by human pets?'

Rattle of puzzlement.

'Of course,' Palforma answered. 'Talins don't wear things like this because it would interfere with the plates at the back of our neck.'

'You guys are the strangest, most wonderful, yet shittiest species ever,' she declared. Then she pointed at the collar before speaking again. 'After this is all over and we're far from other Talins, I'm going to keep wearing this, but it's a necklace. Not a collar. Got it?'

Rumble of amusement.

'Yes, understood. My Zia wears a necklace, not a collar.'

'And if I ever call myself a princess, I need you to go along with it,' she continued. 'Even if I'm covered in dirt and wearing coveralls, this necklace makes me a goddamn princess. A tool using, bad-ass princess.'

Rattle of agreement.

'Whatever a princess is, I'm sure you'd be the best among them,' Palforma answered. 'Would you like me to call you princess?'

'Maybe.' Delighted with him, she stood up on her tiptoes and framed his face with her hands. A little pressure had him bending over so his face was close to hers. Closing her eyes, she pressed her lips to his. He returned the kiss eagerly.

She must be a princess because she'd found her prince.

CHAPTER 22

Zia's mouth was watering by the time the squat server bot set their food on the table. Although not as large or elaborate at the transport they took to get to Oglin station, this ship still boasted several nice eating establishments, one cantina, and a handful of shops. They'd already visited a clothing store to buy Palforma some new pants, a pouch, and a belt. Although she tried to get him to buy something nicer, he opted for the plainest items they had. But she decided that was fine because it would allow her to buy him something nicer later as a gift.

With that small bit of shopping done, they picked a place to eat that boasted a menu fit for human pets as well as Talins. Already several Talins who worked there had introduced themselves to Palforma and then interacted with her.

Not a single Talin looked twice at her "collar." She expected at least mild curiosity that a pet would be wearing an outrageously expensive item of jewelry as a collar, but everyone was much too interested in talking to her to bother commenting on what she thought was an inappropriate collar.

It was apparent quickly that spending this amount of funds on a collar for a pet wasn't out of the norm for Talins at all.

One Talin passing them outside their room even sounded an excited rattle as she said how "pretty the little human looks in her sparkling collar."

The comment made her grin, and that grin delighted the Talin. Even if she spent years among these Talins, she'd never get used to the way they interacted with her. She had never met another species that viewed the showing of teeth as anything but a threat display, but these Talins were so familiar with humans that they wanted her to smile and show teeth!

The one thing she absolutely didn't like is the way many of them tried to casually touch her, just like when they were on Oglin. She was forced to turn down her implant sensitivity to Palforma's rattles because he was making so much noise as he warned off those trying to pet her.

Most of them sounded regretful rumbles and backed away when Palforma rattled aggressively. A few tried to make an offer to buy her, but with one growl from Palforma, they all gave up. And just like at Oglin station, by the time they got to the eatery, she had a pocket full of candy that random Talins kept insisting she take.

She knew she could ask Palforma to make the candy-givers keep their treats to themselves, but Zia didn't have the heart to refuse them. They were excited when she accepted the treats, even if she tucked the candy away to "eat later." Her simple thank you smile was received as if she'd handed out a major award or precious gem.

One Talin even walked away proclaiming loudly to his partner, "She smiled at me. I saw teeth! That's a sign of real joyfulness."

By the sound of the number of rumblings she left in her wake, these small interactions made the Talins far happier than she could have ever predicted. It felt oddly empowering to be able to make them jubilant by simply accepting a small square of sugary food.

But now it was time for her and Palforma to enjoy a real meal. She was starving and couldn't wait to taste some new foods.

'Try the somba first,' Palforma suggested as Zia reached for a piece of the black flat bread that Talins served with every meal. 'Scoop bite size portion up with the bread.'

Palforma had explained that a few dishes came with special utensils, like janpi fruit that needed a specific knife to cut it open and pull out the seeds. But otherwise Talins didn't use eating utensils. All their food was meant to either be scooped up with the bread or eaten with fingers. Lack of utensils didn't bother her after so many years living among Nimons who simply held their plates up to their faces and scooped the food into their mouths with their palps.

The somba looked like chunks of moldy cheese but tasted like an Old Earth meal called Tikka Masala. After the first bite, she'd eaten half the plate before guilt caught up with her hunger. They'd offered her food back in medical on Oglin station, but she'd been too tense to eat anything. Still, that was no excuse for denying Palforma his share!

'Eat this,' she ordered as she nudged the plate of somba to Palforma's side of the table.

Rumble of amusement.

'We can always order more,' Palforma said as she cast him an apologetic look. 'But try everything before you fill up on one dish.'

'Sure thing,' she agreed as she reached for the next dish.

As she popped an orange ball into her mouth that tasted a lot like beef, Palforma started chowing down as well. She doubted they'd fed him when he was being held in the brig, so he must have been as hungry as her.

While she chewed a third mouthful of the orange-ball-beef-tasting food, she gave into the impulse and pressed a morsel to Palforma's lips. He startled at the gesture at first.

Rattle of surprise.

Rumble of affection.

Then he opened his mouth. But he didn't let her pop the bit of food in. He leaned forward and sucked her fingers into his mouth. He made her laugh as his tongue got busy licking off every bit of food from her digits. When she tried to pull away, he grabbed her wrist and kept her there, causing her to laugh even more as he pulled her fingers from his mouth and then licked up her palm.

When he finally let her pull her hand away, she leaned over to kiss him, only to remember last minute that it was taboo. She was a pet. According to Palforma, it was barely acceptable for Talins to even have sex with each other, let alone someone of a different species.

But then again, it couldn't have been that acceptable for him be licking all over her hand!

She tried for a serious expression. 'Don't get us in trouble.'

Rattle of agreement.

'You're correct that we need to be more circumspect. I'll try not to lose myself in the moment, but it's hard to remember that around you. You're the sun after a long winter, and all I want to do is wrap myself in your warmth.'

Her heart melted. 'You should write poetry or romantic prose.'

'Poetry or romantic prose?'

She forgot that some species never evolved creative writing. Humans were unique in the universe for being one of the only species to not only have fiction but create large volumes of it in many different ways.

'Poetry is a type of writing involving short, descriptive verses that sometimes rhyme,' she explained. 'Humans on Old Earth loved it. Some poetry was even set to music and then they were called songs.'

They chatted about poetry and song lyrics as they ate. It turned out that not only did Talins lack fiction, but they didn't have music either. Palforma knew what she was talking about because he'd come into contact with other species that had it, but it wasn't something Talins had developed in their own culture.

'What about the human pets?' Zia asked. 'They don't sing or make music.'

Rattle of interest.

'I think they do, but I never paid attention. The humans on Kalor didn't like me coming too near them, so I've always kept my distance,' he explained.

Zia felt anger on his behalf. 'What do you mean they didn't like to be near you?'

'They thought my inability to talk indicated a poor mental state. I think they feared I would lose control of myself. Only one human would spend time with me, but she never made any musical sounds.'

Knowing Palforma as she did, she couldn't imagine anyone being wary of her giant. Not with the way he instinctively treated humans, even when wounded and in pain. 'Anyone who didn't want to be with you was an idiot,' she declared. 'And my family will adore you. I promise.'

'Tell me about them,' Palforma requested. As they nibbled at the last of the food, she regaled him with stories of her family and some of the adventures she and her sister had while growing up.

When the food was all gone, Zia was tempted to ask Palforma to carry her back to their room because she felt so full. All she wanted to do was snuggle up in their bunk with him and fall into a food coma.

Suddenly Palforma went perfectly still, his head tilted to the side as if he was trying to hear something. That put Zia on alert, but she didn't look around. She knew better than to be obvious.

Keeping her movements small and close to her chest so it would be hard for anyone to see what she said, she focused on Palforma. 'What is it?'

Palforma did the same with his hands. 'I caught the sound of a familiar voice. The last time I heard it I was barely conscious, restrained, and being dragged onto a barely functioning ship.'

'You mean the ship that exploded? Right after you got out of it by using the inoperable planet hopper we picked you up in?' she asked.

His answer was quick, the movement of his hands decisive. 'Yes, and now that I think about the situation, it makes sense that they'd be here.'

'Why?'

'The other survivors of that ship would have been picked up by other Traditionalists or a friendly species. Either way they wouldn't want to travel as a group, which would be too conspicuous if the authorities were out looking for them. Splitting up into pairs and taking different ships to get back to Talarian would be the most logical thing to do. Transports might be slower, but they're more anonymous.'

'And going through Oglin station without the full security set up yet would make it easy to keep a name off official logs, ' Zia pointed out as she remembered the guy guarding the gate to the bay was checking for weapons. He wasn't doing any type of passenger identification or recording.

Rattle of agreement.

'You make an excellent point.' Palforma moved his head a little, as if he was having difficulty hearing. 'I can only make out a word or two. Not enough to know what they're saying. I think I might try to move closer. I need to know it's them and not my mind playing tricks on me.'

Zia was quick to intercede. 'Don't move yet. Let me try something first.'

Using the finger motions the Talin healer showed her, she accessed the menu of the implants and turned on the feature they'd told her about but she hadn't tried yet. Dropping her hands back to the table she looked at Palforma. 'Where are they?'

'Behind and to my right,' Palforma told her. 'One has a blue belt and the other has a gray belt.'

It was easy for her slide her gaze over and pick out the Talins. Then she moved her jaw and blinked in the right sequence. The feature came live with a 3-D arrow pointing to the Talin with the blue belt and then the one in the gray belt. Suddenly their words were scrolling across her right eye as if she was standing right next to them. None of the other conversations or ambient noise around her registered.

"…doesn't matter. The plan is still a good one, even if we find out Halieni isn't with us."

As the words scrolled across her vision, she tapped them out to Palforma, keeping her hands low and shielded by the two of them leaning in close. She had to keep her eye trained on the Talins, but her peripheral vision told her that Palforma was paying close attention to what she was repeating.

The Talin wearing the gray belt spoke, and as she moved her eye to him, the 3-D arrow shifted and his words were displayed. This worked even better than she expected.

"What if Halieni proves to be a Reformist like her brother and mother? Then killing the Monarch and Prime Son Searin gets us nothing."

Blue belt leaned closer to gray belt. "Then we simply wipe out the whole family and the Apogee Assembly can pick another lineage and start a new royal line."

Gray belt's crossed arms made it obvious that he wasn't convinced yet. "That gets us nowhere if the Apogee Assembly picks another Reformist family. Then we would've broken all these laws for nothing. We'll have the same issues as now."

Blue belt slid an information square across the table. "I already have a list of acceptable families ready to present to the Apogee Assembly." He pointed to the screen. "This one has military heroes, pets, and is highly esteemed by most."

Gray belt studied the list. "I know this family; they are outspoken Reformists."

Blue belt pulled the information square away and tucked it into his belt pouch. "That is what they wish everyone to think. But a member of this family got us the intel to successfully capture Holian. The head male of that family is true to our cause and will appeal to both sides. Once in power, he can undo the damage the monarch and Prime Son Searin have caused and help us strengthen the Traditionalist laws."

Gray belt sat back and picked up his drink. He was silent for a moment as he sipped and then finally sat the drink down and addressed blue belt. "But assassinating Prime Son Searin and the monarch is extreme. Don't you think?"

"Extreme is called for right now. Look what is happening! With the way the monarch and her son are persuading assembly members to their side, it won't be long before parents will be raising their own children. Think about the kind of damage that would do. They could be teaching their children anything. And unnecessary emotional attachments would be formed that could harm the child as an adult. This can only lead to disaster. It could mean the end of Talin superiority and expansion."

"Perhaps," was all gray belt said.

Blue belt pressed. "We can't afford not to take advantage of this opportunity. It's rare Prime Son Searin is vulnerable, especially after the failed attempt to take Holian captive last Solar. It needs to be now."

Gray belt wasn't done arguing. "Your plan is sound, but I'd feel better if we hadn't lost the information Holian's idiotic messenger Palforma was carrying when our ship deteriorated."

It took a lot for Zia not to react to that and keep her eyes on these nasty Talins. Palforma wanted information, and it sounded like these guys wanted to give it to him with the help of her implants.

"You speak the truth," blue belt conceded. "But I believe we must be bold. Now is the time to strike. We Traditionalists have let the Reformists gain too much ground, and we no longer have the luxury of time. I've been in contact with Brilanian. He's prepared the bomb and has found the perfect place to put it."

Gray belt's body went stiff. "Do you plan to carry this out even if I don't agree?"

Blue belt was quick to deny the accusation. "Of course not, but I like to be prepared. If you decide against it, I'd simply contact Brilanian with different instructions."

Zia wasn't sure how she knew, but she was sure blue belt was lying. Even if gray belt didn't agree, blue belt was set on murder. She'd met men like him before—zealots focused on a course of action and unwilling to be dissuaded. They were the most dangerous kind of individual because they truly believed they could do no wrong.

It made her sick to listen to them blithely planning out murder. It was inconceivable to her to be casually discussing slaying people because of political differences. And to make it worse, they were using a bomb that wouldn't discriminate between innocent bystanders and the actual target. Blue belt was an evil man.

Looking away from the two Talins she popped her jaw, ending the eavesdropping and refocusing her attention on

Palforma. 'This is wrong. They plan to use a bomb. That would kill a lot of people! Even if this Searin person deserves to die, how could they justify using a weapon like that? The guy with the blue belt is a psychopath.'

'Searin doesn't deserve to die, but what is a psychopath?' Palforma questioned. Because there was no equivalent word in Norka, Zia had used the modified Norka alphabet to spell the word out in Common. It probably didn't even come close to sounding like the Old Earth word, but that didn't matter.

'Someone who has no regard for other living creatures. They are cruel and unfeeling,' she explained. 'They will hurt others for gain, even if it's a harmless, innocent person.'

'That describes most of the militant Traditionalists,' Palforma answered. 'I need to know what room he is in. Do you think you can make it back to our room by yourself? Or you could wait here for me. I can ask one of the attendants to keep others away from you. They'd be happy to do it.'

Zia narrowed her eyes at her Talin. 'Go back to the room? I don't think so. Do you really think you're going to go off and have an adventure without me?'

CHAPTER 23

He should have known his human wouldn't be left behind. Zia had the same spark as Lakin and Nalia. The same fierce loyalty too. He didn't know how he could be so lucky as to find such an amazing human, but it made him determined to be true to her as Dalt was true to Lakin.

If his human wanted to help, it wasn't his place to say no—at least not when the help was as simple as observing and following. Besides, her advanced implants gave them an added advantage he hadn't anticipated.

'They know what you look like. Right?' Zia asked as the two Talins continued to drink at the table behind him. Using the reflective surface of the drinking flask in front of him, he observed the Talins. His memories of his abduction were fuzzy at best, but while he didn't recognize these faces, the voice he'd heard when the one had spoken in a loud, shocked voice triggered his memory.

'They must,' Palforma admitted. 'I was transporting an information square with false documents on it to draw out the militant traditionalists. They were supposed to steal it from me so they would think the lies we were telling them were real. It would make them reveal themselves to Prime Daughter Halieni and make it easy to identify and then bring them all to justice. But instead of simply stealing the square, they knocked me out and took me prisoner along with a small human named Nalia. I got her to a life pod and ended up in that planet hopper you rescued me from before the ship exploded. By the sound of it, the square was destroyed with the ship.'

Zia was quick to catch on. 'That means they'll know you by sight. We need to keep you hidden.' Palforma started to protest, but Zia's nimble fingers cut him off. 'No! I mean it! If they figure out you're still alive, their first priority will be to kill you. Think about it. They don't know there's a long game at play with fake documents and false trails. If they see you, they'll be concerned you'll identify them.'

'You're right,' he agreed reluctantly. 'We could wait until they're alone and I could take them both down. We could, uh, persuade them to tell me everything.'

Zia's grin turns wry. 'As much as I love the idea of you beating on these two bastards, we can't risk it. I'm sure whoever that Brilanian guy is, he's ready to blow up your leaders without blue belt needing to contact him.'

'Why would you say that? He told his companion that Brilanian was waiting for them.'

'He was lying to gray belt. This bombing is happening with or without them. And even if you tortured these two, that wouldn't guarantee truthful or accurate information because zealots are like that.'

'You speak the truth, and taking these two out might not save Searin and the monarch.' They were going to need to be sneaky and clever if they wanted any chance to stop this. And it already sounded like Zia had some ideas. 'What do you think we should do?'

She pointed to his head and then asked. 'First we need to hide your face. Would any Talin outfits do that?'

There weren't many garments a Talin could wear to hide his face outside of armor or a space suit, and that wouldn't be appropriate to wear inside the transport. Really, there was only one option. 'I could wear a Lamentation Cloth.'

'What's a Lamentation Cloth?'

'It's a long dark-colored tunic with a cowl that Talins wear to denote they've decided to formally enter a time of deprivation.'

Zia tilted her head to the side. 'Because someone died?'

'It could be because of death, because they were outcast from their family or clan, or because they lost a battle and feel responsible. When you wear it, you're not supposed to engage in any activity that is enjoyable or even satisfying. The time spent in the Cloth is supposed to be unpleasant, and when you emerge from the Cloth, any guilt you might feel is absolved. It's an old tradition that most don't bother with anymore because it's considered indulgent. Those who put on the Cloth are useless because they don't sleep or eat enough.'

'Only you guys would make mourning an indulgence,' Zia said with a gentle smile. 'But if the Lamentation Cloth hides your face, that's what we need.'

Palforma was quick to tell her the problem with this plan. 'While I'm wearing it, I can't touch you. Even having a human while wearing the Cloth would be suspicious, but some might dismiss it because humans still need care even if an owner decided to wear the Cloth. But I can't touch or hold you in public.' The thought made his chest feel tight.

Reaching across the table, Zia took his hand in hers and used simpler Norka to talk with one hand. 'That doesn't mean we can't do whatever we want in private. And remember, it's only for a short time.'

Her words made him feel better. 'You're right. But I can't very well go off and then come back to this table wearing a Lamentation Cloth. That would be too noticeable. How do we keep track of these two right here and now?'

Letting go of his hand, Zia sat back and looked around. When her eyes settled on something, Palforma turned his head slightly to see what she was looking at. It was a glass of imported Malvia wine. The moment he saw it, he knew what she was thinking.

'It wouldn't take much,' he agreed when their eyes met.

Smirking, she nodded her head. 'Reading my mind now?'

'I think so. If I'm correct, you're thinking that a few drops of Malvia wine on their clothing would leave a trail of molecules we could follow with even a low-grade enviro-sensor,' Palforma answered.

'I knew there was a reason I loved you,' she commented with a familiar cheeky grin. 'You order the wine and then leave. I'll stay here and figure out how to get it on their clothes. Then I'll meet you out front. Stay hidden because if they see you, it's all over.'

After a few taps on the table display to order the wine, Palforma met her gaze. He didn't want to leave her, but they really didn't have a choice. 'Be careful. I'll tuck myself in that little alcove next to the contract's kiosk. I'll tell the attendant here not to let anyone close or to bother you because you're sensitive. If anything goes wrong, toss the glass to the floor. I'll hear it break and come running.'

She waved him away. 'Don't worry, I've got this.'

From his hidden spot he watched the two Talins leave the table. They didn't head for the cabin section and instead made their way to the front of the ship where guests could enjoy the viewing port. That area had a large seating area where travelers could sit and watch the stars or consult a large display. It gave exact timetables for arrival and departure at various destinations along the ship's route in addition to data on those destinations including exchange rates and weather.

With those two gone, he hurried back to their table to find a full container of Malvia wine sitting in front of Zia. Her satisfied expression told him she'd been successful.

'Sit down,' she instructed with a big grin. 'I guess you saw them leave.'

Taking a seat, he pointed to the still full wine container, wondering how she'd gotten some on the men.

'How?' he asked simply.

She gave him an impish grin and then dipped the middle finger of her right hand in the open water flask next to the wine. Then she held her hand palm up with the wet finger trapped under her thumb. When her finger released from her thumb, droplets landed dead center on his bare chest.

'My sibling and I would do it all the time during meals,' she explained. 'I ended up with a really accurate flick. It took me a few times, but I got it on both of them and no one else.' She made her silent huffing laugh. 'We might end up trailing the other Talin who drank the Malvia wine, but it would be only one false trail to follow. Now it will be easy to figure out which room they're in, and we don't need to risk being seen following them.'

Her plan was brilliant and should prove to be effective.

'You're amazing,' he commented and felt a rumble of admiration sound from his chest box.

Her expression softened even as she retorted. 'I sure am!' Then she got up from the table. 'We need to do a little more shopping and then we'll track these guys down and figure out what room they're in. I need an enviro-sensor and a few other tools. And we need to buy you that Lamentation Cloth thing.'

Leaving the expensive wine, he got to his feet and picked Zia up from her seat. Her eyes went wide with surprise as he cradled her high on his chest. Rumbling out a soothing, sound he carried her out of the restaurant and tucked the two of them in the alcove he'd been hiding in earlier. Once they were mostly hidden from view, he brushed his aching scent glands across the top of her head. He didn't worry overly much about anyone catching him engaging in such unseemly behavior. They would assume Zia had gotten upset and needed to be comforted.

But in truth, he needed the contact as the oil soaked into her scalp and their combined scent filled his nose. Once he put that damn Lamination Cloth on, he wouldn't be able to touch her in public. It was a minor thing, and it would only be for a few more rotations, but for some reason it hit him hard.

As if sensing he needed this, she wrapped her arms around his neck and squeezed.

"L-l-love you," he whispered in her ear.

Letting go with one hand, she made the single motion that denoted deep affection and adoration and then went back to hugging his neck. That helped settle the small bout of anxiety at the thought of not being allowed to hold her outside of the room.

He wasn't sure how long they stayed like that, but when she finally withdrew her arms from his neck, the tightness in his chest was gone.

When he met her gaze, it felt like her eyes were seeing into his soul. 'Want to tell me what that was all about?' He remained silent even after he'd set her gently back on her feet. 'Fine,' she relented. 'You don't need to tell me what's going on in your head, big guy. But if you need me, I'm here. Always.'

Those words made him want to snatch her back up again. He kept from doing that, barely. 'I'm sorry I'm weak.'

Her lips pressed into a thin, angry line. 'Don't you ever say anything like that ever again. Ever! You're a survivor, Palforma. All of us end up with some scars, inside and out. Those aren't flaws. They're marks of endurance and strength. Besides, you're my Talin, and that means you're perfect.'

He sounded a rumble of happiness. 'I like it when you call me *your Talin*.'

Her lips curve into a smile. 'Well, it's the truth. You're mine so don't even think about trying to get away from me.'

'I wouldn't,' he assured her.

'Good, because I'll hunt you down,' she teased. 'Now, we need to go shopping *and* then track those guys down.'

Taking him by the hand, she led him away from their small, sheltered area and into the busy main area. It would never occur to him not to follow Zia wherever she might lead him.

CHAPTER 24

First they visited the only clothing store on the ship. They had only two Lamentation Cloths for sale, and he bought both to be on the safe side. When Zia added a few pairs of junior-sized pants to the pile he sounded a questioning rumble.

She shrugged. 'I only have one coverall, since Tamerin didn't include the rest of them. Instead he packed these wraps.' Her expression turned annoyed. 'I'm sorry but these wraps suck. No pockets! I think these pants might be small enough to fit, and I could wear them under my wrap. Maybe even cut the bottom of the wrap to make it more like a shirt.'

'Our pants don't have pockets either,' he pointed out. 'You'll have pants but still no storage.'

'But I could put on some adhesive pouches, and then I'd have all the pockets I could want,' she said with a flourish of her hand when she tapped the word *all*.

Her dramatics caused him to sound an amused rumble. 'What about putting adhesive pockets on the wraps?'

She gave him a look he'd seen Lakin make when she thought someone was being deliberately obtuse. 'Have you ever handled one of these wraps? The fabric they are made out of won't hold up under an adhesive pouch. I'm amazed this thing hasn't disintegrated while I've been walking around.'

'Then it's a good thing you're wearing the omnie or you'd end up naked,' he teased her and then eyed some of the junior pants still on the rack. 'Even the smallest size here might still be too big.'

'Don't worry. I can modify them,' she assured him. 'I'm a woman of many skills.'

Before he could reply, the clerk was there shoving a sweet at Zia. "What a pretty human! Don't you look nice in your omnie! Would you like a treat?"

Zia took the offering with a little smile and then ducked behind him so she could stow the sweet somewhere without anyone seeing. She was the first human he'd ever met who wasn't fond of the candy Talins often carried around specially to give to human pets. But what he found adorable was the fact that she didn't want to hurt anyone's feelings by rejecting the offerings.

Four more Talins gave her candy while he purchased the items from an automatic system next to the door. Once done, he slung the clothing over his shoulder so he had both hands free. With one hand, he tangled his fingers with Zia's. He kept the other hand free so he was ready to slap away any Talins who tried to reach out and touch Zia without permission.

Unlike the other transport they'd been on, this one was only Talins, so offering entertainment or gambling would be pointless. Few Talins would bother indulging. But far more shops were geared toward practical things that Talins might buy before they started their next assignment.

Zia led them to that kind of shop next. The small store sold various tools, parts, and technical manuals. No one was in the main area, but he could hear someone moving around in a back room.

It was obvious by her expression she was excited to be here. Although he wasn't familiar with the vast majority of the items in the shop, she seemed to know what everything was and flitted from shelf to shelf with a happy smile on her face.

'This is a good brand,' she commented after handing him an enviro-sensor—one of the only things in the place he recognized. The moment he had it in his hand, she was reaching out for something else and handing it to him as well. 'I don't need it for this job, but it might come in handy later. Oh, and this one too. And maybe this. It's got the dry setting so it can be used without added lubricant.'

Soon his hands were full of the things she was picking out, and it occurred to him that she was enjoying this. His little human liked tools.

After she reacted so favorably to the jeweled collar, he realized she liked sparkly things. He hadn't expected his practical and competent human to enjoy such frivolous items, but her reaction to the collar made him want to buy her more jewels. Not from this transport because the selection was abysmal but later when they were someplace with a proper market, he would buy her all kinds of jewelry.

Now he thought her love of tools might be as strong as her adoration of gems. What a delightful contrast his human was. And from the comments she was making as she picked out items, what this transport lacked in jewelry selection it made up for with a surprisingly good selection of tools.

When she realized he probably couldn't hold anything more, her expression turned mournful. Her eyes fixed on the things he was holding instead of his face, she tapped. 'I should probably put some of this stuff back.'

"No." He filled the silence around them with his refusal. "Get all. No put back. You have all."

A smile blossomed across her face at the same time his words drew the attendant out from where he'd been doing something in a hidden area of the shop.

"Greetings and welcome to my store," the male announced as he hurried up to Palforma. "If you're going to buy those, I can take them for you and start a running total so you don't need to carry them around."

Rumbling in agreement, Palforma dumped the mess into a box the attendant was holding. Zia watched with suspicion as the attendant moved away with the box, almost as if he was stealing all her tools.

'Keep picking out what you want,' Palforma told her. 'Once we've finished shopping, enough time will have passed to start tracking blue belt.'

With a little nod she went back to perusing the shop. No sooner had she turned to look at a display of some kind of small cutting tools than the attendant was back.

"I have sweets if your human would like one. I keep them for when my sister and her pet Neff visit. They're his favorite kind," the attendant told him. "Neff is always eager to see me. He's a sweet male." It was interesting to note that while this Talin named the human, he didn't bother identifying his sister by name. The human pet was more important to him than his sibling.

Palforma wasn't surprised.

Before Palforma needed to explain that Zia wasn't fond of candy, the attendant sounded an indulgent rumble. "Oh, she's holding a dornollian repercussive. She probably likes the bright casing on the dome."

Palforma reached out and took it from Zia, assuming she'd want to add it to their pile. She let him have it with a little nod and continued exploring.

The attendant made a reproving rumble. "The dornollian repercussive wouldn't have hurt her. She could keep holding it. You didn't need to take it away." He sounded so sincere while he talked that Palforma didn't interrupt him. "Your human is very tactile, but then again most of them are. They're adorable when they're inquisitive like this. Aren't they? Does she have enough toys? You know humans require things to keep them occupied or they can have mental issues. It's very important we provide them with enrichment."

Palforma grunted instead of trying to speak, pretending he was preoccupied with paying attention to Zia. When she reached for a tool on a shelf at her head level, the attendant was quick to reach around and snatch it away.

"Oh no, you shouldn't touch that one. That has a sharp end, little human," he explained as he ignored her outraged expression. "You shouldn't play with it because you could accidentally hurt yourself."

Before he could put it back on the shelf, Palforma deftly plucked the tool from the attendant's grip and reached back to drop it in the box of their items on the nearby counter. When Zia saw what he did, her expression cleared a little, but she was still eyeing the attendant with mild annoyance.

The attendant was completely unaware of her ire as he continued to talk to her as if she were a child. "You must need more things to play with. Your master probably couldn't pack enough toys for this trip. But I have some fun Peno syphers you would enjoy. They change color every time they hit each other. Neff loves his set!" The attendant looked up at Palforma. "Watch her carefully and I'll go fetch the toys from the back. I've bought an extra set for when Neff visits, but now I can see how perfect they'd be for her. I can also acquire more before he's here again."

It was probably good that he hurried away because Zia looked ready to kick the male. 'Did he really just talk about me like I'm a kid?'

'Many humans indulge their Talin owners by acting much younger than they are,' Palforma explained. 'Among us, humans are valued for their joy and unbridled emotions. I've watched humans interact among Talins who understand how intelligent your species is. Even with the knowledgeable Talins, those humans will still act with child-like glee or enthusiasm. It's a small indulgence many of your kind give us.'

'That's kind of sweet, actually,' she said.

Palforma couldn't keep himself from teasing her a little. 'Besides, you're so tiny he might think you really are young.'

'And now I'm annoyed with you,' she told him, but he could tell by her expression she knew he was joking. 'I might not be as giant as you Talins, but I'm bigger than a few other species out there.'

'This is true,' he conceded. Some single-celled organisms are smaller than you, but only a few.'

She mock-scowled at him. 'I'm going to put corks on all your quills and glue your back plates down if you're not careful,' she warned him. 'Don't anger me. I might be small, but I'm mighty!'

He pretended to capitulate by putting his hands together and executing a small formal bow. Once he straightened up, he sounded a rumble of laughter.

'I would never doubt your prowess,' he assured her. 'Now you might want to gather what you want and give it to me or risk the attendant refusing to sell us anything if he thinks I'm going to let you play with one of the tools.'

His words made her start grabbing a few more items off the shelves and shoving them at him. She practically tossed the last one at him as the attendant emerged from the back holding half a dozen colorful stone spheres and sounding a soft rattle of triumph.

"I found them!" he announced and hurried to hand them to Zia.

It was obvious he was proud of having found her a toy. Watching Zia's face, he could tell the moment she decided to indulge the shop keeper and accepted the colorful spheres with a smile. Then she retreated a few steps behind Palforma while he paid for their sizable pile of tools.

"You're very lucky to have her," the attendant commented as he organized everything in the tool tote he'd included with their purchases. It would be too big and heavy for Zia, but Palforma would easily be able to heft it around.

He sounded a rumble of agreement instead of trying to talk. The male didn't even notice Palforma's lack of words. He was much too busy giving advice.

"I should warn you not to be quick to breed her. I know everyone is anxious to get pups, but if you breed them too young it can be a strain. And you shouldn't leave them alone ever when they're breeding. Even if you don't keep the male, you should find an elder female that could coach her. It would be even better if you could stay with her. Our mother stayed with Neff's mother all through her pregnancy and the early years of Neffs life. I think that is one of the reasons he's such a happy human and his mother is so healthy. Truly it is…"

Palforma mostly ignored the attendant as the male chattered about humans and grunted when an answer was required. As Palforma held out his Ident to transfer funds, the attendant went still and sounded a sharp rattle of surprise.

Palforma turned to see what had startled the male only to be forced to hold in his own rumble of laughter.

Zia was expertly juggling the syphers while looking at items in a corner cabinet. His little human was full of surprises.

CHAPTER 25

As Zia helped Palforma into the Lamentation Cloth, she tried not to look down at the overly full tool tote at their feet. He had bought everything she wanted. He even purchased a few things she looked at and then tried to put back. She felt spoiled and indulged.

It was amazing!

She probably had a dopey expression as she tugged down the back of the Cloth, but she felt stupid happy. She was in love, she was having the best sex of her life, and she was going on the type of adventure she'd read about in Old Earth spy novels. It didn't get any better than this.

She was especially happy now that they were covering Palforma up with the Lamentation Cloth. The thought of what might have happened if those Traditionalists had seen him made her blood run cold. They could have ambushed him and done all kinds of things, and she probably wouldn't have been able to stop them. She was a confident girl, but she also knew her limits. Trying to take down one Talin would be difficult; taking down two, especially if they were armed, was out of the question unless the situation was dire.

'Tighter,' Palforma instructed her as she helped tie him into the Lamentation Cloth. His motion brought her out of her thoughts and refocused her dressing him.

The Lamentation Cloth was an odd garment. It ended slightly past Palforma's waist and was open on the sides. It had three ties on each side that she was supposed to be tying.

'Still not tight enough,' he said after she'd finished.

'Really?' she asked as she eyed the garment. 'This seems really tight.'

'It needs to be so tight I can't move my back plates,' Palforma explained. 'I'll be regarded with suspicion if it isn't tight enough. The whole point of the Cloth is that I'm not supposed to be comfortable.'

'Dumb,' she commented before she started retying the sides. Now she understood why the Cloth was made of such heavy-duty fabric.

'Most who donned the Cloth wore it all the time, and not being able to move their back plates was part of the penance,' Palforma elaborated after she'd finally gotten it tight enough for him to look stiff and uncomfortable.

Now she felt horrible for insisting that he wear the sadistic garment. 'I'm sure we can avoid them if you'd rather take this thing off,' she offered.

'No, this is fine. And it's better that I can hide in plain sight rather than jumping from spot to spot, trying to keep from being seen if we cross paths.' Palforma lifted the hood to cover his head. Damn, that hood was big, and the top of it hung halfway down his face.

'Can you even see?' she asked.

'Not well,' he admitted. 'But not as badly as you would think. The hood is made of partially transparent material. I can see but not in great detail.'

'But well enough to *hear* and *speak* to me,' she responded.

'Yes. And well enough to discern threats.' Hefting the tool tote on his shoulder, Palforma asked, 'Now, where should we start looking?'

Right, she needed to focus on finding these guys. He was carrying everything in the tool tote, so she reached over and plucked the enviro-sensor out of it. As she walked, she set it up for what she wanted. It was easy to program the sensor to find one of the compounds in the wine that made it so expensive, and soon it was giving her a good indication of what direction to go.

She started to lead him toward the front of the ship, but he stopped her. 'I saw them go that direction to visit the observation lounge. Perhaps we should start closer to the area with the cabins. And once we trace them back to a room, how do we know the room belongs to blue or gray belt when we find it and not the other Talin drinking the wine?'

Recalibrating the machine with one hand, she used the other to point to a seating area not far from where they'd eaten. There sat the only other Talin who had ordered the wine that day playing a strategy game called gav. He'd been there since leaving the restaurant. She'd kept an eye on him as they'd gone from shop to shop.

Palforma sounded a rumble of admiration. 'You're a smart one, Zia. I think Holian should recruit you to help.'

'I only work for you, big guy,' she said, flashing him a grin. Then she pointed to a corridor leading to the cheapest rooms on the ship. 'Let's head that way.'

It turned out to be easy to track the guys to their room once she knew the other direction wasn't going to bear fruit. Once she tracked up and down the hall and was sure this was their room, she studied the door display. She was happy to notice it was an older style, unlike the more expensive display on the door to her and Palforma's room. She debated for a hot second on what to do, but the opportunity was too good to pass up.

'I'm going to mess with the display. Keep an eye out for anyone coming,' she ordered.

She could tell Palforma wasn't pleased with this idea. 'What are you going to do? Those men are probably inside and could come out at any moment.'

'And if that happens, simply pick me up and carry me off while saying something like, *Bad human. Don't run away like that.*'

Rumble of laughter

'Fine, but be quick,' he ordered.

Before she started messing with the display, she felt obligated to warn him. 'I'm not the best at this. I've always worked on bigger stuff, not things this little. I've probably broken-beyond-help more of these things than I've managed to repair.'

Palforma was still and silent for a moment before a *rumble of amusement* came out of him. 'I know another small human female who likes to break these displays. I'll introduce you to her. You two have a lot in common.'

Rumble of affection

A small spark of jealousy hit her, making her shoulders stiff. Whoever he wanted to introduce her to could go hang. She wasn't interested in sharing him with anyone else.

Then she listened to her second thought, which was if Palforma wanted someone else, he'd be with them, not her. With that, her jealousy eased and she was able to face the door display and focus on the task at hand.

She managed to get the display cover off without any issues but then ran into a small problem when one of the components looked like it'd been broken long before she got there. That felt like it wasn't fair. The display didn't even give her a chance to break it. It had come pre-broken.

Thinking fast she pulled apart one of the tools and repurposed a larger but still serviceable component. She was about to fix this stupid transport door display for free. Cheap bastards probably knew it wasn't fully capable but were waiting for it to completely fail before replacing it.

Once the working component was in place, she turned off the safety preset and reset the controls to sync the door display to her implants.

Had she mentioned these implants were amazing?

Tucking everything away, she pushed the display back together and then turned to Palforma. 'Done!' she announced after handing him back the tools she'd used.

Without another word, Palforma tucked everything in the tote and hurried her down the corridor, practically dragging her until they could turn a corner out of sight. Then he slowed the pace, but they didn't stop until they were all the way back in their room. Once safely inside, he dropped the tool tote on the only table and turned to her.

Rattle of curiosity.

'What did you do?'

Zia bit her lip. 'It's more like what I hope I did,' she admitted. 'I'm pretty sure I have access to their door display through my implants now. When they leave, we'll know. And I can unlock or lock the doors with my implant. That means I can sneak in there and go through their stuff.'

Then she remembered the lucky find she discovered in the shop and rifled through the tool tote. Finding it, she held the item up for Palforma to see before setting it down on the table. 'I could even plant a tracker on them.'

'That's a tracker?' Palforma asked eyeing the small disk.

'Not yet. But with one slight modification it will be,' she assured him. 'I've turned these into trackers before when I had to verify where a vent went without climbing in the thing myself. The captain of Red Ore never bothered to keep stuff like that in stock, so I was always having to get inventive, especially since that ship had been retrofitted so many times. No one knew where anything went and none of the schematics were accurate.'

'Clever,' Palforma complimented her as she shrugged out of her omnie. She carefully hung the luxurious garment on a convenient hook and then sat at the table. She pulled out all the various tools, surveying her haul. In this one shopping trip he'd provided her with almost every handheld tool she'd ever wanted.

Palforma took the chair next to her and watched her.

Rumble of interest

Rattle of pride

'Your hands are very nimble,' he commented. 'When this is all over, you'll no longer need to labor unless you want to. But I can see that you might enjoy tinkering or fixing things occasionally. I want you to know I'd never stop you from doing a labor you enjoyed.'

Another feature of her implants was translating Palforma's tapping as scrolling script when she wasn't looking directly at him. The implant programing knew he was talking to her but that she couldn't clearly see his hands, so the program

treated the tapping as if the words were being spoken out loud.
Fancy!

Her hands were busy so she didn't answer, but that
comment did roll around in her head. A life of leisure. What
would that be like? No need to worry about finding work. No
scrimping and saving. No more debating about what necessity to
buy. No more worrying about her family. Palforma had just
offered her a dream.

A dark part of her wanted to know when the other shoe
would fall. When he would become a monster and try to hurt her.

Of course, he had already led her into a situation that
forced her into a collar, so maybe the shoe had already dropped.
Or more accurately had been hurled at her head.

Whatever. She'd consider and debate with herself later.
Right now, she was too interested in playing spy.

Slotting the two sides of the coin-shaped device back
together, she flipped it into the air, caught it, and made it
disappear. 'It's ready,' she announced after showing him her
empty hands.

Rumble of amusement

'Should I search you to make sure you didn't swallow
it?' he teased.

'I promise I didn't, but you're welcome to search me
anyway,' she answered playfully. With a few movements she
compulsively organized her tools on the table before standing up.

Palforma mirrored her movements.

'What's that?' she asked and then palmed the disk from
where she had tucked it into her sleeve.

Palforma blinked. 'What?'

Reaching up she pretended to pluck the disk from his
earhole and made her eyes wide as if she was surprised to find it
there as she showed it to Palforma.

Rumble of amusement

Setting it on the table, she smiled up at him. 'I see you
were hiding it this whole time!'

He tapped his head then answered. 'Yes, I like to store
things in my empty skull.'

That made her laugh and want to show off some more.
Picking it back up, she went through her whole routine. When

they were young, she and her siblings would entertain passengers waiting for their next transport. Their sleight of hand and silly magic tricks usually got them a few tokens. It wasn't enough to even buy a meal, but the things they stole as they entertained the crowd usually resulted in extra food that night.

They almost never got caught, and on the rare occasion they did, the mark usually had to decline pressing charges or making a formal complaint because they had to leave or they'd miss their transport. The authorities on the station mostly ignored them because they mostly ignored all the illegal or shadowy things going on in that station.

As a knowledgeable adult, she winced when she thought about those years. That station had been beyond dangerous, and when they all moved to join the human colony on Wimol station, everything got a lot safer. Less exciting, but also less chance of death!

As she made the tracker disappear and reappear, she marveled at how easily all the skills came back.

Rattle of admiration

'You're highly proficient!' Palforma commented as she made the tracker appear one last time and set it back down on the table. 'If you were a Talin I know of several military sectors that would recruit you, especially the Department of Intel and Awareness.'

She shook her head. 'A few individuals approached my parents and tried to buy me and my sisters.'

Rattle of alarm

'Buy you?'

'Yes. Either because they liked our act and wanted to feature us as entertainers or because they thought we could do stuff like spying or stealing secrets. One time we were almost kidnapped.'

Rattle of agitation

'Why were you allowed to perform without oversight? As pups you shouldn't have been allowed anywhere on your own!'

She gave him a sad smile. 'The whole family was barely scraping by, Palforma. The little we got helped feed and house all of us. Everyone in the family worked. We had to. It got better when we were able to move to be with a bunch of other humans on Wimol station. We still didn't have much, but all the humans there helped each other.'

Rumble of grief

'I mourn for the childhood you couldn't have.'

Nope, she wasn't going to let him pity her. 'Don't get all melancholy about it,' she ordered, her expression light and easy. 'I actually had a lot of fun growing up. My sisters and I ran mostly wild and had a lot of adventures together. And no way were Mom and Dad going to keep me caged.'

Rumble of humor

'I can see you being a willful child.'

She nodded and pointed to an ear. 'I always felt like I had to prove myself because of my deafness. Prove that I was as good or better. I felt like I needed to be fearless. I grew out of that phase, but it taught me a lot about determination.' She flashed him a wicked grin. 'And when we were kids, we all learned how to playact and be sneaky.'

Rumble of interest

Feeling playful, she took one of his hands in hers and brought it to her lips to kiss his palm while she stealthily unclicked his Ident with her other hand. He rumbled with pleasure as she rubbed her cheek on his palm. Letting go of his hand, she stepped back and held up his Ident between them.

With a rattle of surprise, he looked down at where the Ident has been and then up to where she was holding it out.

'Devious little human.' He took the Ident from her and set it on the table next to the tracker.

She grinned up at him. 'It's nice to know I haven't lost my touch.'

Palforma stared at her in silence for a moment, and she couldn't tell what he was thinking. Then he stepped closer to her. A small shiver moved up her spine from the intensity of his gaze.

'What other secrets have you stolen? Will you tell me, or do I need to torture it out of you?'

She blinked up at him. She didn't expect her silly sleight of hand to lead to a role play scenario. She'd never played like this before, not that she was all that sexually experienced. But Palforma was the best lover she'd had by far, so if he wanted to play, she would give it a try. The scent glands in his cheeks glistened with bonding oil, the smell of vanilla hit her, and suddenly she was all kinds of turned on.

'You will tell me what you've done or face the consequences,' he said with dramatically sharp gestures, making his words forceful.

And Palforma had claimed Talins didn't understand fiction? Ha!

CHAPTER 26

This is going to be fun, she thought while she used exaggerated motions to denote a dramatic flair as she pretended to plead with him.

'No, sir! Not torture! I know nothing, so there's no need for something so barbaric.'

Rattle of aggression, volume indication soft

'Now you're calling me barbaric? You're the one working for the enemy. Where do your loyalties lie?' As he spoke, he advanced on her until the backs of her legs hit the bunk. She didn't understand it, but Palforma's aggressiveness was doing it for her in a big way.

But she wasn't ready to simply give in. She wasn't that kind of girl.

'Don't hurt me!' she begged just before she dove sideways toward the room door. Palforma was lightning fast and caught her easily. Lifting her into the air, he tossed her on the bunk. She had to fight the grin as she bounced.

'You brought this on yourself,' he declared as he pulled his pants down to reveal a shaft already thickening inside the flesh pouch. He let the pants drop to the floor and stepped out of them. 'There's only one way to deal with a female like you.'

She felt her face flush with heat as she took in his naked form. She knew he wouldn't appreciate being called beautiful, but he was… in the way a predator was beautiful. All muscles and grace. As her gaze dropped, the tip of his massive cock started peeking out from the top of his flesh pouch. She wanted to run her tongue over that blunt tip, tease her fingers around the taut edge of his pouch, and then tug until his length emerged.

Now that she knew how good he felt and tasted, the temptation was almost too strong to ignore. But she wasn't ready for their make-believe to end yet. She wanted to see how forceful he'd get.

She scooted backward as he put a knee on the bunk in front of her, looming over her. 'How do you deal with a female like me?'

'First we strip them down,' he told her and then grabbed her ankle and pulled. His movement was so fast she didn't realize what he was doing until she was flat on her back and in the middle of the bunk. She kicked out at him with her other leg, but he easily captured that ankle before her foot could connect. Drawing her a little closer, he trapped both ankles with one hand while reaching for the closure of her wrap.

The garment's closure gave under his fingers, and soon he was half hauling her in the air to pull it up so it bunched under her armpits. Because she wasn't wearing anything under the wrap, the cool air of the cabin hit her breasts, making her nipples bead. But instead of begging him to touch her, she flopped around like a landed fish trying to twist away from him.

Aren't I the picture of grace? she thought dryly.

Dropping her legs he straddled her body and reached for the top of the wrap. Thinking quickly, she hooked her feet on the edge of the bunk and pulled herself over. She slid out from under him, leaving him holding her wrap but not her.

Sliding out from between his legs and off the bunk behind him, she landed in a crouched position. From there she sprang up and reached for the bag Tamerin had stuffed her in along with clothing, weapons, and other miscellaneous items.

She only got her fingers into the bag when Palforma was on her again.

This time he didn't toss her. He carried her back to the bunk and laid her out. When he straddled her, he didn't hold his body over her but rested some of his weight on her thighs so she couldn't pull the same maneuver again.

'You can't—' she began but then he had both her wrists in one hand. With only a few movements, he snapped on a set of restraints that were huge on her. Even when they automatically tightened down, they couldn't get small enough to truly restrain her. She could have slipped out of the restraints without much effort, but she played along and let him lock her to a support strut of the bunk. With her arms stretched over her head and his weight pinning her legs, she couldn't move at all.

'You're at my mercy,' he said. 'Tell me what I want to know or clap your hands together and this will all end.'

Palforma's instruction caused her to grin briefly. It was clear he would stop playing and release her if she wanted.

But she didn't want it to stop. She wanted him.

She sneered at him and used one hand to tap, 'Never!'

'Very well,' he said as he scooted back a little and leaned over. His mouth closed around one of her nipples, and her ability to think diminished by a thousand percent. His mouth felt so good. Just the right amount of pressure, and the added danger of all those sharp teeth heightened her excitement.

She gasped when his teeth were almost too much. But even with that little bite of pain, when he pulled away, she tried to beg him not to stop.

'No, please. More please…' she was limited in what she could say with her hands bound over her head. Simple phrases that may or may not make sense were all she could manage. 'More. Give more.'

Raising up a little so she could see his hands, he asked, 'Are you ready to tell me everything now?'

'Know nothing,' she insisted, even as she restlessly shifted her hips under him. Because her legs were trapped by his weight, she couldn't even part them to encourage him to touch her more intimately.

Rumble of desire

Rattle of excitement

These Talins might not have emotive facial expressions, but their noises didn't lie. Even if his massive cock hadn't fully emerged to lie across her stomach, she would've known he was turned on by this game from all that rattling and rumbling scrolling across her left eye.

'Please!' she begged and wiggled her hips again.

Palforma didn't move his lower body at all. 'Your begging won't help. You give me no choice but to act with more force.'

Leaning over, he grabbed a handful of her hair and held her head still as he kissed her. She'd never had her hair pulled before, and if anyone had told her it would have a direct link to her pussy, she would've called them an idiot.

But it did. Good god it did. As he held her head still with one hand and plundered her mouth with his, he finally shifted his weight a little. She parted her legs as much as she could but was still limited because she was caged between Palforma's spread legs. The moment she did that, he slid a broad hand between her feminine folds and start stroking.

The moment he rubbed one of those perfectly callused fingers across her clit, she gasped into his mouth. She was so worked up that all it took was that one motion and pleasure exploded through her. Always before she had to work for her orgasm, even on the rare occasions she had other partners. But this time it happened so quickly and easily it left her shaking and shuddering as her body went limp.

He only stopped stroking her with his hand when she became overly sensitive and tried to draw away from him.

Rumble of satisfaction

Sitting up he looked down at her. 'Now we can really get ready to begin.'

Really get ready to begin? *What?*

Her dazed brain didn't fully follow what he said until he'd moved down and put himself between her splayed legs.

'Remember what needs to happen if you want this to stop,' he reminded her before he grabbed her under the knees and draped her legs over his shoulders. He pressed the tip of his erection at her entrance and then stopped. He moved the head of his shaft back and forth across her entrance, her clit, and then back over her entrance.

It was torture. The touch was too light for her to get any satisfaction from it, only frustration. Especially when she was still tingling from her last orgasm and could tell a second one was waiting in the wings to emerge.

She tightened her legs on him and tried to push her hips up to force him inside of her. She managed to get his broad head into her, but then he grabbed her hips. Pressing her into the bunk, he stopped her from getting him in further. She could feel the vibration of his rattle as he held her down and slowly eased himself inside.

Entire solar systems had been formed in less time than it took Palforma to push himself inside her. It was so torturous she started struggling against him. Her hands kept tapping out the same thing over and over again—'faster!'

Even if he saw her hands, he ignored her plea. He slid himself inside her at a pace that made her want to curse. If she had a weapon, she'd threaten him with it. Straining against the restraints, she bucked under him, not surprised when that got her nowhere. No matter what she did, he wouldn't move any quicker.

When he was finally fully inside her and she felt deliciously full, she thought he'd start moving for real. But he remained still until she opened eyes she hadn't realized were closed. She found him watching her intently, his teeth bared in a growl. Captured by his intense gaze, her breath caught in her lungs.

An intense feeling of connection hit her, and she shuddered as he slowly pulled himself out of her, never once breaking eye contact. When he started to push back at a glacial pace, he angled his hips so he was creating a wonderful friction that made the special tension build. It felt so good she let her lids flutter closed.

A strong grip on her jaw made her eyes pop open. When her gaze connected with his, he growled out a word so low she could feel his voice vibrate in her chest.

"Watch," he commanded. She was helpless to disobey. She kept her eyes focused on him as he started to increase his speed at a measured pace. Anticipation and desire flooded her. Panting in need, she clung to the restraints and didn't look away from Palforma.

His body was perfection in motion. Talins had a muscled physique to begin with, but years of training and discipline had turned him into a flawless example of his species. It made her even hotter to think that this wealthy, skilled, and honorable male wanted her.

As his body hit a rhythm fast enough to make her gasp and start straining to grind against him again, she made sure her gaze never wavered. Even as her orgasm hit and her entire body felt like it had been zapped by a jolt of electricity, she kept her eyes trained on him.

She watched him reach his pleasure as her body started convulsing with her own. He roared and his movements started to stutter. When she couldn't stem her need any longer, she slipped her hands out of the restraints and gripped the hand still holding her jaw. It wasn't that he was hurting her, but she needed to put her hands on him, even if only his wrist.

Breathing hard, Palforma let go of her jaw. He gathered her to his chest as she tried to wrap her legs around his waist, but they weren't long enough to reach all the way.

They were both panting and shuddering. It felt really good to be held so tightly as little aftershock orgasms rolled through her system.

They stayed like that, satisfied to hold each other in the silence. Eventually Palforma laid them out so she could close her eyes and take a nap. The last thing she saw before falling asleep was Palforma, and she was content with the knowledge that he'd be the first thing she saw when she woke.

CHAPTER 27

Apprehension filled him as Palforma watched his little human slip into the Traditionalists' room. Although she assured him the sensor would tell her if anyone was inside, he'd poked his head in before letting her proceed. Then she'd given him a confident grin and slipped past, letting the hatch shut behind her.

He remained in the hall while she went through the Traditionalists' belongings and found a good place to plant the tracking device. Leaning against a hallway wall and trying to appear inconspicuous, he unclipped his Ident from his belt and pretended to be reading something off of it, all the while keeping an eye on the sparse foot traffic.

Worried for Zia, he was hyperaware of every Talin who passed. He was wearing his Lamentation Cloth, so most passengers slid their glances over and past him. It was rude to stare at someone wearing the Cloth and considered bad luck to be in their company for long. Some even went so far as to step to the opposite side of the corridor as they a passed by. It was an added benefit of the Cloth he hadn't considered when he'd first suggested wearing it to Zia. Two other Talins on board had donned the Cloth, which was a helpful anomaly.

They were due to dock within the next rotation at a colony planet that would have an interstellar comm array powerful enough to reach Holian. All he needed to do was give Holian all the information on the Traditionalists as well as the codes to the tracker, and the Commandant could take it from there. Then Palforma and Zia could move on to wherever she wished to go.

He couldn't wait to move on.

As much as he was thankful that she was willing to help him with this, he wasn't thrilled that she was so close to these dangerous men. If it was just these two, he wouldn't be worried. He could neutralize them in his sleep. But there would be more. Many more. The Traditionalists had learned to hide their numbers and intentions well. He worried that others were on the ship waiting in the shadows, and he had no wish to risk Zia's well-being any further than this one act of breaking into a room.

A loud rattle of surprise from a passing Talin made Palforma lift his head too quickly and caused the hood to slide back enough to reveal his face. He met the man's gaze and winced when he recognized the Talin.

"Palforma! I thought that was you, but I wasn't completely sure. It's good to see you, my old friend," he declared jovially.

The male was named Lorian. Not only had they been raised in the same cresh, but they'd gone through early training together before the warriors were split up into specialty units. He remembered this man as kind and helpful both as a youth in the cresh and later while in the military. And obviously Lorian remembered him as well.

"G-g-greetings, Lorian," Palforma stuttered out with a quick look around to make sure the Traditionalists weren't near them. He needed to get this male away and then return quickly.

Lorian pointed to the hood of the Lamentation Cloth and sounded a rumble of sympathy. "Is this because of your family? I heard that they had outcast you. But that was solars ago. You can't still be in mourning for that."

"Y-y-yes," Palforma said with an impatient rattle. "Still mourn."

Lorian's reaction to his rattle and his stuttering words was to sound a soothing rumble. "That was wrong of them. When I found out what they'd done, I wanted to contact you, but Kalor doesn't have a central comm array, and I wasn't sure how badly Commandant Holian would react if I tried to reach you through his household array."

It seemed that Lorian wanted to stand there and talk to him, and the last thing he wanted was for the two Traditionalists to turn the corner and see them standing there. Pulling his hood back in place so it covered half his face again, Palforma started to lead Lorian away. Hopefully he could get the man to depart with a promise of meeting up later, and then he'd hurry back.

"I f-f-f-fine. Good."

Lorian fell in step with him as they walked down the hallway, deeper into the cabin section of the ship. "I know it can be hard without a family or clan, but now that I've found you, I can ask you about something important."

Palforma couldn't think of anything Lorian needed to ask him.

"Important?" Wow, he got that word out without a single stutter.

Before they could turn the corner of the corridor, Lorian stopped him and sounded a rumble of encouragement and a soft rattle of excitement. "I want to ask you about marriage. My sister hasn't picked anyone yet, and I know both my family and clan would be joyful to have a warrior as esteemed as you join. Someone who was awarded five Mattil medals should be celebrated, not cast aside," Lorian continued.

Palforma felt struck dumb by the offer. Finally he got out, "Marriage?"

Lorian sounded an amused rumble. "Yes, marriage. To my sister. She's an honorable female ready to settle with a male of good standing. She has a small business setting up comm satellites and training repair staff. I notice that in the professions registry your status is still retired. That means that if you wish, you could join my sister in her travels. She is knowledgeable, patient, and could use someone to watch her back at some of the more remote locations she goes to."

When Palforma didn't answer right away, Lorian sounded a rattle of worry and continued. "Do you think you aren't worthy of marriage, my friend? It's not true. You probably don't remember, but I visited you in the recovery center. You couldn't speak at all, but you kept trying to get the staff to send you back to your unit. You were confused and believed they were still under attack. You were in incredible pain but all you could think about was protecting your fellow soldiers. That's the kind of male I want in my family, and my parents and sister agree. I already inquired about putting you on the list of acceptable males to my sister. She is open to your offer. It's truly fortuitous that we met here today!"

Palforma was overwhelmed by Lorian's generosity but also frustrated at the male's poor timing. Under normal circumstances he'd be overjoyed to connect with someone who thought so highly of him, but with Zia in the—

A distressed rattle came out of Palforma as he watched gray and blue belt coming down the hall from the opposite end. They must have gone to check the boards again. By the look of their body language, they were happy with whatever they found out.

He had no chance to get Zia out before they were at their cabin and blue belt was pressing on the display to unlock and open the door.

This whole plan had been a terrible idea, and when he managed to get Zia back in his arms safe and sound, he was never letting go of her again!

As she'd hoped, her implants interfaced with the door perfectly. It was easy to gain entrance to the room. Once inside she did a quick search of their belongings and hid the tracker in one of the bags. Then she started searching the room for real. Unless you had experience with hiding items, no one realized how many little places there were to hide things. It didn't take her long to find several weapons and one information square that must have fallen into its hiding spot by accident long ago because it had a thick layer of dust all over it.

Each time she found a weapon, she would disable it if she could without anyone being the wiser before putting it back. The last thing she wanted was for these guys to be able to use a weapon on Palforma or anyone on his side.

When she heard the door display chime, she froze for half a second before diving into the tiny elimination room. She squeezed her body into a small, recessed area next to the door. It was the best she could do to hide without closing the door, which would've been a dead giveaway that she was in there. If they walked into the elimination room they'd find her, but if they stayed out in the main cabin, she was at least hidden from view.

She could only hope she put everything back exactly as it had been. She didn't need them searching the room and their bags because they found a disturbed item and got suspicious. She tried to keep her breathing even and stay perfectly still.

"The ancestors favor us."

"At the moment I must agree. Why else would our timing be so perfect. We arrive only a rotation after Prime Son Searin, and your friend Brilanian is already prepared and waiting for us. It's all so perfect that I know the ancestors approve of our actions. I don't need anything else to convince me that now is the time to strike."

Because she never assigned identity to the voices, her implants scroll the words across her right eye without distinguishing if they come from blue belt or gray belt. They have a small capacity to record, so with one little movement of her hand she set her implants to remember all the words relayed as script to her eye.

"The time and place have already been decided. Brilanian has successfully set the stage for the demise of Prime Son Searin and his mother. He told me he found the perfect spot so it will end their lives just as they're about to give a speech. There shouldn't be too many causalities."

"Even if there are, I'm sure if they're seated close, they are loyal to the family, and we are well rid of them. But if all the plans are set, why are you so eager to be there? Aren't you worried that your presence might be considered suspicious?"

"We should be there to witness this moment, as it will be significant. Monumental. I'm going to want to be able to add my personal experience to the historical record."

Someone's a little full of himself, she thought.

"You make a good point. I'm pleased to be with you for this."

"Not just with me but a part of it!"

As they talked, Zia realized this was turning out much worse than she or Palforma were prepared for. She thought they'd be able to track these two to the bomber, but it looked like they didn't even know where the guy was going to set up his explosives. If these Talins were anything like other species with royalty, a lot of stuff would be going on down on the ground to welcome a monarch and one of her children. That meant a clever guy with a little inside knowledge and access could hide a bomb in a lot of places.

Now the hard part. She needed to get out of this room so she could get back to Palforma and tell him everything she'd learned. Unfortunately, she might be trapped in here until the guys left. She couldn't even get to her information square because that would require her shifting her entire body out of the recess.

If she wasn't worried about one of these guys hurting Palforma, she might go for the door display to get him in here. She was sure he was strong enough to take these guys down in a fair fight. But she might not have found all their weapons and no way did these guys even know what the word fair meant.

The door display chimed and she held her breath. Was Palforma coming to her rescue?

"Greetings," a new voice called out once the door was open. "I'm afraid your presence has been requested by the ship's steward."

Her implant told her that she hadn't heard this voice before. Did these guys come up on some wanted list and were about to be detained? It would make sense because they were close to the next stop, so the ship was probably receiving all kinds of transmissions that had been waiting in interstellar com queues. This could be a major stroke of luck for her.

"This ship will be landing soon. What could he possibly need to speak to us about?"

"I don't have that information, but I was told that you should hurry."

Rattle of aggression, volume indication high. "This is ridiculous."

They kept grumbling but her implant registered the door closing and then no more voices or sounds. Time to get out of here!

It took a bit of wiggling to get herself out of the recess, and when she popped free, she almost fell on her face. Taking a few stumbling steps, she swung around and awkwardly scrambled through the elimination room door just as the door to the room opened and gray belt came walking back in.

They both froze for a moment, staring at each other.

Rattle of surprise. "Human?"

There was no point in tapping. Not only was it unlikely this guy had that language in his INT, but what could she possibly say?

Sorry, I got lost looking for my Talin. Don't mind me, I simply wandered into the wrong locked room.

Yeah, that wasn't going to win her any excuse awards. She felt up her arm and remembered she'd taken out the punch-stick to fill her pockets with tools. Idiot!

All she needed was to get out of the room and then she was home free. She was sure Palforma was lurking nearby and would help whisk her off to a convenient hiding space.

Hell, the guy was so big she could just hide behind him!

Rattle of aggression, volume high. "I don't know how you came to be in my room, but first I'll punish you and then I'll sell you. Annoying species, I don't understand why your kind is so popular. Why keep such weak and self-destructive creatures, even as pets?"

Nothing in that speech made her any less afraid. One of the hiding spots for a weapon was right next to her and she dived for it. She'd disabled the weapon before putting it back, but he didn't know that. Still rattling, he lunged forward and grabbed her by the back of her omnie before flinging her against the far wall.

The impact knocked the breath out of her, and she slid gasping to the floor. He stalked to her, claws out and quills up. His was rattling so loudly she could feel it vibrating in her chest. She tried to suck air into her lungs and at the same time cast her eyes around the room looking for one of the other weapon caches.

Then another figure barreled into the room, sounding an even louder rattle of aggression, and tackled gray belt. The rattling coming from both Talins was so intense as it echoed around the room that her implant decided it was loud background noise and no longer registered it in her left eye.

Strangely, gray belt was fighting with a Talin she'd never seen before. It wasn't Palforma coming to her rescue but a stranger. Whoever this guy was, she silently thanked him as she stood on shaky legs. Her back hurt and would probably be covered in bruises. She was a little dizzy, but thankfully nothing felt broken. Time to slip out before the wrestling titans accidentally got her while they fought in the small room.

Before she could even step away from the wall, blue belt rushed into the room. "What is going on here? Nelium?"

Neither man answered him, and he didn't even glance her way as he went to join the fight between gray belt and the stranger. Two on one was shit odds. Right, new goal—find Palforma and get his skilled butt back here to even up the odds.

As if that thought conjured him up, Palforma barreled into the room and tackled blue belt before he could land another blow on the stranger's head. For some reason when he entered the room, the door shut and now the rattling coming from the four Talins was intense enough to vibrate an information square off the edge of the table.

Even though she wanted him here, fear for Palforma jolted through her. She wanted to help, but there was no point in adding her small body and puny strength to the battle.

But weapons were hidden around the room, and a few of them she could return to working order if she got her hands on them.

She edged sideways toward one of the hiding spots. She didn't even make it two steps before Palforma filled her vision.

"Z-z-zia?" His arms were around her before her implant even finished scrolling his stuttering word across her right eye. After a brief hug, he put her at arm's length and started patting her down. At first she thought he was looking for a weapon, but then she realized he was checking for injuries. "Hurt? Broken?"

Waving her hands to get his attention, she waited until he looked up to start speaking. 'I'm not hurt. Only some sore spots where my back hit the wall. It knocked the breath out of me, but a stranger charged in before I could be hurt more. Are you injured?'

Because the rattling stopped with the fighting, her implants no longer registered it as background noise. So when the stranger started rattling angrily, it drew her attention up to see him standing over the unconscious blue and gray belted Talins.

The stranger was looking down at the unconscious Talins as he spoke. "Traditionalist monsters! They are everything that's wrong with our species. Abusive, cowardly, and underhanded. I saw him toss her against the wall from out in the corridor. Who does that to a human? They're so fragile. He could have killed her."

Palforma sounded a rumble of agreement, which drew the stranger's attention to the two of them. He stepped up to stand behind Palforma, speaking rapidly.

"If she is injured, we can take her to a healer on the colony. We're almost docked. If I move everyone out of the way, and you carry her, we can get there quick."

'Tell him I'm fine,' Zia urged Palforma before the stranger became more upset or talked Palforma into taking her to a medic.

"Zia unhurt," Palforma announced, stopping the stranger's angry rattling. "L-l-lorian meet Zia."

Rumble of gentle reception. "Greetings, little Zia," Lorian said. "Are you sure you're not hurt? Sometimes humans don't realize how injured they are until later. It would probably be safer to visit—"

She cut him off by slashing her hand through the air. 'There's no time for that. We have to save your monarch!'

CHAPTER 28

She wasn't surprised when Lorian didn't move because he probably couldn't understand what she was saying. However, she'd expected Palforma to spring into action, but he didn't even shift in place. His focus was still on her.

'Move each limb individually and make sure you have full range of motion,' he ordered her.

Her lips tightening in frustration, she spoke quickly. 'Forget about that, I'm fine. But your Prime Son person and monarch are going to die! Don't you want to save them?'

Rumble of concern. "Why is she moving her hands like that? And why isn't she talking? Did she hit her head?"

"No hear. No talk," Palforma explained absently as he continued to run his hands over her limbs. "Norka. T-t-t-tapping. Tapping-talk."

Rattle of comprehension. "I see. What a clever little human. I'll download the language right away so I can talk to her as well. But we should really get her away from here. Please tell her I'm not a threat." He started fiddling with his belt pouch. "I think I might even have a sweet in here."

"Can read you. Read in eyes. No hear but read," Palforma told him as he looked up at Lorian. Holding up a hand, Palforma showed him the gesture for yes. "This yes." Then he did a different motion. "This no. Now can simple talk."

She couldn't believe that Palforma wasn't doing anything about the news she shared. 'We need to get moving! Get down to the planet. There's a bomb.'

'We knew that already,' Palforma pointed out.

'Right, but we didn't know that Brilanian is going to set it off even if these two assholes aren't there.' That finally got Palforma's attention.

His body stilled and he met her eyes. 'How do you know that?'

'I was hiding in the elimination room and heard them talking before your friend came in to fight them,' she said and then pointed at Lorian. 'Was that a lucky coincidence or what?'

For Lorian's benefit, Palforma answered out loud. "Lorain passing. Offer help. Know before, trained. Military. With me. Early trained."

"My clan is like Palforma's," Lorain explained, earning Zia's approval by the way he didn't sound an annoyed rattle at Palforma's halting speech or blink at the jumbled words. "Both our clans are famous for our soldiers and military leaders. We went through earlier training together, but I wasn't good enough to make it into his unit."

Palforma rolled his eyes up to meet Lorian's. "To smart for unit. Did smart things."

'Tell Lorian hi and thanks for the save. Maybe he can sit with these two and wait for ship security, but we need to go!' Normally the motion for go was two fingers moving a few times back and forth, but she made the motion big and fast, indicating the need for haste.

Pulling her into his arms, Palforma stood up and cradled her to his chest. Turning to face Lorian, he tilted his head a little as he spoke. "Long story. But need act now. Want help us? Be hero? Save monarch and s-s-s-son?"

Rattle of anticipation/eagerness. Lorian held both arms out from his sides, his hands in fists and quills fully extended. "Do I have quills? The answer to both questions is yes!"

Palforma nodded his head at the two unconscious Talins. "T-t-tie up and then leave."

Lorian jumped to help restrain the males, his excited rattle never stopping. Looked like they had a new member to their team!

The ship had just finished docking as the three met again in the main gathering and entertainment area. Unlike most transports, this one could withstand the rigors of atmosphere and had landed at the colony's only port.

She and Palforma had gone to grab their things from the cabin and Lorian said he had to visit one of the kiosks. The moment they drew together she realized what Lorian had been doing while they'd gotten their stuff. He was rubbing his head slightly over where the INTs were implanted.

He'd downloaded Norka.

Grinning, she tested him. 'I don't think Palforma told you earlier, but thanks for coming to my rescue. I have really great implants so if you talk, I'll know what you're saying. You don't have to tap back. If you want to practice, that's fine. But if we need to exchange info quickly, just say it. Don't bother trying to tap in an emergency situation. Unlike verbal languages, Norka takes longer to integrate.'

"I think I got most of that," he said and tried to tap at the same time. His tapped words however said something along the lines of *I've received communications*.

That made her huff out a laugh. 'Just talk for now.'

The ship around them shuddered slightly, telling them that the exterior hatches were opening.

"Follow me. I worked here for a solar when they were first building the infrastructure to this colony," Lorian told them as he started leading them to the main doors where several dozen Talins had gathered to disembark. "While I was waiting to get my download, I checked on local news and information on the colony's UniBase. Prime Son Searin and the Monarch will be speaking at the Clan Assembly Hall in about a mark. That should give us enough time to get down there and warn their guards."

Although she hoped it would be that simple, Zia had her doubts. She fell in step between the two Talins, who did an excellent job of keeping others from trying to touch her or asking if they could give her candy. With his better talking capacity, Lorian told most of them that she couldn't eat it and every single one expressed sympathy. A few even sounded *rumbles of mourning*, her implants translating the sound as similar to a deep sadness. As if finding out she couldn't have sweets was akin to someone dying!

She wanted to assure them it was just sugar, but she knew better than to try and engage. Instead, she clung to Palforma and pretended to be overwhelmed.

They cleared the port and were making their way into the city when Lorian started to speak, his voice mildly embarrassed. "I want you to know that I wouldn't have told you about my sister if I'd known you had a human. I was worried that perhaps you were alone and in need of companionship. But I realize that's no longer the case."

Zia narrowed her eyes up at Palforma suspiciously. 'Sister?'

"I wanted him to marry my sister and join my family," Lorian explained, his tone dismissive. "But I can see now that—"

Zia didn't bother to pay attention to anything more Lorian had to say. Digging her heels in she made Palforma stop and then pulled him to the side so they weren't impeding other pedestrians and had a little privacy. He could have easily forced her to keep moving, but he abided by her unspoken request without resistance.

Possessiveness filled her. Along with a small bite of fear. 'You're mine,' she told him firmly. Better to make sure there wasn't any confusion, so she looked to Lorian. 'He's mine. Your sister can't have him.'

Rumbles of humor from Lorain.

Rumbles of adoration from Palforma.

'Yes, I'm yours,' Palforma agreed quickly as he dropped to his knees in front of her. 'Lorian was trying to be a friend, but I wouldn't have ever taken him up on it. I don't need a political marriage to have a family again. I have you.'

'Good!' she declared and pretended she hadn't been worried at all. Then she felt a little guilty for how forceful she'd been. 'I'd let you go if you really wanted it, but I wouldn't like it.'

Leaning over, Palforma swiped his cheek across the top of her head. The comforting smell of vanilla filled her nose. When he straightened up, she ran her fingers through her hair to help spread the oil as he tapped. 'I wouldn't want you to ever let me go. It's you and me, Zia. You and me together against anything and everything. No matter what.'

'Yeah, that's true. Anything and everything. I like that,' she agreed with a confidence she didn't really feel. She might be a fighter, but she was also only human. Smaller, weaker, and a member of a species with no homeworld or political power. Palforma might think she was perfect now, but later when he wanted better connections, she would be no help at all.

Sliding her eyes over to Lorian, she realized he'd been privy to this whole conversation and could get Palforma in trouble. 'He means I'm his pet and he's my master,' she told him quickly, not sure what the proper protocol would be between human pet and Talin owner. She shouldn't have worried.

Rumble of laughter. "You can't fool me, little Zia. I can see what's going on here." Leaning in close Lorian whispered, "And I've known others like you two. You know they call it our worst-kept secret?"

Zia didn't know how to answer that, so she remained silent as Lorian straightened up and regarded Palforma. "Humans will be our saviors, not the other way around. Everyone with any common sense knows that."

'Many of us think the same,' Palforma told him, his movements solemn. 'But our society will be slow to change.'

"We either need to change or we will die out," Lorain stated dismissively. "It's the way of all species."

Zia waved her hand to draw their attention to her. 'So you're not going to get us in trouble?'

Rumble to soothe. "Of course not. But this answers some questions I had earlier such as how a pet accidentally wandered into someone else's locked cabin? Now I realize that you're like Yarmin's human."

Rumble of inquisition. 'Who?'

"My cousin Yarmin has a small business where he builds custom docking platforms for small space stations. His human helps him when no one else is around." Lorian lowered his voice and ducked his head a little. "He scent-bonded to her. And she loves him. Most of the family doesn't know, and we need to keep it that way. She's the reason he never went into the military. They were both young when Yarmin finished at the cresh and returned home to pick a career path. Jalli fell in love with him at first sight and was so inconsolable when he wasn't around that the family that owned her finally sold her to Yarmin." *Rumble of amusement.* "I think she played up her emotional distress because in all other respects she's a level-headed human. But all that is to say I know and don't judge. In truth, my friend, I'm envious."

While Palforma sounded a rattle of surprise, Zia grinned. It was looking more and more like all these laws and taboos were rapidly crumbling under their own weight. As with many societies, if they couldn't grow and change, they stagnated and died. The Talins were at a turning point, and although the Traditionalists were fighting change tooth and nail, it was very likely a losing battle.

Especially if the three of them were successful in keeping anything bad from happening to the royal family. That meant they didn't have time to stand around talking about this stuff any longer. They needed to get moving.

'Guys, did we forget about the bomb? Imminent death and destruction?' she reminded them.

"Right, of course," Lorian said as he and Palforma moved to take their previous positions on either side of her. As they walked, Lorian pulled two Idents off his belt. They'd left the two Traditionalists bound up in their cabin with an information square recording telling whoever found them to contact the authorities. They'd included Zia's recording of the men's conversation, and that would be enough to hold them until a more formal investigation could be launched.

They'd tried contacting the royal family's guards to warn them of the attack, but all channels were being blocked to keep anyone from disrupting the events either by accident or on purpose. That meant they needed to get close and personally warn the guards.

Lorian started fussing with the Idents, glancing back and forth between the two. Zia was impressed with his ability to walk and tinker at the same time.

"I unlocked both Idents before we left and sent out response requests. The only one that has pinged back here on Mondron colony belongs to a low-ranked member of the Cil Clan, named Brilanian."

'That's him,' Zia confirmed with excited movements. 'Can you track him using his Ident?'

"Yes, but we should give all these things to the authorities," Lorian told her. No sooner had he said that than they found themselves facing a dense crowd of Talins.

Beyond the crowd were guards and beyond that the Colony Governance Hall. Zia shook her head in disbelief. No way were they getting through that.

"Let me see if I can speak to a guard," Lorain said and then slipped the Idents back into his pouch.

'We'll wait here,' Palforma agreed.

Even though Lorian wasn't particularly short or small for a Talin, he managed to move with ease and soon disappeared into the thick crowd.

Everyone was so excited about the visiting royals that most didn't notice her. Still, without Lorian there to help hide her, she stepped in front of Palforma so he could better shield her from view. When he wrapped his arms around her and drew her back against his front, she felt even more secure.

Lorian was back before long.

Rattle of frustration. "I got to a guard, but they said all issues needed to be submitted to the head of the royal guards. But all com channels are shut down so I can't contact that person until the event is over."

Zia was astonished. 'What did he say when you told him there was a bomb?'

Rattle of anger. "He scoffed and said there was no chance that could be true. That they swept the area thoroughly and then posted sentries and sensors."

'The Traditionalists back on the ship were sure that Brilanian could get access,' Zia argued. 'So they must have missed something.'

'You helped with this colony,' Palforma pointed out. 'You might know where Brilanian could've planted the bomb. Optimally it could be under or over where the royals will be located for the event. And he might—'

Rattle of excitement. "I think I know!" Lorian announced. "This Government Center is a transitional building, meaning it doesn't have a hardened foundation. Instead, they installed a stabilization system similar to grav pushers on ships."

'Why would anyone build something like that?' Zia asked. It sounded like a horrible idea to her. When grav pushers went offline on ships, everyone floated around a little and everything was fine. But if they were relying on the same kind of tech to hold up a building, if the machines shut down or had issues, the whole thing would collapse.

"Because of supply chain issues they couldn't build Colony Governance Hall fast enough," Lorian explained. "My contract was over a few days after they decided a stabilization system was a fast way to have a building ready for the royal visit. They plan these things out half a solar in advance."

Zia shook her head. 'Won't they have to completely dismantle the building after?'

Rattle of agreement. "Yes, but they didn't care because it was more important to the colony founders that the royals see everything as on track."

Rattle of annoyance. 'Hubris is a bad way to govern,' Palforma commented.

"I agree with you, my friend. But it's even worse. These stabilizers are powered by infinity drives."

Zia jerked in surprise at that. 'Tell me you're joking,' she responded but then added, 'Never mind. You guys probably don't do that. This is so bad.'

'Why is this news bad?' Palforma asked.

Zia was quick to answer. 'Blowing up a bomb, even a small one, near a running infinity drive would make it powerful enough to level this entire colony.'

"Planet," Lorian countered. "There are three infinity drives because they wanted to make sure the stabilizers would never be without power."

'Three? Damn, there goes the planet and maybe even the two moons,' she agreed. 'I always wondered how I was going to die.'

CHAPTER 29

Palforma's first instinct was to grab Zia and run. Get off the planet by any means possible. But he could hear the sound that indicated they were getting close to the time of the speeches. They had no chance to get a minimum safe distance away if the bomb was as powerful as Zia and Lorian were telling him it would be.

That meant the only way to keep Zia safe was to neutralize the threat.

'I'm going to find a place for you to hide while—' Zia's fist impacting the tough skin of his belly stopped his words. Not that the blow hurt him, but she must want his attention to hit him like that. Looking down, he gave her his full attention. 'What?'

Her expression was part stubborn, part mad. 'We're in this together.'

"It would be safer if you didn't come with us," Lorian said, backing up what Palforma wanted to do. He sounded a rumble of thanks to his friend without taking his eyes off Zia.

'It won't be safer anywhere on this colony if you can't get the bomb defused,' she countered. 'I've got skills. On top of that you might need me to wiggle into a tight place to get to the bomb. Leaving me behind only makes it harder for you to succeed.'

It was a valid point, and as much as he hated to admit it, she was as safe with him and Lorian as she would be anywhere else in the colony.

'Besides, I've almost been blown up a few times. I can show you how not to get blown up,' she stated with an impish grin. She reminded him so much of Lakin right then that he wondered if there were any free-born human women out there who didn't like getting into trouble. Even Nalia with her sweet disposition had learned very quickly how to be brutal with the little dagger he'd given her.

"You need to listen to Palforma," Lorian began to argue, but Palforma stopped him.

'No, she's right. We might need her help.' Palforma pointed to the tool tote he was carrying. 'All of these belong to her, and she knows how to use them. Besides, trying to find a secure place for her to hide would take up time we don't have.'

Lorian considered for a moment before he rattled out an aggravated sound. "I don't like it, but you're correct. Follow me, I know a way into the sub-basement."

Lorian strode off at a pace that was only slightly slower than a run. Zia fell behind quickly, and without a word, Palforma picked her up with one arm and swung her onto his back. She grabbed him around the neck and tried to get her legs around his waist. He was quick to push her feet back so she could rest them at his hips where the armor plating flared slightly and created natural foot pegs.

When she had her balance, she reached one hand out in front of his face. 'This works.' Then she made a gesture that would translate phonetically to something along the lines of *giddy-up* in Common. It must have been a term that wasn't familiar because no translation came through. He'd ask her about it later, but at the moment he was busying keeping their duffle and tool tote secure and away from her legs as he kept up with Lorian.

His friend led them around the crowd and to the far side of the building. This planet was made up mostly of massive rock formations with small, tangled vines growing on the ground and covering everything except the highest peaks. That made the entire place look like a sea of green interspersed with gray islands. This port and city were the only places settled so far on the planet. The colony was so sparsely built-up that the rear of the Colony Governance Hall backed up to the vine forest, and Palforma realized that the smallest of these vines was as thick as his body.

No one was back here because the vines reached all the way to the wall of the building, forcing them to scramble over and under them. Zia seemed to cling to his back with little effort. When she could, she'd even pet him with her little hands as he followed Lorian. He had the most inappropriate urge to scent mark her right there but forced himself to keep his movements smooth so as not to suddenly jostle her.

Eventually Lorian found what he was looking for and ducked down to crawl under a vine on his belly. Palforma gently pulled Zia off his back and set her down. Before he could say anything, she stripped out of her omnie and dove under the vine to follow Lorian.

Growling, Palforma pulled off the duffle and tool tote. He pulled some weapons from the duffle but then left the bag behind. He shoved the weapons in the tool tote and then wrangled it with him because he wasn't sure what tools Zia might need. It was awkward, and he was greatly inhibited by his own size, but he finally managed to find where Lorian and Zia had disappeared to. He saw an access tunnel with the hatch already pulled off and set to the side. Eyeing the tunnel, he barely kept from rattling in distaste. This was going to be a very tight fit. Holding the tote over his head, he rolled to his belly and wiggled his way in.

This wasn't the first time he'd cursed his above average size. The warriors he trained with often only saw the advantage his size gave him in battle, but they didn't realize that for almost everything else his size made life difficult. When his shoulders got stuck, he wondered if he would even be able to get loose. He briefly considered panicking, but then two sets of hands grabbed his legs and started pulling.

He popped free and found that the tunnel had only been a little longer than his body. Otherwise, he might have been stuck there until Lorian climbed back up to get him.

Blinking a little to help his eyes adjust to the dim light, he looked around. They were in a small room surrounded by machines. The noise level was loud enough to make vocalization impossible.

'Are these the infinity engines?' he asked Zia when she looked up from checking him for injury.

'No, this is a basic bio systems room,' she explained. 'The stabilizer would need to be more dead center of the building and they would want to put the infinity engines close so as not to risk running long conduits between everything.'

'Center would be this way,' Lorian told them, pointing through a large access hatch he'd already opened.

Palforma stopped Zia before she could go through. 'We don't know if anyone stayed behind. Let me lead.'

'Sure, big guy,' she agreed. 'That's your area of expertise anyway.'

Grabbing the weapons he'd shoved into the tool tote, Palforma checked charges and then secured them to his body. Once he was satisfied, he took a deep breath and then dived through the access hatch, rolling before coming up in a crouched position, ready to sight and fire.

He was in an empty corridor. Looking back at the access hatch, he saw Lorian and Zia watching him, and he gestured for them to follow. Once they were both in the hallway, he caught Lorian's gaze and used simplified Norka with one hand.

'Which direction?'

Lorian pointed and Palforma started moving with Zia and Lorian falling in step behind him. Soon they found themselves in a massive room ringed with pillars and notably hotter than the corridor. The center of the room was empty except for one rectangular machine in the middle and three glowing cylinder-shaped machines spaced equally around it. This must be the stabilizer and the infinity engines.

Attached to the side of the infinity engines was an all-too-familiar yellow-striped box. The standard-issue demolition kit was used to destroy sites the military was abandoning during conflict so the enemy couldn't make use of them. Once the timer was started, it couldn't be stopped.

This demolition box was meant for space stations that didn't take much in the way of explosions to make them inoperable. But if Zia and Lorian were correct, by setting it off so close to the infinity drives, the original small explosion would be increased exponentially.

Something didn't feel right, so when Zia began walking toward the center, he grabbed her by the back of her coveralls and pulled her behind him. She didn't fight him, but he did catch her annoyed look in his peripheral.

This room wasn't as noisy as the bio systems room they'd entered through, but it was still too loud to hear the five men before they appeared from around the stabilizer. All of them were holding energy weapons, and two of them looked like they might actually know how to use them.

In one fluid motion Palforma moved himself and Zia back behind a pillar. Lorian wasn't nearly as fast and took a hit to one of his legs. Landing behind the next pillar over, Lorian tried to stand back up, but his leg gave out under him.

That meant it was down to him to neutralize these men. With only five of them, it shouldn't be an issue.

'Stay here,' he told Zia. 'I'll be right back.'

Watching Palforma charge into danger caused Zia a moment of déjà vu. She debated for a brief second but then crouched low and peeked around the pillar. The blast from an energy weapon hitting the pillar slightly higher than her head made her scramble back. Damn, that was close.

Looking over, she saw Lorian propped up against his pillar. The lower part of his left leg was bent at a strange angle.

She needed to get to him and see if she could help, but how?

Despite the sound of fighting registering loudly in her left eye as Palforma engaged the men, at least one weapon was trained in her direction, waiting for her to make a move. Right, well then, she had no choice but to give them a move. Any light-fingered magician knew that distraction was the key to all tricks. Upending the tool tote, she got to her feet and then flung it out from behind the pillar. Then she sprinted in the opposite direction toward Lorian.

Her implant registered the sound of an energy weapon being fired, but it also noted that the rounds were *outside her personal safety margin*—meaning the thing wasn't being fired at her.

She was landing next to Lorian as her implant registered a round impacting *within her personal safety margin.*

Thanks, implant, but the chunks of flooring kicked up by the weapon's blast were clue enough!

Rattle of fear. 'You shouldn't have done that!'

She ignored him and leaned over his leg. As she examined him, more blasts took chunks out of the pillar, but the thing was made of something sturdy enough to take the hits and remain mostly solid.

'Your leg is broken,' she told him.

Rumble of amusement.

Rattle of pain.

'I'm aware.'

Although she couldn't hear his tone, she was pretty sure he was giving her some sass, which made her smile. 'I don't have anything we could use to stabilize it. You're going to have to remain still until Palforma's done showing off by taking on five armed men at once. Then he'll carry you out of here.'

Rumble of laughter. 'Showing off? You're a witty one, Zia.'

A blast close enough to create a jagged crescent on the edge of the pillar made both of them jump. Whoever was firing on them was getting closer and changing his angle of attack. He was probably moving around until he could get a line of sight on them.

Standing up, she scrambled to Lorian's side. 'We need to move!'

He'd already come to the same realization and was doing his best to drag himself around the pillar as another blast hit the ground way too close to his broken leg.

"Make your way around the pillar and shelter yourself," he ordered her, probably shouting to be heard over the noise of firing and ambient sounds of machinery. "I'll stay here to draw fire."

Like hell she'd abandon him like that, but she did realize that staying with him would only get them both killed. She was sure only one guy was coming after them. The quick peek she'd seen of the room as she'd dashed from one pillar to the other told her that two men were already down, so Palforma would be the major threat they'd focus on.

Unfortunately, everything happened so fast that Palforma didn't leave them with any weapons. Slipping her fingers in the sleeve of her coveralls she pulled out the punch-stick. It was a familiar and comforting weight in her hand but of little use unless she could get close to their attacker.

Leaving Lorian to "distract" the guy, she slipped around the pillar. She caught sight of Palforma performing an impressive leap from the top of the stabilizer onto another guy. Then she found the male who was trying to kill her and Lorian.

He was slowly moving out from around another pillar and hadn't seen her yet. She froze, watching him. She would need to time this perfectly or Lorian would end up dead and maybe her as well.

The idea of skittering off to hide never occurred to her. She wasn't a *run away when friends were in danger* type of girl. She was more of a *let's fuck shit up* type, just like her sisters. Besides, if Palforma managed to take out four guys by himself, she could handle one.

Forget about the fact that he was a Talin and she was human. That he had a distance weapon and she only had a punch-stick. She had the element of surprise, which was invaluable.

Right?

The guy was at Lorian's pillar now and moving around it. She couldn't see Lorian at all, and by the way the Talin was progressing, he was wary that Lorian had a weapon.

Her heart was racing, and she could feel adrenaline flooding her system. It was now or never. Holding the punch-stick ready, she took a deep breath and sprinted.

She planned to get him in the lower back with the punch-stick. A slight seam in the plates there might be the perfect place to press the tip of her weapon.

She didn't even get to touch him.

He couldn't have heard her with all the ambient noise, but he must have sensed her somehow. With a speed she couldn't match, he swung around and leveled his weapon at her. She'd like to say she artfully dodged, but all she did was try to stop. She lost traction and slid to the floor, landing hard on her butt and sending the punch-stick flying. The round passed overhead, grazing a few strands of hair and creating a fist sized crater in the floor behind her.

Before the Talin could drop the muzzle of the weapon to sight on her, Lorian was there. He managed to grab one of the guy's legs and pull him to the floor, sending a round into the ceiling. Using his hold on the Talin's leg, Lorian started pulling him, trying to bring the weapon close enough to grab.

Kicking Lorian with his free leg, the male sat up and brought the butt of the weapon to his shoulder, ready to aim and fire on Lorian.

Scrambling to her feet, Zia launched herself. She managed to grab one arm and send the shot wide. Wrapping her arms around the weapon, she held on for dear life.

Rattle of surprise, volume indication high.

Rattle of anger, volume indication high.

"Get off me, you stupid human!" the guy screamed as he grabbed her by the hair and tried to peel her off his weapon. Gritting her teeth, she held on, watching as Lorian moved up the guy's body through watering eyes.

Abandoning the weapon to her grip, the Traditionalist threw her and the weapon away. She hit the floor hard and rolled once before she stopped herself. Getting to her knees she mimicked how the guy had been holding the weapon and tried to fire.

Nothing.

Lowering the weapon, she saw the symbol near the trigger that denoted a bio-sig was required for operation. This weapon was keyed to work only for him. Frustrated she thought briefly of trying to use the weapon as a bludgeon but dismissed it. The last thing she wanted to do was hand the Traditionalist back a weapon he could use against them if he managed to wrestle it away from her.

Getting to her feet, it took her a second before she could walk because the world swayed a little. Lorian was fighting, but with his broken leg limiting his movements and probably causing him intense pain, he was losing. The Traditionalist was on top of him now, pummeling him with three blows to Lorian's one.

Seeing her punch-stick on the ground near Lorian's head, Zia dived for it. She snatched it up and performed a tumble roll she and her sisters had perfected when they'd been young. Unlike when she'd done it in her youth, this one hurt, and if she survived all this, that shoulder would be one giant bruise later.

The Talin trying to kill Lorian roared and swiped a clawed hand at her. As she ducked away, Lorian took advantage of the distraction and landed a solid blow to the enemy's face. The Traditionalist roared again and tried to eviscerate Lorian.

Without thinking about it, Zia lunged at the Talin, aiming the punch-stick at his eye. He moved his face out of the way, but that gave her a clear path to that small slip of unprotected flesh at the base of his neck. Slamming the tip of the punch-stick down, she slapped her palm against the other end, firing the weapon.

Because she had it angled slightly up, both his neck and head exploded, showering her and Lorian with brain matter and blood.

Slumping down, she blinked owlishly at the gore. So that's what it looked like when you used a punch-stick. Good to know.

CHAPTER 30

Fear roared through his body as Palforma dashed around the pock-marked column to find a Traditionalist missing his head and both Lorian and Zia covered in blood. He'd seen the male moving on Zia and Lorian's position as he dispatched the last of the four men he was fighting. Worry for them made him act recklessly to end the battle so he could hurry to their sides.

Only now he stood there stunned. He was overjoyed to see that they were both alive and whole but also impressed that they'd managed to take out a well-armed male with nothing more than a punch-stick.

He said the first thing that came to mind. 'I would have both of you at my back in any fight.'

Lorian was struggling to sit up, his broken leg hampering his movements, so he didn't see what Palforma said, but Zia's eyes went wide and then she grinned. Seeing her white teeth flash under all that blood and gore would be a startling sight for anyone who hadn't served the Talin Empire in several wars.

Palforma simply thought she looked fierce.

'Next time leave me a gun so I can kill from a distance,' she ordered and then pointed to her coveralls. 'The blood will probably stain and this is my only pair!'

By now Lorian had managed to get himself in a seated position and caught Zia's words. He let loose with a rattle of astonishment that Palforma could barely hear over the loud machinery in the room.

"Zia, you're an extraordinary human! You were so fast and aggressive," he exclaimed as he spat a bit of blood and keratin plating out of his mouth. "I know he must have hurt you, but you never stopped. You're savage in the best way possible."

Palforma watched Zia preen under Lorian's compliments. 'I'm a princess of action,' she declared.

"What's a princess? Is that a human term for soldier or warrior?" Lorian asked.

Zia looked over at him and started to respond, but then her eyes latched on to his crooked leg. 'Crap, you need a doctor!' she exclaimed.

As she scrambled to Lorian's side, Palforma dropped to a knee next to his fallen comrade. The bone hadn't pierced the tough skin of his leg, but that wasn't uncommon in Talins. Their skin was so strong and armored that it was rare for a bone to protrude, but that didn't mean it any less painful.

Brushing Zia's hands away, Palforma manipulated the break until he was mostly sure he had it back in place. Lorian rattled loudly from the pain but remained still. They both had basic med training, so he knew what Palforma was doing. Unlike most species, Talin bones had a type of "hooking" structure around them. That meant once you put the bone back in place, the limb could be used again, although not vigorously until fully healed.

Once Palforma was done, Lorian slumped a little. The pain would rapidly recede now that the bone was back in place, but Lorian might feel a little wobbly for a bit from what Palforma had done to him.

He hoped they could find a different way to get out of the basement because he wasn't sure Lorian would be able to make it out the duct they came in through.

'I hate to do this, but I need to check out that bomb,' Zia reminded them. 'After all our hard work to stay alive, I'd hate to get blown up.'

"I'm fine," Lorian lied as he tried to get up. He almost fell, but Palforma snaked out a hand to grab him under the arm to keep him steady. Palforma hated to admit it, but he'd gotten so caught up in battle and then concern for Lorian and Zia that he'd forgotten about the bomb.

In an effort to expedite things, he picked Lorian up, tossed the wounded Talin over his shoulder, and then walked them to the stabilizer with Zia following. Lorian smacked him on the back and let out a rattle of outrage at the undignified assist.

When Palforma set him down next to the machine, all that indignation was forgotten as the three of them examined the bomb.

Lorian pointed to the display at the top of the bomb. "It's active and counting down. We don't have much time."

Zia's reaction was blasé. 'Don't worry, I've got this.'

Her heart thundered in her chest even as she tried to project an air of nonchalance for Palforma and Lorian. No point in getting them worked up. If they ended up dying, their last moments didn't need to be ones of extreme anxiety. Nope, better off to go out with hope than fear.

Turning her attention to the two men, she talked rapidly. 'Here's what we're going to do. We can't simply turn off the infinity drives and run. The stabilizer will fail the moment we do that. The building collapses and everyone still dies. That saves the planet but still kills off your royals.'

'So what should we do?' Palforma asked, his body language telling her he was calm and ready to follow her orders.

'Cycling the stabilizer will shake the building. I'm going to do that a couple of times and hopefully that will get everyone out of the building. Then we turn off the infinity engines. There's one issue, though. The moment I turn them off, the stabilizer stops working and the whole building comes down around our ears.'

Lorian cast a look at the closest infinity engine and then back to her. 'Will turning the engines off be enough to keep the bomb from causing a cascading effect and destroying the planet?'

She nodded. 'Infinity drives are made to be stable while off. They can get knocked around a lot during transit and installation, so when they're powered down, they don't react to anything. Even if the outside casing gets demolished, nothing will happen. I watched a demo vid were the company that makes them deliberately set off an active engine next to an inert one. The inert one blew apart but didn't explode.'

'What do you need from us?' Palforma asked.

'Go gather all my tools. I'll need them to shut down the infinity engines. Lorian can help me cycle the stabilizer.'

Palforma's response was to sprint off to get her things as Lorian limped over to the stabilizer. 'Get them off,' she told him and then pointed to the panel that covered the display.

Casually Lorian reached up, sank his claws into the metal, and ripped the panel off. Well, that was handy.

Stepping forward as Lorian threw the panel away, she pulled up the display menu. Thankfully the stabilizer worked almost exactly like her bigger sister, the grav pusher. It didn't take her long to set the stabilizer to cycle three times as close together as the program would allow.

The first cycle started as soon as she hit the execution key, making everything around her shake so violently that both she and Lorian lost their footing. Palforma seemed to magically appear with her tool tote slung over his shoulder. He steadied both of them with a hand under her arm and Lorian with a hand looped through his belt.

She could see the display showing a diagram of the cycle and the countdown to it being done. Dust and small debris rained down from the ceiling above them, forcing her to duck her head and close her eyes. Palforma pulled her in close, trying to use his body to shield her.

Then the shaking stopped and the display on the stabilizer counted down to the next cycle. With the room still, she pulled away from Palforma and rushed to the first infinity engine with the two Talins right on her heels.

She'd only ever shut down an infinity engine once, and that had been in a safe, calm, and controlled environment. If she messed up the shutdown sequence, she could set the infinity drive off before the bomb had the chance.

Palforma stood next her, so she reached over and pulled out the first tool she'd need. Holding the tool in one hand, she scrolled the menu of the drive with the other. She then initiated the first set of steps from the menu. It worked for a moment and then stopped and indicated it was ready for her to do her part.

Crouching low, she carefully removed a small panel and reached in with her bare hand to feel around. Finding the tubes she was looking for, she carefully inserted her tool and then pulled out the tubes. Nothing sparked and the drive didn't explode, so she dropped that tool and the tubes in her tote and scrutinized the display for the next step.

By the time she'd successfully finished the shutdown sequence on the first drive, the stabilizer was starting its second cycle. The moment the building shook, Palforma grabbed both her and Lorian. When the stabilizer finished cycling, he picked both of them up and carried them to the next engine. When he was sure neither of them would fall over, he sprinted back for the tool tote.

Having done it once, Zia was much faster shutting down the second drive, and both Talins helped by handing her the things she needed while holding hatches open or taking tubes from her. Six hands made quick work of it, and the engine powered off to enter safe mode.

She'd started the shutdown on the last engine when the stabilizer started its next and final cycle. Lorian was braced, but Palforma still acted as a helping hand to him and a shield to her. She could only hope that by now everyone had either left or were in the process of evacuating the building because very little time was left.

Once the shaking was done, Zia straightened up to face the men. 'This is the last drive, so when I shut this down, the stabilizer will stop working, and it won't take long for the building to come down around us. We need to be ready to run the moment I'm done,' she warned them.

Palforma eyed Lorian. 'I'm going to carry you.'

"I can make it," Lorian argued. "You need to carry Zia."

'I can carry both of you. But if you're on your own feet and slow, Zia will be slow because she'd never leave anyone behind. That means you'd be the death of all three of us.'

Zia winced at Palforma's harsh statement and was about to add something when the bomb on the first infinity engine flashed. 'What was that?'

"It's a warning," Lorian explained grimly. "It tells the soldiers that they need to get to a minimum safe distance because the bomb will be going off within the next fifteen submarks."

Eyes going wide and heart racing in her chest, she pointed at Lorian. 'Palforma will carry you, end of discussion, or I will knock you out and then he will carry you.'

She didn't even wait for his response. Turning back to the machine, she went through the shutdown process as fast as she felt comfortable. Before she initiated the final sequence, she looked over her shoulder and signaled the guys.

'Ready?'

Palforma took a look around the room, then examined Lorian, then her. Finally, he answered. 'Ready.'

With that she turned back to the machine. She sensed movement behind her as she hit the final key and the infinity engine wound down, all lights going off.

Two things happened at once. The building started shaking, and Palforma wrapped a powerful arm around her waist and lifted her to his side. Then he was running.

She was dangling from his arm, facing forward, and everything around her was moving by at a startling speed. Looking over, she saw Lorian folded over Palforma's shoulder and his arms wrapped around Palforma's waist to try and maintain his balance as Palforma moved.

They approached a closed door at the opposite side of the room from the access panel they'd entered through. That must have been what Palforma had been looking for when he'd examined the room before declaring himself ready. He didn't even slow as he approached the door but barreled into it with the shoulder that wasn't carrying Lorian.

Trying to make herself small, Zia curled into herself and wrapped herself around Palforma's arm. Unlike when the stabilizer cycled and the building shook a little bit, the place was now bucking and moving violently around them. Large pieces of the ceiling were raining down as huge cracks opened up in the floor.

Palforma ran, leapt, dodged, and avoided every hazard as if he'd been given a map of where every crack would form and detritus would land. The man was a marvel of movement. Thankfully they didn't have any choices to be made when trying to exit. There was only one corridor, one set of stairs, one set of doors with light shining through them before they were in the main lobby area of the building. It filled Zia with relief to see no one was around. Everyone must already have evacuated.

Palforma sprinted to the large ornate entry doors, the floor crumbling behind him as the entire building started collapsing in on itself. He passed through the door in a cloud of dust and debris.

He kept going past the cloud until Zia could see a ring of people all standing at a distance from the collapsing building. Palforma was about halfway to them when the bomb when off, knocking them forward. Not even Palforma's superb balance and quick reflexes could keep him on his feet, and the three of them went tumbling.

Somehow Palforma managed to tuck her close to his chest and shield her from a hard landing by putting his body between her and the ground. It wasn't until they stopped rolling that she saw Lorian on the ground not far away, sitting up and looking a little stunned. His leg was crooked again.

Before she could stumble to her feet to go to him, they were surrounded by heavily armored guards with weapons already drawn and pointed. One of them stepped a little forward, his armor slightly different than the rest of the guards.

Rattle of aggression, volume indication high.

"Who are you and why did you do this?"

CHAPTER 31

Zia was snuggled in Palforma's lap happy to be alive but still mourning the loss of all her tools and her necklace. She was exhausted, dirty, still covered in gore, and completely uncertain of her fate. They'd been in this windowless room for a long time, and except for the guards who put them in there, they'd seen no one. She should be worried that they might all be summarily executed for destroying the building, but all she could think about was losing her tools and gems. She hadn't even had them that long, and now they were all gone.

At least the guards hadn't tried to take her away from Palforma and Lorian. She wasn't sure why because a few of them had commented that a healer should see her, but no one made a move to pull her from Palforma's arms.

Lorian lay on the floor next to them. Palforma had reset the bone again, and after going through so much trauma, Lorian's body decided it was time to pass out during the process. Zia was amazed he hadn't fainted earlier. The guards' rough treatment had been hard to watch as they forced Lorian to hobble along without Palforma's help. By the time they'd gotten to the room, Lorian had been in so much pain he'd collapsed the moment he got past the threshold.

Palforma had assured her that Lorian would be much better after his "nap," as if Lorian was simply tired and not suffering from a major medical issue. But then again, these Talins were a tough group, and maybe a broken leg was painful but not that big of a deal. She could only hope that was the case.

Palforma hadn't escaped the battle and collapsing building unscathed. He had a massive gash in his shoulder where he'd rammed the door and one of his back plates was ripped half off. Almost all the quills were broken or missing from his left arm, and he had a laceration on the sole of his right foot.

Despite all that, he was far more concerned about her. After setting Lorian's leg, Palforma had checked her over for injuries. She had some shallow cuts and a lot of bruises but had fared much better than the two men. After he was assured she wasn't grievously injured, he had settled them on the floor. Holding her close to his chest, he'd leaned against the wall and gone to sleep.

It had been a tough day for all of them.

Zia's body might be exhausted, but her mind wouldn't stop. She nestled against Palforma and stared at a bit of flooring with a slight dent in it as she thought of the last few marks. She had no idea how much time passed as she eventually slipped into sleep.

She woke when Palforma jerked under her. Groggy, she straightened up in Palforma's lap to find several Talin and one human walking into the room. Palforma stood with her in his arms. Gently he lowered her to her feet, never taking his eyes off the new people.

Zia didn't really bother looking at the Talins. She was too busy staring at her fellow human. The woman was wearing a plain, utilitarian collar and looked healthy. What was weird was that she was smiling and crying at the same time.

"Palforma! We thought you were dead!" the woman yelled as she flew across the room to hug Palforma.

Rumble to soothe.

"Alive," he stated simply, and the woman sounded a sobbing laugh.

As much as Zia could understand someone being overjoyed to find out that Palforma was alive, she didn't like this woman touching her Talin. With a firm grip on the back of the woman's omnie, she pulled her away from Palforma.

The woman blinked at her in surprise as she drew back. 'I know Palforma is wonderful, but he's mine,' Zia explained. 'You need to get your own Talin.'

Her face registered confusion as she watched Zia's hands move, but Lorian and Palforma both sounded rumbles of amusement as they watched her words.

"She said that Palforma belongs to her and you can't have him," Lorian explained from his spot on the floor. He hadn't tried to stand up. Glancing down, Zia winced at the sight of his leg. It was swollen and looked painful. Lorian needed to see a healer more than any of them.

"What?" the human asked Lorian.

"Zia can't hear or verbalize," Lorian explained. "But she speaks very well using Norka. And she has implants that can tell her want you say, so you can all speak normally. I'll translate her words for you."

Moving her gaze back to the woman, Zia was surprised to find the stranger grinning even wider, the tears all gone. "I'm going to get Norka downloaded right away because we need to be able to chat without needing an interpreter," the woman declared. "Because you're pushy and possessive and I like it!"

"She same. Zia and Lakin," Palforma told the woman and pointed to the locked door display. "Like to break."

So this was the woman Palforma had spoken about with such affection. Zia felt a scowl form on her face.

Unperturbed by Zia's expression, Lakin nodded and grinned. "So you liked messing with door locks too? For me it started out as a necessity, but now it's a hobby."

The Talins standing behind the woman burst out in amused rumbles and Palforma joined them. She knew there must be a joke here she wasn't privy to, but that didn't bother her. What was bugging her was that Lakin was still standing within arm's reach of Palforma. Slipping herself between the two, Zia grabbed Palforma's arms and pulled them around her. Then she met Lakin's gaze. The woman held up her hands, palms out and took a step back, the grin never wavering.

"Palforma's a buddy, nothing more," Lakin assured her. Looking over her shoulder, she waved at one of the Talins behind her. The one that stepped forward was smaller than Palforma and was missing all his quills, but he moved with the same grace and confidence.

He stepped up behind Lakin and wrapped his arms around the woman in a mirror of her and Palforma.

"This is Dalt. He's my Talin so you don't need to worry about me making any moves on Palforma." Lakin pointed to another Talin who took half a step forward. "That's Commandant Holian. He's kinda a big deal among the Talins. The four of us had an adventure together last solar. Then we got word that Palforma had died, and as you can guess, we were pretty heartbroken. So it feels like a gift to find him alive and well."

"And he's as lucky as always," Dalt added. "He found a human who is as fierce and loyal as him." Then he looked up to meet Palforma's eyes. "I'm overjoyed to see you alive, my friend."

"I'm also filled with relief and happiness," Holian added. "And not at all surprised to find that you've managed to put yourself in the middle of trouble."

Zia clapped her hands to get everyone's attention and frowned at Holian. 'We saved your monarch's life. How about a thank you and access to some medical care?'

The moment Lorian finished translating, Dalt, Holian, and the two Talins with them jolted and all started speaking at once.

"Where are you hurt?"

"I'll send those guards that ignored you to the coldest, most desolate outpost I can find!"

"Can you make it to Searin's royal ship? He has an excellent healer there. Or maybe we should bring the healer to you."

"This is outrageous! Did they not even check you over? How much of this blood is yours? Where is the worst injury?"

Zia clapped again to get their attention. 'Not for me, for the guys,' she explained, a little bemused by their reactions. 'Lorian's leg is broken and Palforma has cuts that need a flesh knitter. I've only got some bumps and bruises.'

That calmed everyone down right away, which she found a bit annoying. Before she could get upset on Palforma and Lorian's behalf, Holian turned to speak to one of the men next to him.

"Gravian, we're going to need transport off this colony. The monarch is already on board, but I believe Prime Son Searin is still planetside. Can you send my request to Searin for passage on the royal family's ship and access to their healer?"

Rattle of assent. "Of course," Gravian responded and hurried out the door.

Holian swept his gaze around the room. "While we wait for permission, why don't you give me the abbreviated version of what happened because I know you weren't trying to kill the Monarch and Prime Son Searin.

Many marks later they'd all been transferred to a luxurious ship, seen by the healer, cleaned up, and given new clothes. Zia reluctantly dressed in the wrap Lakin brought her but only after she was promised her coveralls would be cleaned, repaired, and returned. It was unlikely that the duffle of her stuff left at the back of the building survived the demolition, so along with her tools she lost almost everything. The only things she had left was her small personal information square and those coveralls.

She made sure to dig the square out of the coveralls before Gravian took them from her with a rattle of disgust and disappeared out the door.

'He'll return them,' Palforma assured her. 'He's a royal guard. He'd never give a false promise.'

No sooner had Gravian disappeared than enough food to feed an army was delivered. 'How much do they think we can eat?' she began and then the door opened again and she realized the food wasn't only for the three of them.

Holian, Dalt, and Lakin all trooped in followed by several more Talins Zia hadn't met yet and another human. Before she could start asking questions, both Lorian and Palforma scrambled to their feet, banged their fists against the hard plating of their chests and bowed their heads.

Oh shit, one of these new arrivals must be important. Unsure what to do, Zia edged closer to Palforma and mimicked his bowed head.

"I'm pleased to meet all of you," one of the Talins said and stepped forward, the other human at his side. "I'm Prime Son Searin, and this is Sora."

Looking up Zia caught a smile and little wave from Sora. Small and delicate looking, she was wearing an ornate collar and a red and gold decorated omnie. The sight of the beautiful omnie made Zia long her for blue and silver one.

As if reading her thoughts, Sora held up a bundle of clothes. "Gravian said you lost everything, and it's always so cold on these ships, so I brought you this. You can have it."

Zia accepted the garment and shook it out. It was a green omnie with navy blue trim and no embroidery, but it felt as plush as her old one. She'd gotten spoiled wearing the omnie Palforma had given her and now felt cold without one. With a grateful smile at Sora, she slipped it on. The nanos in the omnie started warming her right away.

'This is nice, thank you.'

She expected Lorian to translate, but before he could talk, Sora spoke again. "Oh, that felt odd! We all downloaded Norka, but using it feels a little different in the brain," she said with a laugh as she rubbed a spot over her INT.

It might not be a big deal to get the download, but Zia was surprised this royal and his pet bothered. It seemed very unroyal like. Before she could comment, the sound of an infant wailing stopped her.

Baby? What was a baby doing on board this ship? Hadn't she been told that Talin children were raised in creshes?

As a Talin hurried in with a bundle in his arms to hand to Sora, Zia understood. When Palforma had been trying to convince her it was safe to travel into Talin-controlled space, he'd told her the Prime Son had a child with a human. This was the proof that Palforma hadn't lied to her about that. The child Sora held was obviously a human-Talin hybrid with features from both parents. The little girl had her mother's mobile human face, and she was telling the world with her expression and voice she wasn't happy.

Rumble of affection. "She missed you, my heart," Searin commented as Sora settled the girl in her arms.

Zia almost got misty eyed at the sight of these three huddled close together. Looking around, she noticed everyone else was transfixed by the sight, including Palforma who sounded a soft rumble of longing.

Taking in his unwavering gaze on the baby, Zia decided he'd make a good dad. She wasn't entirely decided if she wanted to have a kid or not. The universe felt too dangerous for her to create a tiny, vulnerable life that could be snuffed out so easily. But if they did have a child together, she knew by the way he watched Sora's baby, their offspring would be cherished beyond measure.

It was a comforting feeling.

The Talins standing closest to Sora were quick to grab chairs and urge her and Searin to sit. Then the tables of food were moved closer to the couple. Sora laughed and protested, but everyone was too busy sounding indulgent rumbles to hear her. Soon they were all seated around the food with Searin feeding Sora as their daughter fell back to sleep in her arms.

So much about this ran counter to how she'd seen people wearing collars treated in the past that she was too distracted to reach for any of the food. Instead, she watched everyone interact with Sora, Searin, and the baby while absently accepting the morsels Palforma pressed to her lips.

Lakin moved to a seat next to Zia. "They can take some getting used to," the woman commented.

Zia nodded and then wrinkled her nose in distaste. 'They've been nothing but kind to me. Even when Palforma was being dragged off and I was drugged, they were still gentle with me. But how can you stand to wear that collar around your neck?'

"Ah, but mine is special," Lakin said with a laugh and reached up to unlatch it herself. Then she pulled the thin lining out to reveal a set of small tools that could easily be used to manipulate electronics. She even had a tiny key coder hidden in there.

Zia leaned in closer to examine Lakin's hidden marvels. 'No shit yours is special.'

Grinning, Lakin put the lining back in and secured the collar around her neck. As she talked, she tried to tap, but it was clumsy with the wrong words interspersed. It didn't matter, though, since Zia would read and watch what the woman was saying so she caught everything.

"All of us humans on Kalor, and a lot of humans on homeworld, can take off our collars. But I wanted something special on mine. I don't like to be without at least a few tools," Lakin explained. "Kalor is a gorgeous place and full of Talins and humans like those in this room. But even though I'm usually safe on Kalor, I like to be prepared."

'Are you trying to sell me on Kalor?' Zia asked.

Lakin's expression was unrepentant. "Of course. Mostly because any girl who can destroy an entire building is someone I want to get to know. But also because I want Palforma to be happy."

Zia ignored the comment about destroying the building. 'And Kalor would make him happy?'

Was she going to have to live among the Talins? It wasn't a horrible prospect, but it would feel strange to know that every Talin she met who wasn't in the know would treat her as if she had the intelligence of a very small child.

Then Palforma was there, kneeling in front of her. 'I don't need Kalor to be happy,' he told her. 'I need you. We'll go where you will be happy.'

His word made her feel both cherished and guilty at the same time. 'We can talk about it later.'

"I'm inclined to disagree with you, Zia," Searin said, and that's when she realized that all the background chatter that had been scrolling nonstop in her right eye had gone silent since Palforma moved to his knees.

Warily she looked up at the Prime Son. Palforma twisted around so he could see Searin as well. Lowering himself, he sat between her legs and pulled one of her feet into his lap, petting her calf. She could tell he was a little nervous about what the Prime Son wanted to say to them.

"I have an offer to make," Searin continued. "A new colony is being started on the border of Delorta space and near their colony planet Ki-Jol."

'That seems like an unlikely place for Talins to set up a colony,' Zia pointed out. 'Delorta despise any kind of slavery and I'm pretty sure Ki-Jol has a high population of runaway slaves. If humans found their way there, and you tried to get them back, you'd end up at war with the Delorta.'

"That won't happen," Searin assured her.

Zia tried very hard to keep her expression from revealing her annoyance. 'Because it's inconceivable that humans could successfully run away?'

Rumble of amusement. "I have quite a bit of experience with humans running away, so no, not for that reason. The reason that escape isn't a concern is because if they truly wanted to go to Delorta, they could. This colony will be special because it will be a place where humans and Talins can live freely without being governed by archaic laws or outmoded taboos."

She felt and saw Palforma tense up before he let go of her leg to talk. 'Prime Son, isn't that dangerous?'

Rattle of assent. "Very, which is why I'd like to ask you and Zia to move there and help me build it. I can only have those I absolutely trust, so I don't have many I can send yet. There's almost no infrastructure and the two merchant ships I can trust can only transport goods so fast."

Rumble of interest. 'That sounds like a haven, Prime Son. Better than even Kalor.'

Palforma might have been in awe, but Zia was suspicious. 'What is the end goal of this colony if it has to be kept so secret? It will be discovered eventually, so you can't think to keep it hidden indefinitely.'

"You're correct, Zia. But keeping it hidden permanently isn't my intention. My hope is that eventually the political climate will be such that I can reveal Sorana to all Talins as proof positive that we can thrive even when scent-bonding and living in family units."

'Uh, correct me if I'm wrong, but didn't we just save you from an attempted assassination down on the planet? That doesn't strike me as a political climate that's going to change their mind any time soon.'

At her words, rumbles of surprise and amusement broke out from everyone in the room. Lakin laughed but Sora looked pissed.

"Assassination attempt? You said a building stabilizer failed. You said nothing about someone deliberately trying to kill you!" Sora spoke so loudly that the baby in her arms woke and started fussing.

Rumble of worry. "I didn't want you to feel unnecessary anxiety. As you can see, I'm perfectly fine. The attempt was unsuccessful, and the men who tried it are all dead thanks to these three." He waved at Lorian, Palforma, and Zia. "That's why I want them on Sorana."

"We're going to talk about this later," Sora grumbled as she started rocking the infant.

"Searin might be Prime Son," Lakin whispered to her. "But he's as malleable as inactive plastifilm in Sora's hands."

"Aren't we all when it comes to our humans?" Dalt quipped as he swept Lakin up in his scarred arms. He took her seat and then settled her on his lap. She snuggled back against him with a content expression.

"So, will you do it?" Lakin pressed. "Will you go help out on Sorana? When all the bad business with the Traditionalists is done, Dalt and I plan to move there. I'm told the temperature and plant life are similar to Kalor, so it'll be a nice place to live."

Zia thought about the question for a moment and then looked around to find everyone silently staring at her. She met Searin's gaze and then answered. 'We might. But if I do, I'm going to want a contract and I'm going to need tools. Lots of tools.'

CHAPTER 32

Sorana Colony

When Zia felt the vibrations around her, a tired smile broke out on her face. She'd been battling with the old repeater station for rotations and might have finally found all the issues keeping it from talking to the com array satellite in orbit around Sorana. That was a good thing because she was close to taking a blunt object and pounding the repeater into submission!

Crawling out from under the machine, she found four people waiting for her. They must have moved incredibly stealthily for her implants not to pick up their footfalls. She waved and smiled at them as Palforma stepped forward to help her to her feet.

Once she was standing and mostly brushed off, Palforma introduced her to the new arrivals. 'These men moved here from Kalor,' he explained. 'This is Iansif, Tisuran, and Narmolo. They're all honorable men who served with me under Commandant Holian.'

So these were more of the retired soldiers from Kalor. When they'd gotten to Sorana, only one Talin had been here trying to set things up as best she could. Soon after she and Palforma arrived, men and women from Kalor started arriving. Now the Sorana Colony was sixty strong with almost all of them coming from Commandant Holian's colony.

'Welcome, guys!' Zia greeted them with a smile. When they gestured back with the simple greeting in Norka, Zia's smile got even wider.

'And they arrived with more modular domiciles,' Palforma told her. 'It won't be long before we can bring your whole family here.'

"I was told your family lives in a colony of about a hundred humans, and we could bring them all here," Iansif pointed out. "We've brought enough modular domiciles to accommodate many families."

'Let's start with my family,' Zia countered, amused by these eager Talins. 'Then we can see if any of the others want to come. And remember, we ask. We don't kidnap.'

"Yes, of course," Tisuran responded, but she got the feeling he wasn't entirely sold on the no-abduction policy. She wasn't surprised, because the more Talins she met the more she realized they always thought they knew what was best, even when they acknowledged human intelligence. She'd need to keep an eye on him.

Rattle of excitement. 'I want to show you some other things in the shipment,' Palforma told her before he started gathering up her tools.

She didn't bother asking him what had arrived with these men. She simply bent over and helped shove items into totes. The men followed suit, and soon everyone was burdened with totes overfull of all the tools and old parts she'd replaced on the repeater. A new one was coming, but it wouldn't get here until well into next solar, so for now she had to do battle with this old one. She wasn't sure, but she'd estimate that forty percent of the repeater was new parts now!

'Did the reconditioners get here?' she asked once they were all walking the well-trodden path back to "town." Palforma's hands were full so he couldn't answer her, but he sounded another rattle of excitement and a rumble of amusement.

With so many bodies to help carry her tools, it didn't take long for all of them to walk back. After dropping off all the gear in her shop, the men headed to the communal building where most gathered for an evening meal. But Palforma picked her up and sprinted back to their private domicile, making excited rattles the entire way.

Once there, he set her on her feet in front of a small table that held some nondescript packages. 'These are too small to be reconditioners,' she stated, feeling mildly disappointed.

'Open them, my heart,' Palforma urged.

She couldn't understand why he was so excited, but she reached for the smaller of the packages. She gasped once she got the cover off to reveal the contents. It was a replacement for the necklace she'd lost. It was almost exactly like the original but with even more gems!

She shoved it at Palforma. 'Put it on me!'

Rumbling with happiness, Palforma gently took it from her and draped it around her neck. As much as she didn't want a collar, she *did* want this. Reaching up to stroke the gem sitting at the base of her throat, she met Palforma's eyes.

'There's more,' he told her and pointed to the other package. With clumsy hands she snatched it up and ripped it open. Then she stared at the item inside, flummoxed.

Pulling the item out, she held it in one hand as she spoke. 'You got me a tiara?'

'I read some Old Earth literature and it said princesses wear crowns. So, I got you a crown,' he explained. 'I found some images and had this made for you.'

Eyes tearing up, she shoved it on her head with so much haste she probably would have to detangle it from her hair later.

'You're the best Talin a girl could ever have!' she declared and then jumped into his arms.

'No. You're the best owner a Talin could ever have,' he teased as he sounded a rumble of affection.

'I told you I'd void that contract,' she reminded him.

'Absolutely not! I'm yours and you're never getting rid of me.' He started rubbing his cheek on the side of her head to avoid the crown. With the scent of vanilla in her nose, a tiara on her head, and Palforma's arms around her, Zia couldn't imagine life getting any better than this. She tightened her arms around him and said the words she'd been practicing verbalizing since they landed on Sorana.

"I love you, Palforma."

Rattling with surprise, Palforma pulled her a little away from him so their eyes could meet. "True gift," he said. "Your voice, gift. My heart. My love."

Then he drew her back in and held her tightly, purring hard enough to vibrate her chest. She never thought her life would end up like a fairytale complete with a happily ever after ending.

She was never so happy to be proven wrong.

Dear Readers,

Thank you for reading *Fighting Captivity*. I hope you enjoyed it enough to leave a review! As an indie writer without the support of a publishing company, I need all the help I can get. Your good reviews keep me writing.

The next book in the series is available! You'll get to meet Zia's friend Lasha and the sweet Talin who rescued her *in Craving Captivity*.

Have you gotten a copy of *Tender Captivity* or any of my free novellas yet? Visit my website for all the great offers:
www.rk-munin.com

Have a Fruitful Rotation,
Rye

www.ingramcontent.com/pod-product-compliance
Lightning Source LLC
Chambersburg PA
CBHW060435310726
48977CB00001B/195